FLAME

A H E N R Y H O L T M Y S T E R Y

A H E N R Y H O L T M Y S T E R Y

FLAME

John Lutz

H E N R Y H O L T A N D C O M P A N Y
NEW YORK

Published by Henry Holt and Company, Inc.,
115 West 18th Street, New York, New York 10011.
Published in Canada by Fitzhenry & Whiteside Limited,
195 Allstate Parkway, Markham, Ontario L3R 4T8.

Library of Congress Cataloging-in-Publication Data
Lutz, John, 1939–
Flame / John Lutz. – 1st ed.
    p.   cm.
ISBN 0-8050-0968-X
I. Title.
PS3562.U854F5   1989
813'.54—dc20   89-7562
                                                    CIP

Henry Holt books are available at special discounts
for bulk purchases for sales promotions, premiums,
fund-raising, or educational use. Special editions
or book excerpts can also be created to specification.

For details contact:
Special Sales Director
Henry Holt and Company, Inc.
115 West 18th Street
New York, New York 10011

First Edition

Designed by Paula R. Szafranski

Printed in the United States of America
10   9   8   7   6   5   4   3   2   1

FOR ELLEN

A little fire is quickly trodden out;
Which, being suffer'd, rivers cannot quench.

—William Shakespeare,
Henry VI

FLAME

A H E N R Y   H O L T   M Y S T E R Y

Chapter 1 .

~~ Outside the window the sun bore down with the brilliance and blanching effect of a cosmic tanning lamp. It made the eyes ache. Magellan Avenue was a wide, pale ribbon of pavement. The white stucco combination court-house and jail across the street looked as if it were constructed of meringue skimmed from the richest of pies. Beyond it, the sun-sparked sea undulated with a shallow glitter that suggested sequins suspended just below the surface like mischievous half-formed thoughts.

Inside the office, Carver sat quietly in his new chair, leaning back with his lame leg propped up on his gleaming new desk. Through the silence in the office he could barely hear the surf breaking on the narrow white beach beyond the buildings on the other side of Magellan. The fetid fish scent of the sea seeped into the cool office with the sound of the waves.

He'd been content working out of his home—Edwina's home actually—a few miles north on the coast highway, but Edwina was in real estate and had mentioned a possible good deal in a building in downtown Del Moray. At first he had resisted the suggestion. Discussion ensued. Positions wavered. Some dangerous situations had developed in the recent past, and Carver thought it might be a good idea to separate his business from Edwina as much as possible, to protect her. So in the end it was Carver who'd insisted, and who now sat in the quiet office with nothing to do except organize paper clips and rubber bands, though they were already pretty well whipped into shape.

He'd had one client during the month he'd been located here, in this cream stucco building that also housed an insurance broker and a car rental agency. The client had been a wronged husband. A Volkswagen dealer named Wayne Garnett, who, as it turned out, was dealing in murder, as well as drugs smuggled into the country in new cars. Options not mentioned on the sticker.

Carver was getting a headache sitting here staring into the searing clear light beyond the window. He dropped his leg from the desk with a solid *thump!*, levered himself to his feet with his walnut cane, and limped across the carpet to close the drapes.

He was about to yank on the cord when he saw the dark blue Cadillac pull into the gravel lot. It was a sedan De Ville, one of the last of the block-long models, and was waxed and buffed to a deep shine that gave back the sunlight and danced with the reflected images of palm trees and pale buildings. The driver, obscure behind the dark-tinted side window, looked like a man, but that was all Carver could determine.

Guy must need insurance, he told himself. Or wants to rent a car to carry as a spare in the trunk of that one.

But something kept him from pulling the drapes closed. He stood motionless instead, leaning on his cane, his free hand on the cord, watching while the dinosaur on wheels maneuvered through a wide turn and parked halfway between his office entrance and the entrance to Golden Future Insurance next door.

A man in his sixties climbed out. He was about six feet tall, well built except for a large stomach paunch, and was wearing lime-green pants with a white belt, a pastel green shirt. He had a full head of white hair combed to the side and down low on his forehead, as if he might be disguising a receding hairline.

Before slamming and locking the car door, he slipped a pair of tinted glasses on and adjusted them with a tap to the bridge of his nose. Even from the office window they didn't look like sunglasses, but light pink prescription lenses. White shoes flashed beneath green pants cuffs as he veered only momentarily toward Golden Future, then set a course straight for Carver's office, plodding in the puddle of his dark shadow.

He glimpsed Carver standing at the window. Gave a slight nod to acknowledge his presence but didn't smile or wave. Sunlight shot rays off the round lenses of his glasses as he passed from sight.

Carver heard the door to the small anteroom open and close. The door to his office was open, but the man didn't barge in. Carver waited a few seconds, then said, "C'mon in," and limped back toward the desk.

He was taller than six feet, Carver saw when the man stepped into the office. Maybe six-three. He was also closer to seventy than sixty. Once he'd been a powerful specimen, and he still had the wide frame, but age had sapped his body of sureness and power. He moved with the kind of tentative slowness indicative of arthritis. His eyes flicked to the cane and Carver's stiff left knee that was bent at a thirty-degree angle for life. Souvenir from a shooting when he was on the Orlando police force.

The man said, "You Fred Carver?" The remnants of a Southern accent lingered in his voice. Maybe long-ago Tennessee.

Carver nodded, edging up to stand behind the desk. He noticed that the white shoes were soft patent leather and had ornate silver-tipped tassels.

"I'm Bert Renway." A thick arm dusted with white hair was extended. Carver shook hands with the man, surprised by the coolness of flesh and strength of grip. "Phone directory says you're a private investigator."

Carver motioned for Renway to sit in the chair near the desk. Sat down himself. Said, smiling, "The yellow pages wouldn't lie."

"Hard to get a recommendation for somebody in your line of work," Renway said. "Don't know anyone who ever hired a private detective. Coulda gone to the police and asked them to recommend somebody, but I didn't wanna do that."

"Usually the people who hire me have already been to the police," Carver said, "and came away dissatisfied. How can I help you, Mr. Renway?"

"By figurin' out what the hell's goin' on. I promised I wouldn't get too nosy about it, but, dammit, I just gotta know!" He leaned forward and parted his white hair with his fingertips. Surprised Carver by tugging at the hair and removing most of it to reveal a large bald spot. Held the toupee out as if it were a small animal he'd just slain. Said, "This ain't my real hair."

Carver said, "Hope not."

Renway tapped one of the lenses of his glasses with a broad fingernail. "One thing never went bad on me's my eyes. I don't wear specs; these are ordinary tinted glass, though they don't look it. Wouldn't wear these floppy white shoes, either, 'cept they made me. They're not even my shoes. Givin' me blisters. Walkin' around in the damn things is part of the deal, though."

"What deal?"

"To be somebody else."

"Who?"

"Got no idea, other than a name don't mean a thing to me."

Carver leaned forward and placed his elbows on the desk. The wood felt cool on his bare arms. A hint of vulnerability.

He said, "Mr. Renway, we better start you-know-where."

Chapter 2

Renway absently drew a pack of Winstons from his shirt pocket, then looked down at them as if seeing them for the first time. He peeled off the tinted glasses and raised his gray eyebrows inquisitively at Carver. "Okay if I smoke?"

"Sure." Carver was guilty of an occasional cigar, so who was he to object? He stretched out an arm and handed Renway the seashell ashtray from the corner of the desk. Its occupant was long gone and wouldn't complain.

Renway placed the ashtray in his lap, then got out one of those cheap disposable lighters that encased a fishing fly as if it were an insect in a kill bottle. Touched flame to cigarette and inhaled deeply. He said, "I guess the beginning's back when I retired from the railroad up north and moved down here to Florida with my wife, Ella, to live on my pension. It was gonna be the beginnin' of the good years." He picked a shred of tobacco from his lower lip and flicked it away. "Things didn't work out. Pension money didn't go as far as we thought, then six months ago cancer took Ella. After she died, I kept livin' in the mobile home we'd bought east of town. Beach Cove Court. You know the place?"

"Been past it."

"I didn't see any reason to move away from Del Moray. Didn't see any reason to do much of anything. Kinda went on automatic pilot, if you know what I mean."

Carver said, "I know. I've been in the same flight pattern."

A long blue-and-silver tour bus rumbled past outside. Exhaust fumes wended their way into the office, maybe through the air-conditioning system, and competed with the scent of tobacco smoke.

" 'Bout a month ago," Renway went on, "I was invited down to Fort Lauderdale to visit another old railroad man retired and moved to Florida. Fella I used to work with in the Alton and Southern switchyards. He lives in this little one-bedroom apartment with his wife, so I stayed the night at a motel. We had a nice visit, and when I went back to the motel, this fancy-dressed guy stopped me in the parkin' lot. Called me by name. Said he had a business proposition that was perfectly legal and would earn me a lotta money. I figured I didn't wanna see a condominium or time-share project, so I politely told him I wasn't interested. That's when he peeled off five one-hundred-dollar bills and handed them to me. Said all I had to do was listen and I could keep the money."

"What'd you do?" Carver asked, knowing it was a silly question. He wanted to keep Renway rolling so everything would come out and his words wouldn't be so carefully chosen.

"I invited him for a drink in the motel bar. We had some daiquiris, and he laid out the plan for me."

"Plan?"

"Well, too simple to be called a plan, really. I was supposed to stay in Fort Lauderdale and live in this condo-minium unit on Ocean Boulevard. Call myself Frank Wesley, if anybody was to ask. Drive this guy Wesley's car and even wear some of his clothes. As for my other duties, all I was supposed to do was leave every morning before noon and drive around a while. Stop off for lunch. Drive around some more. Go to the movies if I wanted. Spend some of the money I was gettin' paid."

"How much money?"

"Two thousand dollars a week."

Carver studied a bluebottle fly crawling straight up the edge of the window. It reached the top, made a sharp right turn, and began moving horizontally, as if there might be some purpose to what it was doing. "You didn't think there might be something off-center about the deal? Impersonating this man Wesley?"

"I said two thousand a week, Carver. And, sure, I figured somethin' wasn't right, so I asked Palmer—"

"Palmer?"

"Sorry. Ralph Palmer, the fella who hired me. I asked him to sign a paper I drew up proclaimin' that what I was doin' was perfectly legal. A contract. We both signed it." Renway drew a sweat-damp, folded sheet of white paper from his hip pocket and handed it across the desk to Carver. "Bear in mind I ain't a lawyer," he said apologetically. No need to apologize for that.

The "contract" was typewritten, with a lot of whited-out mistakes. What it said, basically, was that Palmer had hired Renway to live in Wesley's condo as Frank Wesley for three months or until his services were no longer needed. It also stated that nothing illegal was occurring and that the real Wesley was aware of the impersonation and approved of it. The financial terms were also spelled out. Renway's clumsily scrawled signature was at the bottom alongside Palmer's tight neat one.

Carver handed the paper back to Renway. "This probably doesn't mean much legally," he said.

Renway carefully refolded the paper and slid it back in his hip pocket. "I know, but it gives me some measure of protection."

"Not enough."

"Well, yeah. That's why I'm here. Why I wanna hire you to find out what's goin' on. I drove back up to Del Moray to get some of my stuff outa the mobile home, and I figured I oughta hire an investigator here, seeing as Palmer and his friends must have been watchin' me before I went to Fort Lauderdale."

"Why do you say that?"

"Palmer knew a lot about me the first time we talked in the motel lounge. Even knew about Ella. That it was cancer took her."

"You said 'Palmer and his friends.'"

"Yeah. I never met anybody but Palmer, but he says 'we' now and then and talks like there's others involved."

Carver toyed with the crook of his walnut cane for a moment, then propped it against the desk. "What's happened to you while you've been wandering around being Frank Wesley?"

"Nothin' outa the ordinary. I might as well be Bert Renway, same as always, only I wouldn't be gettin' a couple thousand a week." He leaned forward. "Whole thing, Carver, it makes me uneasy."

"Know anything about Wesley?"

"Nope. Palmer wouldn't tell me nothin' about him. Lives in a nice place though. Man's for sure got money. That's his car out there, the big Caddie. Me, I usually drive an Escort."

Carver said, "They give you any idea where Wesley is while you're being him?"

"Not a hint. That's why my feelin' is that part of this two thousand a week oughta go to findin' out *why* I'm collectin' it."

"Could be money well spent," Carver agreed. He told Renway his fee. Got an advance in cash. The way to do business. He said, "What's this Palmer look like?"

"Man about forty," Renway said, "kinda handsome. Got straight black hair, dark eyes. Maybe part Cuban."

"Spanish accent?"

"Just a trace, I'd say. Dresses like a million; always got on an expensive suit and tie. Drives a little gray car—don't know what kind. Somethin' foreign, maybe. I been livin' as Frank Wesley for a little more'n three weeks now, and I only seen Palmer four times: when he hired me, and when we met the next three Friday nights and he paid me."

"Where'd you meet?"

"We got an appointment every Friday evening at seven at a spot on the public beach. A bench near where Sunrise Boulevard meets Ocean."

"Pay you in cash?"

"Yep. All in fifties or smaller bills. Money looks real enough. That's some of it there on your desk. Him to me to you."

Carver lifted the top two bills from the stack of fifties in front of him: Renway's retainer. He snapped the bills through his fingers, rubbed the ink, held them up to the light, compared serial numbers. "Real stuff, all right." He replaced the bills. "Can you give me your—Wesley's— address and an extra key? I think I oughta look the place over while you're out driving around. That way whoever might be watching you wouldn't be near the condo."

"I don't think anybody's watchin' or followin' me; I checked on that. Doubled back a few times. Kept a careful eye on my rearview mirror."

"There are people who are very good at following," Carver said. "Better write down Wesley's phone number, too. I probably won't use it, and it'd be best if you didn't call here. For that matter, don't make any call from the condo you might not want overheard."

"Huh? You think the phone's tapped?"

"I think we need to find out. If the people who hired you are pros, they might be doing all sorts of things without you being aware."

Renway didn't argue. He wrote down Wesley's address and said he'd have an extra key cut that afternoon and drop it by Carver's office. As if to emphasize his intention, he fished a key ring from his pocket. A bulky gold letter *W* was attached to it by a chain. He worked a brass door key from it and dropped the key into his shirt pocket. Sat clutching the gold ring with its car keys in his right hand.

Carver told him he'd type up a contract and trade it to him for the duplicate key when he came back. Gave him a receipt for the money. All above-board and businesslike. Unlike the Wesley deal.

Renway tucked the receipt in his pocket and raised himself out of his chair. "I feel better after talkin' to you, Carver. I couldn't go on not knowin' and not doin' a thing about this." He snubbed out his cigarette in the seashell ashtray he'd been holding, then placed the pink-and-blue-tinged shell on a corner of the desk. A thin wisp of gray smoke continued to curl from it. Caught the draft from the air conditioner and dissipated.

He said, "Thanks, Carver. See you about two o'clock, okay?"

Carver said two was fine. Watched Renway walk from the office in his stiff, slow gait that said he was a senior citizen and taking it easy. No rush to be anywhere or do anything. Time was running out and he was going to be selfish and enjoy what was left. Only trouble was, he needed money and had to bend a little to get it. Like getting involved in something he didn't understand.

Life kept demanding compromises, Carver mused. Never stopped.

He heard the Cadillac's powerful engine turn over and roar.

His ears popped, as if he were in a plane climbing through changing air pressure. That was odd, but he didn't have time to think about it.

The blast blew in the window and knocked him out of his chair.

Chapter 3

He was dancing, whirling on two good legs. The woman he was with was wearing heady perfume. A scent he couldn't place. Diamonds shot sparks off her black velvet gown.

Carver opened his eyes wider.

There was no woman. He wasn't dancing. The diamonds were fragments of glass. The velvet wasn't a gown, wasn't black, and wasn't even velvet; it was the blue carpet in his office.

He was disappointed.

Why was he lying on the floor? Staring at a thousand glittering glass shards and wondering where the hell was his cane? A curl of blackness broken by light washed over him, then receded. Like a dark surf rushing in, rushing out. He tried to gather his senses.

What's going on here?

Not sure.

You fully conscious, Carver? Reasoning straight?

Dumb question. How would I know? But yeah, I think so.

Where *was* his cane?

Stretched out on his stomach, he propped himself up on his elbows and looked around.

Whoa! The office was some mess. All the papers that had been on his desk were spread over the floor and up against the far wall, like leaves tossed by the wind. Nothing was left on the desk, not even the ashtray or the incredibly complicated Japanese-made combination answering machine, telephone, recorder, and Dictaphone Edwina had talked him into buying. The drapes hung limply at the window and were so shredded they admitted narrow sunbeams that dappled the floor and caused the broken glass to glitter.

Diamond, diamond.

Carver saw his cane lying on the floor near the desk. He started to drag himself toward it, then felt a shard of glass penetrate the heel of his hand and stopped and lay still.

The sharp pain cleared his mind. Gingerly, he pulled the splinter of glass out with his thumb and forefinger and dropped it off to the side.

Then he moved more carefully, picking glass out of the carpet before him. Like a fastidious maid removing dangerous lint.

He reached the cane and gripped it tightly, feeling the hard walnut warm to his grasp. But he didn't try to stand up. The way he felt, that could wait a minute or two. Instead he worked his way to a sitting position and leaned his back against the wall, his stiff leg angled out in front of him, and wondered what had put him here, what had happened.

He heard the singsong wail of a siren, way off in the distance, yet red and blue light danced off the glass fragments remaining in the window frame. Roofbar lights. Odd. A police car had turned into the lot and was parking out front, but the siren seemed miles away. Sound and sight didn't coincide. Didn't make sense.

Then he realized there was something wrong with his hearing. And there was a high, steady buzzing in his ears, hardly noticeable because it was so monotonous it seemed part of normal background noise. He'd been ignoring it the way people ignore crickets screaming.

Then the sky outside the window darkened, lightened, darkened. Smoke drifting on the wind. He could smell it. And he could smell something else. Something sweet and cloying that was burning and creating the black smoke.

And he remembered.

Said, "Holy Christ!" Grabbed the edge of the desk, planted the tip of his cane firmly in the soft carpet, and pushed himself to his feet.

His head ached and he was dizzy. And now that he'd remembered, he was trembling. He could feel the vibration running like electricity through the cane.

He leaned hard on the cane with both hands and waited, his body swaying. Finally the dizziness passed. The trembling ceased. The headache decided to stay.

Another siren wailed outside. Much louder than the first. Through the window, Carver saw the roof of another police car and its flashing red and blue lights as it braked to a halt outside.

Renway. It had to be Renway who'd triggered the explosion when he started the Caddie. Carver remembered how the sound of the big car's engine turning over had preceded the blast. Renway, who'd been pretending to be someone else. Who? Oh, yeah, guy named Weston, or Wesley. That was it—Frank Wesley.

Carver hobbled to the window to make sure he was right about the source of the explosion. Peered outside and saw the long Cadillac burning despite the frantic efforts of two uniformed cops with fire extinguishers. The car's twisted hood was lying on the ground nearby; its doors were blown open or had been opened by the cops. One of the rear ones hung crazily by only the bottom hinge, like some kind of injured wing.

The car's interior was pure orange flame, fed by gasoline and not in the least affected by whatever the cops were spraying on it. The tires were already melted to globs of rubber. What Carver had smelled were the mingled odors of rubber—and Renway—burning. The sickening stench of charred flesh that lodged in the nostrils and lay thick on the tongue to become taste.

Through the pulsing, constantly unfolding orange blossom trapped in the car, a wizened black form could occasionally be glimpsed bent over the steering wheel as if trying to coax speed from hurtling steel, like Renway's narrow shadow. Only it wasn't his shadow, it was Renway himself. What he'd become in the blast furnace of the Cadillac.

People were standing across the street and on the edge of the parking lot. Staring, knotted close together as if for protection. Death was always an unpleasant reminder. Another uniformed cop was over there, strutting back and forth like a storm trooper and waving his arms, motioning for everyone to stay well back, though no one was moving. Carver knew there was no danger of another explosion. Everything explosive or flammable in the car was already blazing.

Sirens. Very loud now. And a clanging bell.

A yellow-and-chrome Del Moray fire engine, gaudy as a jukebox, belched black smoke of its own from its diesel exhaust, slowed down with more bell clanging, and turned off of Magellan into the driveway. Another patrol car arrived, following the fire engine like a pilot fish trailing a shark. No other vehicles moving out there; Magellan must be blocked to through traffic.

The breeze caught the smoke and the sweet odor again, carrying them Carver's way.

He swallowed the syrupy taste at the base of his tongue and backed away from the window. Limped over behind his desk. Sat down hard in his chair. Dizzy like before. Not feeling well at all. His headache flared, pounded. Jesus! Soon as he felt like standing again, he'd root through the locked bottom drawer of the file cabinet, where he kept his gun and some Extra-Strength Tylenol. Needed three of four tablets to block this baby.

What happened next didn't help his headache at all.

The office door opened and in stepped McGregor.

Chapter 4

Del Moray Police Lieutenant William Mc-Gregor was probably six-foot-six. In his early forties and skinny but with the kind of wiry, coiled strength seen in pro basketball players. He had straight blond hair, combed severely sideways and beginning to thin, a lock of it lying raggedly down his forehead. A long, narrow face with tiny and close-set blue eyes, a jutting jaw. He looked more Scandinavian than Scottish. His thin lips parted in a smile to reveal the wide gap between his front teeth, and he shut the door behind him and stepped all the way into the office. Like many very tall men, he seemed to move lazily, in sections. Broken glass crunched beneath his boat-size black wing-tip shoes.

He said, "Looks like your cleaning woman ain't been in yet today."

Carver said, "I'll tidy up myself just as soon as you're gone. I'd like to get to it."

McGregor hitched his thumbs in his belt and stood with his legs spread wide. A colossus straddling anything he could bully. Not going anyplace. "This is police business, Carver.

Let me ask, you notice a car explode right outside your window?"

Carver's headache throbbed. "It didn't escape my attention."

"Now, the guy who's barbecued in the driver's seat might have come to this building to rent a car, only he arrived in what looks like it was a pretty new and nice car before it got all bent and scorched. Or he might have driven here to buy some insurance next door; that'd be a classic case of bad timing, hey? Or he might have come here to see you, a private investigator sitting with his thumb up his ass in his brand-new office. That seems most likely of the three. Incidentally, what made you rent an office? Edwina get tired of you and throw you outa her house?"

The last thing Carver felt like doing was talking to McGregor, the most self-involved, ambitious, and unscrupulous person he'd ever met. Add to that bad grooming. Even from a distance of over five feet, he could smell McGregor's foul breath and cheap perfumy cologne. The afternoon Florida heat was pushing in through the blown-out window, too. Almost enough to turn the stomach.

"You didn't answer my question, fuckface."

"I thought you said police business."

McGregor brushed glass fragments off the chair by the desk and sat down. Draped one long, long leg over the other. There were deep creases behind the knees of his cheap brown suit. Lint and dandruff littered the shoulders. Suit needed to go in for its yearly cleaning. He said, "Okay, you know the guy that got blown up?"

Carver trusted McGregor about as far as he'd trust Charles Manson with a badge. The lieutenant often worked outside the police department and outside the law itself in his pursuit of personal glory, wealth, and promotion. It had led to his dismissal from the Fort Lauderdale police, but he'd come north to Del Moray and quickly lied and cheated his way up the ranks in that small department.

"I knew him," Carver said. He leaned into his cane and stood up. Limped idly around the office, extending his bad leg out in front of him now and then, with the heel on the floor, and doing a kind of cane-supported deep knee-bend to pick up things from the carpet. A file folder. The ashtray. The third thing he picked up was the Japanese-made combination phone, answering machine, recorder, and Dictaphone. As he did so, he pressed the record button. Casually placed the machine on the desk corner with the built-in mike aimed at McGregor. Lifted a nine-inch shard of window glass and tossed it over near the upended wastebasket. Just tidying up. The conversation in the office would be recorded now, without McGregor's knowledge.

"So go on, tell me about it," McGregor said. "Gonna make like a shy talk-show guest and force me to drag every answer outa you?"

"His name was Bert Renway. He came here to hire me."

"That figures. Guy musta been a loser from the get-go. Everything in that car's been burned or melted, so you're the main source of information. Don't lie or hold anything back, Carver. This is a murder investigation."

"Maybe the car exploded by itself. Gas fumes."

"Don't give me your coy act. First thing I smelled when I drove up was cooked meat. Second thing was cordite from a blasting-powder charge. It was TNT or something sent your client on his way, not super unleaded."

Carver knew McGregor was right—this was a murder investigation and no time to play cute. Not unless he had some other occupation in mind. Which he didn't; he had a love-hate relationship with investigative work.

He sat back down behind the desk and told McGregor every detail of Renway's visit.

When Carver was finished, McGregor sat rubbing his thumb along the side of his long jaw. He said, "You and I both know the likely reasons somebody'd hire some fool to take over an apartment and car."

Carver said, "I was gonna approach it from that angle."

McGregor's close-set, beady eyes took on an intense look. Carver had seen that expression before. The lieutenant was thinking hard, turning it all over in his mind, figuring how to use to best advantage what he'd just heard.

Then he smiled, poking the pink tip of his tongue through the space between his front teeth. It lent him a thoroughly evil, lascivious air that perfectly matched his character. He said, "Fort Lauderdale, huh? I got no use for any of the worthless fartbrains in that department."

"They feel the same way about you," Carver said. "Difference is, they're right."

"The murder happened right here in Del Moray," McGregor said thoughtfully. "You've fulfilled your professional obligation and informed the police of what you know. From now on, I think you better keep the story to yourself. So it'll be just between the two of us."

One part of Carver couldn't believe it. The other wasn't surprised. He'd seen too much of McGregor to assume limits on his deviousness or unethical behavior. Where ethics should be, McGregor had a vacuum.

Carver said loudly, so the recorder would be sure to pick it up, "You mean you're not going to tell the Fort Lauderdale police about Renway living in Wesley's apartment? Getting blown up in Wesley's car?"

"This is a Del Moray matter," McGregor said. "We'll see what the Fort Lauderdale police find out for themselves. See how they play this thing. See if *they* share with *us*."

"You sound like a schoolkid arguing on the playground over whose turn it is to be It."

"*It* was Renway, and if he could, he'd tell you we ain't playing schoolyard games." He slumped his lanky frame to the side. His suitcoat fell open to reveal a wrinkled lining, a brown leather shoulder holster, and the checked butt of a Police Special. "Maybe now it's your turn to be It, Carver. You say this Renway gave you two thousand dollars?"

"That's right."

"So you've been officially hired. Bought and paid for."

"Thing is," Carver said, "my client's dead."

"You still better do what you were hired for," McGregor said. "Go to Fort Lauderdale and figure out what the Wesley impersonation's all about. Let me know what's going on, but don't let anyone else in on it. Not even anybody in the Del Moray department. Our little secret. Ain't it deliciously fun?"

"No."

"But ain't you curious?"

"Yeah," Carver had to admit. He knew he'd have gone to Fort Lauderdale even if McGregor hadn't suggested it. The police wouldn't think kindly of a private investigator mucking around in an open case, but McGregor was solving that problem. The police were requesting Carver's help, and it was all on tape. Carver decided to put up some resistance anyway, for the recorder. The reluctant virgin. "Being curious doesn't mean I'm on my way to Lauderdale."

McGregor began making obscure but unmistakable threats about pulling strings and having Carver's investigator's license revoked if he didn't cooperate. Carver tuned him out and let him talk in the direction of the microphone. McGregor was right, this was fun.

"I dunno," Carver said, stringing him along, "this is an open case. I can wind up in the wringer."

"You're in the wringer now," McGregor said. "Balls and all." He leaned forward and smiled with all the earnestness of a Yugo salesman. "Listen, Carver, we both know this smells like something big and important. The kinda thing where there'd be plenty of credit to spread around if we broke it. Fame and money for you, and a career maker for me. Be fucking captain someday."

"Another way for you to make captain again might be old-fashioned good police work."

"Screw good police work. Sticking parking tickets under windshield wipers, standing and waving traffic through on streetcorners too hot to touch, peeling dead winos off the sidewalks—*that's* good police work. If you'd stayed with the Orlando department instead of pulling a dumb-ass stunt like getting your knee shot away doing good police work, you wouldn't've gone higher than patrolman. It's 'cause of the way you think. Way you see the world. Like you got some kinda mission and can't bend with the wind. Kinda dumb hero who dies defending the bridge and then gets marched over and forgotten. Small-time shit, that's you."

"No way to talk to a man whose help you want."

"Hey, it's a two-way street, fuckhead."

"Until you decide to put up a new sign."

"I'm not asking you to cut off your dick, Carver. And this way you keep your client's two grand instead of it gets confiscated for evidence. Use it to cover expenses in Fort Lauderdale. Figure out what's happening down there and keep me tuned in. We'll be the kinda goddamn heroes that collect medals, we play this right."

"Let me think about it."

McGregor snorted and looked disgusted. "It ain't like you got a choice, Carver. Not a real one, anyway. I gotta know now, or I got no recourse but to put your story in my report. Haul you in as a suspect, maybe. Hey, why not? You were the last person to see the victim alive. You and him argued."

"I don't recall an argument."

"Then why'd you tell me about it? I gotta put it in my report. Hell of an argument. Over some money you owed him, I think it was. Root of all evil, hey?"

"And I excused myself, ducked outside, and planted a bomb in his car?"

"Who's to say you didn't have help?" McGregor flashed his gap-toothed, Satanic grin. "You're over a barrel, Carver. You don't wanna get fucked, you best do as I tell you. Either you drive down to Fort Lauderdale, or you go for a drive to headquarters and log some jail time. Get muddied enough to lose the privilege of taking people's money for uncovering dirt and screwing up their lives. Which direction you wanna travel?"

Carver pretended to think about it. Finally said, "South to Fort Lauderdale."

"Very sensible," McGregor said, unfolding up out of his chair to loom over the seated Carver. Guy probably hadn't trimmed the hair in his nostrils for years. "Kinda rare for you, to be so reasonable."

"As you pointed out, I don't have much choice."

McGregor grinned and took two long strides to the door. Paused and said, "Keep in touch, assface. Don't forget that part of our arrangement."

"You'll know what I know," Carver said, in the mood to be agreeable. He wanted McGregor to leave as soon as possible, before the combined odors of cheap cologne and scorched flesh became too much for his stomach.

"*When* you know it," McGregor added, and ambled out the door, swinging his long arms wide.

Carver waited a few minutes, then pressed rewind on the machine to make sure the conversation was recorded. He could put the cassette in his safe-deposit box, conduct the investigation his way, and tell McGregor to go fuck himself if push came to shove. Serve the dumb yahoo right for not keeping up with Japanese technology.

Something was wrong. The tape wasn't rewinding.

Carver flipped open the machine's plastic lid and saw that there was nothing to rewind; the tape hadn't moved. The green "Power On" light wasn't glowing. He lifted the receiver and heard no dial tone. Jiggled the cradle button up and down. Nothing.

He punched every button on the complex control panel. No result. The circuitry was dead.

The machine's contact with the floor had broken something in its delicate, microchip-stuffed interior. Damn the Japanese.

Chapter 5

 Soft. Warm.

Carver was aware of Edwina kissing him on the lips. He sat up in bed and saw she was fully dressed, even carrying her blue vinyl attaché case, smiling down at him. On her way to turn real estate.

She said, "You overslept."

"I was tired," Carver said. "Bomb going off nearby made me exhausted."

"Guess it would."

He had an erection. "Sure you have to leave right away?"

Something in her gray eyes; she wanted to stay. " 'Fraid I do. I have an appointment to show a condo."

"Can't you be half an hour late?"

"It's beachfront property."

Ah! Big commission. Not that it was the money that primarily motivated Edwina; this was her game, the symbolic and real means to her independence after her divorce and then a crushing love affair with a man now deservedly dead. She didn't trust Carver completely. He didn't trust her. He'd gone through a hellish marriage and divorce himself. His ex-wife Laura and their seven-year-old daughter Ann lived in St. Louis. In a way, that was worse for him than if they didn't exist. In a way.

Edwina bent down again. Kissed him lightly on the forehead this time. She smelled like roses. Fresh shampoo and perfume. She had on her gray pin-striped blazer and matching skirt. Dark hose and black high heels. It was real-estate biz this morning, all right. She smiled again, as if kissing him brought that on automatically. Gave a kind of shrug and said, "Sorry, but I have to go. Will you be here this afternoon?"

"No. Gotta drive to Fort Lauderdale." When she'd come home late last night, he'd told her everything about yesterday. Let it all flow from him, and then he could finally relax. "One stop I have to make first."

"Bert Renway's mobile home?"

She was ahead of him. "That's right."

"Why do you think he was hired to impersonate Wesley?"

The why of it was something they hadn't discussed last night. Carver had been too tired to talk for very long. She'd urged him to forget the day, to sleep. To blot out everything and think about it again when he was rested. Good advice. Irresistible, coming from Edwina. Much about her was irresistible.

He fluffed his pillow against the headboard, sat up straighter, and leaned heavily back into it. The maneuver brought him eye-level with a shaft of morning light spearing through the gap in the drapes. Made his head pound. "My guess is that Renway fit Wesley's general description close enough so that whoever was hired to watch Wesley would be lured into tailing Renway. Hell, why not? Wesley's apartment, Wesley's car, even some of Wesley's clothes."

"So the idea was that Wesley knew someone was out to kill

him and arranged to have Renway murdered in his place?"

"Not necessarily," Carver said. "It might have been nothing more than a setup that'd allow Wesley freedom to do what he wanted while his watchers were wasting their time following Renway."

"Isn't there some law against that?" Edwina asked.

"Not as long as everybody knew where they stood and Wesley wasn't doing anything illegal. Renway was playing a role for pay. Like an actor."

"His first and final role," she said.

"Turned out that way, poor bastard. He didn't know the script or all the players. Or the danger. Maybe, for that matter, neither did Wesley."

Her lips parted, then she pressed them shut; her pink lipstick seemed to bond like glue. She'd been about to ask him to be careful, but had thought better of it. Their love for each other was obsessive and they both knew it. Two obsessive personalities. She about whatever real-estate deal she was working to close, he about whatever case he was on. They needed to be that way. It was their oxygen.

The air conditioner clicked on and sent a wave of cool air flowing across the room. Felt good on Carver's bare chest.

He said, "If you need to get in touch, I'll be at the Carib Terrace."

She said, "I'll need to get in touch," and swayed from the bedroom. She had the most elegant walk Carver had ever seen; maybe he was especially awed by it because of his lameness. Even her long auburn hair, swinging gently in syncopation with her hips, was mesmerizing. When she was gone the room felt larger and emptier.

He listened to the rumbling whine of the automatic garage door opener. Heard the snarl of her Mercedes. Listened to her shift gears as the car rolled down the long, curving driveway and then accelerated up the highway. She was in a hurry. Determined. Sometime soon, papers would be signed and a condo would change hands. Another triumph.

He got up and took a lukewarm shower, staying under the needlelike drive of the water for a long time. Then he dressed in lightweight brown slacks, a black pullover shirt, and his brown moccasins that were easy to get on and off even with the stiff knee. Poked his left hand through the band of his gold Seiko watch and fastened the clasp around his wrist.

Ready to joust with windmills, he told himself, checking his image in Edwina's dresser mirror. Guy too harsh-looking to be called handsome. Bald on top, with thick curly gray hair in a fringe over his ears and at the back of his head well down on his neck. Catlike blue eyes in a tanned face. Scar that gave a permanent sardonic twist to the right corner of his lips. Made him look like a cynic, which wasn't far from the truth. But a cynic with hope. Carver was forty-four now, and he knew he'd look much the same at fifty-four. His arms and torso were lean and muscular from dragging his lower body around with the cane and from his morning swims in the ocean. When Carver swam, strokes long and powerful, legs kicking freely from the hips, he was as whole as anyone. He relished that feeling.

Edwina must have gone out and bought a newspaper. The morning *Del Moray Gazette-Dispatch* lay folded on the sofa in the living room. Carver limped over and reached out with the tip of his cane to flip the paper so he could see the front page. There was the story about the car bombing, featuring a color photograph of the burned-out Caddie being hoisted by a police tow truck. What was left of Bert Renway had already been removed from the front seat and transported to the morgue.

Carver moved closer, picked up the paper, and read. The

Cadillac's license plates had been legible, even though burned black, because of the raised numerals, and the car had been quickly traced to Frank Wesley of Fort Lauderdale. McGregor was letting the press and the Del Moray police think the charred body behind the steering wheel was Wesley. Carver remembered the force of the explosion and the intensity of the fire. Possibly even dental records wouldn't work to identify the victim. But eventually, Carver knew, the medical examiner's office would glean from forensic evidence that the corpse wasn't Wesley's. Give them time and an infinitesimal sample of bone or tissue and they could tell you about the victim's family tree. Science. And surely Bert Renway would sooner or later be reported missing. Two and two would equal the inevitable four, and some cop with a mathematical mind would stumble upon the equation. McGregor was buying time and nothing more with his silence.

Carver read the entire news item quickly but thoroughly. His name wasn't mentioned. Good.

In the kitchen, he rooted around and found a day-old cinnamon Danish. Brought a cup of water to a boil in the microwave, then spooned in some instant coffee. He tested the brew's temperature with his little finger and figured it would have burned the tip off his tongue if he'd been foolish enough to take a sip.

He carried the Danish and steaming coffee out onto the veranda and sat at the white metal table in the shade of the umbrella that sprouted from its center. The breeze off the sea made the umbrella's long fringe sway and tangle. It would cool his coffee nicely.

The Atlantic was sending in large breakers this morning. He could hear the surf crashing on the beach, but he couldn't see it because the house and brick veranda were built on a rise the developer had calculated would expand the ocean view. That meant Carver had to negotiate steep wooden steps down to the beach almost every morning for his swim, something that had given him difficulty at first. Now he took the steps easily, knowing exactly where and when to plant the tip of his cane.

On the narrow strip of beach, he'd thrust the cane into the sand like a spear. Then he'd scoot backward into the rushing waves until they lifted him and carried him seaward and the water was deep enough for him to swim. The jutting cane was his marker when he was tired and stroking for shore.

After about ten minutes, he ate most of the Danish and drank all the coffee. Glanced at the Seiko. It was only nine forty-five, and he wasn't on a schedule, so he fired up a Swisher Sweet cigar and sat watching a determined sailboat tack into the wind and zigzag its way out to sea. Far beyond it, near the horizon, a grayish, hulking oil tanker, ghostly in the morning haze, moved almost imperceptibly northward.

The breeze picked up, carrying landward the fish smell of the sea and the real or imagined scent of crude oil. Just off the shore, a pelican, flying low and straight and with almost mechanical wingbeats, flapped across Carver's line of vision and headed south. The bird was fishing, he knew, watching for movement in the dark, dancing waves. There was a world beneath the surface out there. In here, too.

He heard a low, sonorous humming, different from the rest of the faint traffic sounds from the highway. Familiar.

Edwina's Mercedes.

The tone changed as she downshifted to turn into the driveway, another shift as she took the curving grade. Tires crunched on gravel as the car rolled to a halt near the garage, out of sight from Carver. The deep rumbling of the engine stopped and silence sang between the drawn-out sighs of the surf.

Thunk! The car door slamming.

Edwina walked out onto the veranda. The stiff breeze off the ocean riffled her hair and folded back her unbuttoned blazer to reveal one of her breasts jutting beneath her silky white blouse. She didn't seem to mind being mussed. Tilted back her head and squinted into the wind as if luxuriating in it.

Carver propped his cigar in the ceramic ashtray. The breeze snatched the tenuous spiral of smoke and carried it away like a restless spirit.

"I decided to come back," she said.

He said, "I thought you had a condo to sell."

She dropped her attaché case in a webbed lounge chair. Swayed across the uneven bricks toward him on her dark high heels. Said, "Screw the condo."

He thought, Well, sure.

Chapter 6

Beach Cove Court was nowhere near a beach or cove or the ocean. To reach it, Carver had to drive through the poorer, mostly Hispanic section of west Del Moray, then five miles farther west. The climbing sun blazed through the windshield, heating the steering wheel and softening the vinyl seats. The air conditioner wasn't working. Carver considered putting down the ancient Oldsmobile convertible's canvas top, but that would probably make the heat more intense by turning the car into a convection oven. Might bake him like bread.

The mobile-home court spread for a mile or so north of the main highway. The highway itself seemed to be its southern boundary. Carver steered the Olds in beneath the cypress BEACH COVE COURT sign that dangled on plastic chains from an arch framing the main entrance. Found himself on Beach Cove Drive. Where else?

Most of the mobile homes were double-wides: two trailers joined side by side so they created a semblance of a medium-sized house. They were all fairly new and well kept. In front of each was a neat little square lawn with very green grass.

The undercarriages were disguised by wood latticework, but on the mobile homes facing the opposite street, Carver could see license plates mounted on rear walls. In Florida, if you licensed your mobile home as a vehicle, there was no need to pay real-estate taxes. Many of the homes had small front porches or carports built onto them to make them appear even more permanent. Some had screened-in "Florida rooms" attached to the rear. Palm trees lined Beach Cove Drive, and there were smaller palms in some yards, and here and there a struggling sugar oak or citrus tree. Beach Cove Court, Carver decided, was a pleasant lower-middle-class retirement community, exactly the sort of place he'd imagined the retired railroad man Renway living in, marking diminishing time and coping with inactivity and expenses. Frank Wesley's beachfront condo, exclusive-label clothes, and late-model Cadillac must have seemed like quite a step up for Renway. Stairway to heaven.

Beach Cove Drive wound back toward the highway. Carver finally saw Little Cove Lane, Renway's street, and made a sharp left turn. Many of the trailers were singles in this part of the court, and not so well kept up. At this slower speed, without the wind rushing through the cranked-down windows, the sun was cooking Carver.

Renway's was the last place on the street, not more than a hundred feet from cars and trucks swishing past on the sun-baked pavement. His home was a neat white double-wide with trim the color of egg yolks. A gleaming maroon Ford Escort was parked alongside it, in the deep shade of a carport with a slanted yellow-and-white fiberglass roof held up by white curlicued metal posts. The mailbox out front was black and supported by a thick chain welded together so it looked as if it were snaking up out of the ground and defying gravity in the manner of an Indian fakir's rope trick.

Stenciled on the box in white was THE RENWAYS. Renway hadn't changed it after his wife died. What was her name? Ella. Maybe Renway and Ella were together again. Maybe the moon was Bailey's Irish Cream.

He parked the Olds behind the Escort and climbed out, feeling the back of his sweat-soaked shirt peel away from where it had been plastered to the vinyl seat. Leaned on his cane in the heat. No one was visible on Little Cove Lane, and he'd seen no one on his drive through the court other than a couple of teenage boys in swimming trunks climbing into an old pickup truck with surfboards in the bed. The late-morning July heat was keeping almost everyone nailed indoors in their air conditioning. Looked like the mobile-home court had been struck by a neutron bomb; buildings standing, but no people.

Noticing the grass needed mowing, he limped to the metal steps leading to Renway's front door. For appearance' sake, he rapped on the aluminum door with the crook of his cane.

There was no sound from inside. Perspiration stung Carver's eyes and dripped off the tip of his nose. After a moment he climbed the two steps and peered inside through the door's window. Saw dark carpeting, a dollhouse kitchen with white appliances. Nearer to him, but in dimness, were a recliner chair, console television, and a corner of a plaid Early American sofa. Everything was precisely placed and there was no clutter other than a magazine folded over the arm of the recliner. As if someone had been interrupted reading and would be right back. Renway the widower had been a neat housekeeper.

Carver left the metal steps, then the concrete walk, and limped across sandy soil to the back of the mobile home. The sun was hot on the nape of his neck, and he could feel sand working its way into his moccasins. Had to be careful where he planted the cane, too, in this soft ground. Didn't want to take a tumble.

The back door was locked. And glaringly visible from homes fronting on Beach Cove Drive. Through the line of mobile homes he saw a blue station wagon flash past. He waited, but the car didn't turn onto Little Cove Lane. He caught a glimpse of it beyond the corner of Renway's mobile home, speeding down the highway.

He'd planned on slipping the lock and letting himself in through the back door, but that didn't seem wise, considering its high visibility. And he'd spent enough time snooping around. Might have attracted the attention of some of the cooped-up neighbors, just looking for ways to help pass time and temperature.

He rattled the doorknob, to show whoever might be watching that he was above-board and not sneaking around. Then he backhanded perspiration from his forehead and limped around the wide aluminum structure and back to the street. Then up the grease-stained driveway of Renway's only close neighbor. Willa Hataris, according to the name on the mailbox perched on a rotted cedar post.

The Hataris home was a single. Blindingly white like Renway's but with pink trim and in disrepair. Its front square of lawn was brown in spots, and a stunted orange tree was slowly expiring from heat and lack of water. Brilliant red bougainvillea grew lush and wild along the side of the place, though, loving the sun and twining thick tendrils into the peeling lattice. The white latticework in front, on each side of the door, also needed paint, and was broken here and there as if someone had kicked it. The pink-and-white-striped metal awning over the front door was rusty and canted at a sideways angle.

Carver started to ring the bell but saw there was only a

rust-rimmed hole where the pushbutton used to be, so he knocked three times with the crook of his cane. The rapping sounded muffled and distant in the sultry air. He felt dizzy for a second, his ears buzzing.

The woman who opened the door was about forty, overweight, with bushy, carrot-colored hair and red-rimmed blue eyes. A large wart thrived on the left side of her nose, just above the nostril. She seemed almost to have expected Carver to knock on her door; must have seen him roaming around the Renway trailer. Her eyes took a trip down him, saw the cane, then peered into his eyes curiously and intently. Hers were infinitely sad eyes, deep with self-pity and defeat and yearning. *Are you one of us?* The world's victims have a quiet understanding and recognition of each other; they're resigned to fate and to permanent membership in the losers' club. They want pity from each other. Mock understanding. Most of all, they want to be reassured that it wasn't their fault, any of it. It was somebody else's fault. Or it was bad, bad luck. *I'm not one of you,* he screamed at her with his eyes. *I haven't given up and never will!* She got the message, he could tell. A flicker of respect, then her eyes became shallow and concealing ponds of blue, her features set.

He said, "I was looking for Bert Renway. Know where I can find him?"

"Not if he ain't home."

"You Mrs. Hataris?"

"*Ms.* Hataris." She drew it out, pronouncing it "Mizzz." The rancid odor of stale perspiration hit him. It was hot inside the trailer. Getting hotter as she stood there with the door open.

"I'm Frank Carter, an old friend of Bert's." Carver smiled at her. He had a beautiful smile for such a fierce-looking man, and she seemed to relax somewhat. Her fleshy body, clad in shorts and a white halter, appeared to become a few inches shorter and much heavier as the tenseness left it. Had she thought he was a salesman or bill collector? He wasn't selling aluminum siding, that was for sure.

Now that she knew he wasn't going to give her problems, she was more prone to talk, though she wasn't about to invite him in out of the sun. "Mr. Renway ain't been home for weeks, you ask me. Car ain't budged an inch. Not so far as I can tell, anyways." In the dimness behind her, Carver saw a child's small plastic push toy, one of those clear globes in which colored balls dance when the wheels turn. He wondered what it was like for a child, growing up in this sun-blasted metal box in Beach Cove Court with a mother like Mizz Hataris.

He said, "You mean Bert just disappeared? Didn't tell anyone where he was going?"

"Well, that's a little strong, I'd say. He didn't tell *me*, anyways. And I'd be the logical person he would tell, so I could keep an eye on his place. It ain't that I'm nosy, but there ain't a goddamn thing to look at out my window but Mr. Renway's trailer. I ain't seen him around, and like I said, his car ain't—" Her eyes got wide. "Say, you don't think he's inside? I mean, somethin' happened to him?"

"I don't think so," Carver assured her. "I looked in the windows and could tell there was no one there."

"His wife, Ella, died a while back," Willa Hataris said. "Damned fine woman. Peppery little thing. When she was alive they was always on the go. Drivin' here, drivin' there. Gettin' enjoyment outa what time they had left. Nice old couple, you know?"

"Yeah," Carver said. "It's a shame this happened."

"This?"

"The wife dying, I mean."

"Did you know her too, Mr. Carter?"

"No, didn't know Ella. Knew Bert from when we worked for the railroad up north. I was driving through and thought I'd stop by and see him." A mosquito droned around his face, tried to flit up his nostril. He brushed it away. God, he was hot! Wished this conversation was over.

"Well," she said, "maybe you can catch up with him if you're gonna be around the area a while. But I can tell you, been quiet as a tomb over there at his place till this morning." She leaned heavily on the metal doorjamb, trying not to smile. She had cast bait and was waiting for him to snap it up, show she had control of the situation. Carver was beginning to dislike Willa Hataris.

He took the hook. "What did you see this morning?"

"These fellas went in the Renway trailer, stayed a while, then come back outside and drove away. 'Bout seven thirty, I'd say it was."

Carver moved closer to her. "How many fellas? And what'd they look like?"

"Two of 'em. A black guy and one that appeared like he was maybe Cuban. They had on nice suits, drove up in a gray car. I don't think they was cops, 'cause they sorta looked around and moved like they didn't really belong there, you know? Cops'd walk right up big and loud as you please, but not these two. They weaseled around outside a few minutes, then they let themselves into the trailer."

"With a key?"

"I dunno. Coulda been."

Or they were pros who knew how to slip cheap locks, Carver thought. "How long were they inside?"

"I'd say fifteen, twenty minutes. Listen, *you* ain't a cop, are you? I mean, is somethin' wrong over there?"

"I'm not police, I swear to you. If I was, I'd have to show you my ID, follow the rules. These two men, you remember what kinda car they were in?"

She didn't answer immediately. If Carver wasn't police, who was he really? she was wondering. But it didn't matter much to her; she wanted to talk, after all, and she seemed satisfied he meant Renway no harm. Not if he knew nothing about the early-morning visitors, men she'd decided definitely weren't police. "Make of car, you mean? Naw. Kinda squarish, newer car. Medium-size. 'Bout all I can tell you. Not one of them shoebox foreign jobs. Anybody buy one of them don't know what it's like bein' outa work. Oughta leave this country and go to some foreign place and eat raw fish and get a job buildin' cars."

"I'll say. Can you give me a better description of the two men?"

"Oh, not really. I seen 'em from a distance, of course. They both looked sorta tall. The Cuban one was slim, kinda the dandy. The black guy was heavier. Muscular. Fulla energy and looked all business, like Jesse Jackson pissed off. What I remember about 'em both, they was kinda grim. I could tell that even from here."

"Were they carrying anything when they came out?"

"Naw. Neither in nor out. Seemed like they just went in, maybe looked around a while or sat waiting for Renway, then out they came and drove away. All there was to it. You think they're friends of Renway's he gave a key to, or what?"

"It could be that," Carver said.

"Thought as much, Mr. Carter."

He thanked her for her help and then set the tip of his cane and backed away. When he was halfway to his car, he twisted his torso and looked back at her. Saw her fade into the dimness of her trailer and close the door.

She was watching, he was sure, as he lowered himself into the Olds and drove away into the merciless glaring day. She'd probably seen the old, rusty car when he'd arrived, and figured from the first he wasn't a cop. She was a woman who'd know.

On the highway, heading south toward Fort Lauderdale, he sat in the beating turmoil of hot wind and thought about what Willa Hataris had told him. The Cuban she'd described was probably Ralph Palmer, who'd contacted and hired Renway. Whoever had hired Renway knew he was dead. Murdered. They no doubt wanted to make sure there was nothing in his mobile home that might lead the police to them—when the police inevitably discovered it wasn't Frank Wesley but Renway in the burned-out Cadillac. Covering their asses, all right.

At least two people other than McGregor and Carver were aware of the Renway-for-Wesley exchange: the black man and Ralph Palmer. Carver thought the reason for the impersonation itself would be simple enough and so should be relatively easy to discover.

He didn't realize he was wrong about that.

Didn't realize the Olds was being followed by two men in a medium-size gray Dodge.

Chapter 7

Carver checked into the Carib Terrace late that afternoon. He'd stayed there before; the woman behind the desk, who owned the motel with her husband, seemed to recognize him. She asked if he wanted a corner room for the price of one of the smaller inside units. Carver said sure. She smiled and gave him a registration card to fill out, then handed him a key attached to a large red plastic tag. With a glance at his cane, she asked if he needed help with his luggage. He told her no thanks, trying not to let his irritation show. Telling himself not to take offense—for all the woman knew, he was traveling with a steamer trunk.

His room was on the southeast corner on the first floor. The Carib Terrace, one of the smaller motels on Ocean Boulevard, had only two stories. Each room had a view of the private beach and the rolling Atlantic. On the Ocean Boulevard side of the building was a small heated swimming pool that smelled strongly of chlorine. Two preschool kids were splashing around in the shallow end. A slim, tan woman in a red two-piece bathing suit was lying on her side on a large yellow beach towel keeping an eye on them. She averted her gaze for a second to take in Carver as he limped past her toward his room, carrying his scuffed leather suitcase. She made it a point to turn quickly away from him, as if he'd insulted her. He told himself he'd appealed to her and she resented it, but he didn't really know. Who understood women except other women? Prince?

The room was large, with a small kitchen equipped with a compact white refrigerator and stove. The sink was stainless steel and tiny and had a dripping faucet. Deep red carpet spread to a king-size bed near wide glass doors that led to a patio and a couple of blue plastic-webbed lounge chairs. Beyond that was a strip of barren ground and then the gently sloping beach and the ocean.

The sun was bright out there, glancing off the sand and shooting silver shafts of light off the incoming waves. Made the room seem all the dimmer and cooler. A middle-aged guy in loud striped trunks was walking at an angle toward the beach. Two striding young girls in string bikinis crossed his path and he sucked in his stomach and held it until they were past. A lot of effort for nothing; it was obvious the girls were busy talking and hadn't noticed him anyway. A short woman with lank wet hair, leading a sand-caked four- or five-year-old girl up from the beach, trudged toward the motel. A tired-looking man carrying a wad of white towels, and what appeared to be an inflated life-size plastic alligator under his arm, followed a few steps behind. The woman had on floppy rubber thongs, and her heels kicked up roostertails of sand; the man stayed well back and to the side to avoid them. She and the girl were both smiling and talking to each other. Family. Carver wondered what it would be like to have family around him every day. They veered slightly about fifty feet from his room. He heard the rumble of a sliding door. Then the woman's laughter as they entered the room next door. The faint sound of the little girl bitching about something and tromping around. The father's deep and reprimanding voice as he controlled his temper. A minute later the shower burst on and hissed and gurgled in the bathroom that shared a wall with Carver's. The woman's voice, and the little girl's. Laughing. Sand being washed off. Family.

Carver hefted his suitcase onto the bed and opened it. Got out pants and shirts and arranged them loosely in the closet so the wrinkles would hang out. Then he carried his shaving kit into the bathroom and set it on the washbasin. He left socks, underwear, and miscellaneous in the suitcase. Since he didn't know how long he'd be staying, there was no point in unpacking; it was, after all, only a drive of a few hours north on Highway 1 back to Del Moray.

He closed the suitcase and fastened the clasps, then placed it on the floor alongside the dark wood dresser. Sat on the edge of the bed and looked around. Home. At least for a while.

Leaving his cane leaning on the bed, he used furniture and the wall for support and limped over and pulled the cord that drew the heavy drapes closed. Sound from outside was muted and the room became almost dark.

He made his way back to the bed and stretched out on it on his back, lacing his fingers behind his head. Listened to the noises of the family next door. Missed his daughter. Missed his son, who'd been dead a little over a year now. Lump-in-the-throat time. He tried to push aside his emotions, but it wasn't easy. Wasn't entirely possible. Ever.

The mattress was softer than he would have liked, but it didn't prevent him from finally dozing off.

When he awoke the room was completely dark and seemed cooler. He could hear the surf smashing away at the beach, over and over, ticking away eternity. The swells building size and momentum offshore and roaring in with freight-train speed to spend themselves in spreading white foam on the sand. There were unintelligible voices outside. Laughter. People walking nearby? More likely it was sound carried up from the moonlit beach by the ocean breeze. A distant gull, or perhaps a woman, screeched with a wild kind of joy and then was silent.

Carver glanced at his watch's luminous green dial. Nine forty-five. It wasn't like him to sleep at all during the day, much less almost six hours. His eyes felt grainy and there was a sour taste in his mouth. His tongue was coated and seemed swollen; he was sure he'd have difficulty if called upon to speak. No matter, he'd have nothing to say anyway; his mind was sluggish and didn't want to engage gears.

He swiveled his body, shoving his stiff leg with both arms as if it were a completely lifeless appendage, and managed to sit up on the sagging edge of the too-soft mattress. There was a slight ache in the small of his back. No surprise there.

He switched on the lamp, then located his cane. Limped into the bathroom and splashed cold water over his face. Saw that he needed a shave but decided not to take the trouble. His shirt looked as if it had been wadded up and pressed in a vise, so he peeled it off and got a fresh one from the closet and slipped it on. The clean cotton was cool and soothing against his flesh. Made him feel like giving a detergent testimonial.

When he left his room he saw action in the swimming pool. The kid he'd seen earlier coming up from the beach with her family was straddling the inflatable plastic alligator, windmilling her arms in the water so her mother had to squint and turn away to keep chlorine out of her eyes. The mother glanced back during a moment of calm and the kid got her. Carver smiled. He wasn't sure why.

He *was* sure he was hungry.

After lowering the canvas top on the Olds, he backed the car out of its parking slot onto Ocean Boulevard and drove to the Harp and Shamrock, an Irish pub he knew over on the North Federal Highway.

A thin blond man with a guitar and a beautiful tenor voice sang sad Irish songs while Carver had a hamburger, french fries, and a draft Guinness. He thoroughly enjoyed the calorie-laden fare, and was glad his therapeutic swimming meant he had no problem controlling his weight. After he'd finished eating, he stayed through a haunting song about Galway Bay. He had no idea where Galway Bay was.

Halfway through "Danny Boy," he left and drove through the steamy night back to Ocean Boulevard, the Galway Bay melody still playing through his mind. It was eleven o'clock.

After parking the Olds in the lot of a strip shopping center, he limped across Ocean and made his way down the street toward Frank Wesley's condo. Traffic was still heavy on the seaside avenue, and the rushing sound of passing cars was almost indistinguishable from the sibilant breaking of the surf on the beach behind the towering buildings. There was a depressing sameness to the pale high-rise structures: identical rows of windows and balconies, like stacked ice-cube trays illuminated by floodlights.

Wesley's building, Highcliff Tower, had no doorman, which made things easier.

Carver pushed in through the tinted-glass doors and crossed pale blue tile and then royal blue carpeting to the elevators. The only other people in the lobby were a man and a woman over by a huge potted fern, interested in each other and nothing else. Humming the song about Galway Bay, Carver rode the elevator alone to the fifteenth floor. Limped silently along a carpeted, powder blue hall to the white door marked *15K*. Wesley's unit.

He wished he'd gotten that duplicate key before Renway had been blown up in the Caddie, but life—and death—were seldom so accommodating. He was no good at picking locks, so he'd simply kick the door open with his powerful good leg and trust that if anyone noticed the noise they'd assume it was something other than a door being forced.

Do it fast, he told himself. *Do it to it.* Automatically, before rearing back to let fly his kick, he tried the doorknob. Found the door unlocked.

Damned odd.

He should have known better than to enter. But he stood for a moment with the knob completely rotated to the right, then swung the door open and edged inside into cool darkness. Located the smooth plastic light switch on the sandpaper-rough wall and flipped it upward.

A lamp winked on.

Next to a black leather sofa.

The handsome Latin man seated on the sofa with his tan suitcoat draped across his lap looked over at Carver. Didn't seem surprised that the lamp had come on, even though he'd been sitting there in the dark.

Carver caught movement in the corner of his vision. A black man, about six feet tall and built blocky beneath his well-cut blue suit, stood leaning with his back against the wall. The movement Carver had glimpsed was when the man had uncrossed his arms and lowered them to his sides. They were still swinging in short, lazy arcs, his thick fingers loosely curled. Very relaxed. Very ready. He wore a diamond pinkie ring on his right hand. It caught the light and sent it glimmering in a tightly focused, dancing pattern over the wall.

Leaning on his cane with both hands, Carver put on the innocent act. Let his initial surprise linger on his face as he pretended to glance back at the number on the still-open door. "Say, I'm sorry. I was looking for Frank Wesley. Isn't this his apartment?"

The Hispanic on the sofa smiled and moved the suitcoat off his lap just far enough to reveal the blue-steel revolver he was holding. Said, "Yes and no."

The black guy said, "You're letting the air conditioning out, Carver. Shut the door. Stay on this side of it."

Carver did both those things. Heard the latch click behind him, metal against metal.

It sounded like the cocking mechanism of a gun.

Chapter 8

〰 The black guy did remind Carver of Jesse Jackson, only heavier and broader through the shoulders. Thicker, rougher features. A blue-black scar that slanted through a dark eyebrow. He squared around and took a step toward Carver. Moved with a hint of shuffle, as if he might have done some serious boxing. Said, "The position, you."

Carver knew what he meant but said, "Huh?" Innocent Joe Citizen. Dunno from nothin'.

"Lean against the wall with both hands and spread your legs. Pretend you're standing there gonna take a piss free-handed, 'cause maybe you will. Cop that never made anyone assume the position, is it? Don't smartass us, Carver."

Carver obeyed, keeping the cane in his right hand, pressing it against the wall to prevent it from dropping. The Latino stayed seated on the sofa, watching it all with mild interest, as if it were something on television. He kept the gun in his lap aimed at a point on the floor. Carver figured he was probably Ralph Palmer, but he couldn't be sure.

His black partner kicked Carver's bad leg out to the side so his feet were spread wider. Wide enough to put strain on his groin. Then the partner gave Carver a very skillful patting down. "Ain't carrying," he said to his buddy on the couch.

"You'd think he would be, a private detective," the Latino said. He had a trace of Spanish accent. Cuban, Carver thought. "Some dangerous occupation."

"How about it?" said the one who'd searched Carver. "How is it you're clean?"

"Private investigators don't wander around armed like commandos. What do you think this is, a novel? Read Robert Parker books, if that kinda stuff suits you."

"He's got him some smart mouth," the Latino said.

The man behind Carver said, "Probably his smarts don't go any higher'n that, though. Dumb from the nose up."

"Gotta be," said the voice from the sofa. "Otherwise he wouldn't be here."

"Why don't I straighten up and turn around?" Carver asked. "You know I'm not carrying." He rapped with the cane on the wall. "Bad leg's starting to get sore."

"Sympathy ain't in our line," the black guy said.

"Aw, let him turn around," sofa chimed in. "He don't figure to rabbit on us. What he'd do, he'd fall and bust his ass."

"I wouldn't mind," the black one said. "In fact, that's something I'd like to see. So you go ahead, stand up and turn around, Carver."

Carver pushed away from the wall, caught his balance with the cane, and turned to face the two men. He didn't like this. He was scared, but he had control of himself. Thinking objectively. He said, "You know my name, but I don't know yours."

"Not necessary," said the black one. "This ain't a tea social."

"Business, then," Carver said. He wondered if he could

whack the gun out of the Hispanic's hand with his cane, snatch it up before the black guy could drag his gun out of the shoulder holster bulging beneath his tailored blue suit-coat. Doubted it, but things might come down to having to try.

"That's right, business."

"What are you doing here?" the one on the sofa asked. "And please spare us any bullshit."

"I told you, I came to see Frank Wesley."

"You and him friends?"

"More or less."

"It's less now," the man said. "Wesley's dead. Went boom in his car, right near your office in Del Moray."

"A shock to hear that," Carver said.

The black one scowled; he was meaner-looking than Jesse Jackson ever thought of being. "Remember what I said about trying to jive us, Carver. We know Wesley drove to your office yesterday, talked to you for about half an hour, then came out and did his bang-and-burn act."

"Convincing act," Carver said. Thinking, if these two knew that much, they might have been the ones who planted the bomb in the Cadillac. Almost had to be them. Not a reassuring thought.

The black one smiled, knowing what was running through Carver's mind. He said, "The bomb was set off by electronic signal, most likely from a garage-door opener. The explosives mighta been on board the car for a month."

"You sound sure of that."

"I am. We knew about Wesley. Knew about his car."

"Except for the bomb."

"You're right, that was a surprise. More of a surprise to Wesley, though."

"So you didn't plant the bomb?"

"Something for you to wonder about, Carver. Maybe we got somebody rigging plastic explosives right now in that pile of shit you got parked down off Ocean Boulevard."

"Why would you be so mean?"

"Because we don't know what Wesley told you."

"Ah!"

"But we want to know. And it's time for you to tell us."

The Latino said, "Soon it'll be past time. You don't want that. Really." He was laconic but sounded concerned for Carver's safety. Carver doubted his sincerity. Who were these two? What did *they* know? One thing they didn't seem to know was that Bert Renway, and not Wesley, had been killed in the explosion. Whatever story he told them, he thought it should ring true when the police lab established the identity of the real victim.

"We're busy men," the black one said. He made a show of rotating his wrist in a neat, quick movement so his white cuff rode up and he could glance at his watch. "We're late for night surfing right now. Best you commence to chat."

"Wesley came to my office to hire me," Carver said. "He was uneasy. He thought somebody might be driving around impersonating him."

The black one grinned wide and white. "You sure fulla shit, my man." A parody of ghetto slang. Letting Carver know that while he'd become sophisticated beyond street smarts, still he was unpredictable and dangerous. Not to be messed with unless you were prepared to pay the price.

The Latino muttered something in Spanish, then stood up from the sofa. He was tall and slim. Stood calmly with his arms loose, his left hand resting atop his right one at his crotch, the right holding the blue-steel revolver pointed at the floor. In a gentle and reasonable voice he said, "If Frank Wesley was your client, he's dead and you're unemployed.

So how come you're down here instead of minding your business in Del Moray?"

"Curiosity, I guess."

"You and the cat," the black guy said, no longer grinning.

Carver thought a little offense might be in order. He tried to put some indignation into his voice. "Are you guys friends of Wesley?"

"Get this," the black one said, grinning again. "*He's* asking *us* questions."

"Don't know protocol," the Latino said softly, not moving. "Got himself all tangled up."

The black one glared at Carver. "This ain't fuckin' 'Love Connection,' Carver. We ask, you answer. Know why?"

"Something to do with guns?"

"That's it, all right. Now, here's a question. What address did Wesley give you?"

"This one. His condo."

"He tell you why anyone might be going around pretending to be him?"

"He had no idea. That's why he hired me."

Now the black one drew a gun from his shoulder holster, a .38 revolver. He assumed a shooting stance, feet spread wide, aiming the gun with both hands at Carver's forehead. He said, "So you been hired. Now, you gonna be fired, or is it gonna be Smith and Wesson here?"

Carver swallowed loud enough for everyone to hear. "I suppose you're right, I'm no longer working for Mr. Wesley."

"That's how it is. 'Cause there is no more Mr. Wesley. As of this moment, consider yourself unemployed as regards Frank Wesley or anything having to do with Frank Wesley."

Carver stared into the steady dark tunnel of the gun's bore and felt fear grow in his bowels like a cold thing with claws.

"I'll consider your little speech my pink slip." His voice was higher than he'd intended; irritation that he'd revealed his vulnerability wormed through his fear.

The Latino was studying him with calm, somber dark eyes. With a faintly sad expression, he raised his revolver and poked it into a belt holster on his right hip. A Spanish Wyatt Earp.

"You got no business here," the black one said to Carver. He didn't holster his gun, held it as if it were locked onto Carver with radar.

"Then I suppose I better leave," Carver said tentatively. Damned if he'd say please.

Somehow without moving the gun, the black man shrugged. How'd he do that? "Ain't nothing to keep you here, Carver. Nothing to make you come back. Wouldn't you say?"

"I'd say."

"We got us an understanding?"

"I'd say that, too."

"Go back to following wayward spouses, that kinda thing," the Latino said. "Live longer, man. Maybe even get prosperous, you peek through the right keyhole."

"Don't trip and fall on your way out," the black one said.

Carver turned, limped to the door, and opened it. Trying not to hurry. Salvage a shred of dignity.

The tenseness left his back muscles only after he was in the hall and had closed the door behind him. Out on the sidewalk, he found himself hurrying to where the Olds was parked. Worked up a sweat.

He drove back to the Carib Terrace and locked his door. Wedged a chair under the knob. Made sure the sliding glass door to the patio and beach was locked.

Then he got undressed and went to bed, and was vaguely surprised to feel himself relax.

He knew if the two men in Wesley's condo had wanted him dead, he'd already be dead. They gave the impression they were experienced. Experts at their work. The fact that he was still alive meant they wouldn't come around to see him again unless they thought he hadn't been scared off the case.

Repeating that comforting thought like a mantra, he fell asleep.

In the morning he showered and dressed, then checked out of the motel.

He had a breakfast of waffles, bacon, and freshly squeezed orange juice at a coffee shop on Ocean Boulevard.

It was quiet in the coffee shop, and narrow-slatted blinds were angled to deflect the brilliant morning sun. Carver took his time eating. The food tasted terrific, maybe because he was so glad he was still alive to enjoy it.

When he was finished, he ordered a second cup of coffee and unfolded the Fort Lauderdale newspaper he'd bought at the vending machine outside. Accidentally laid it in some spilled syrup and moved it aside.

A follow-up story on the Del Moray car bombing was at the bottom of page three. That was because there wasn't much in the way of new information.

Only that the victim had been positively identified from dental records as Frank Wesley.

Chapter 9

Though it was only one in the afternoon, it seemed like dusk in Carver's office. The broken window had been boarded up and would be replaced tomorrow. Apparently there was a rash of broken windows in Del Moray, according to the management company that leased Carver's office. So for the time being he had to make do with a sheet of rough plywood lettered BILL'S BOARD-UP instead of glass. It made the office gloomy and claustrophobic.

Even more claustrophobic when the towering, lanky form of McGregor strolled in. The glow of the desk lamp was projected at an upward angle on his long face and made him look even more grotesque than in natural light. A sort of stretched-out Lon Chaney in *Phantom of the Opera*. His cheap brown suitcoat was flapping open, his red tie was loosely knotted, and there were dark perspiration stains around his unbuttoned collar. He didn't look happy.

He said, "Jesus H. Christ, it's hot in here."

"Just seems that way," Carver said. "Because of the window being boarded up."

"The way your landlord jumped to fix the place, you must really have some clout."

"I paid the rent," Carver said. "That oughta be clout enough to have a window."

"That's just how jerk-offs like you think." McGregor puckered his lips as if he might spit. But he didn't. Surprising. "Ninety-fuckin'-five degrees outside and I figured if I had to talk to an asshole like you it'd at least be cool in your office; instead you give me this." He waved a long, encompassing arm; looked as if he might touch the opposite wall. "Damned wreck of a sweatbox."

"Humble but home," Carver said, kind of enjoying McGregor's discomfort.

"Would be home to a shrimp-brain like you." McGregor stood with his fists on his hips in front of Carver's desk. Glanced left and right and said, "Least you picked up around the place. Or do you have maid service?"

"Janitor service," Carver said, "but I did my own neatening up this time."

"Ain't you exactly the type?" McGregor peeled off his suitcoat, revealing his shoulder-holstered Police Special, and dark crescents of perspiration on his shirt below his armpits. No deodorant was a match for him. The movement of air he stirred up brought the unwashed scent of him to Carver. Carver's stomach lurched and the faint ringing in his ears began again. "Let's get to why I came here," McGregor hissed through the space between his front teeth. "You said on the phone you had something to tell me. So get fuckin' talking. And you better explain to me how it is the autopsy report says the guy got blown up in the Caddie actually was Frank Wesley and not Bert Renway, like you said. Play goddamn games with me, shithead, you're gonna lose hard."

Carver felt a rush of disgust, not just directed at McGregor, but also at himself for being involved with the unethical police lieutenant. Carver had taken police work seriously, and, maybe naïvely, had seen it as a service to a beleaguered society. McGregor took only McGregor seriously and saw his job as a service only to himself, at any cost to anyone else. Justice was something to be avoided; she was blindfolded and might trample anyone.

Swiveling in his desk chair, Carver switched on the plastic electric fan on the nearby file cabinet. It gave a low hum and rattle and began to oscillate. The fan was a cheap one without a place to oil the motor. He wondered how long it would last.

McGregor flashed his gap-toothed smile. "Whazza matter, fuckface? I thought you said it was cool enough in this shoebox you call an office."

Carver said, "It is. But this puts me upwind of you."

Not at all insulted, McGregor widened his smile. Got his tongue into the act by thrusting it to peek between his front teeth like a curious pink viper. "You saying I forgot my Right Guard?"

"You smell as corrupt as you are," Carver told him.

Unfazed, McGregor said, "Corrupt, huh? Maybe your price ain't been offered yet. So what? Everybody's corrupt, dumbshit. Even preachers'll tell you that. How they make their living. Original fuckin' sin and all." He crossed his long arms. "You and me are part of the same ooze, Carver. Difference is, you pretend otherwise. If you want your delusions, okay. Just don't bore me with 'em. Hypocritical fuckers like you make me wanna puke all over myself."

"Who'd notice?"

McGregor loomed closer and sat on the edge of the desk, still with his arms crossed. Something about his posture reminded Carver of a perched and waiting vulture. The rancid stench of the man was almost overwhelming. He said, "Sooner we get to the point, sooner I'll be outa your office. Unless you'd rather keep trying to convince yourself you're somehow better'n me."

McGregor was right about getting the conversation over as

quickly as possible, Carver thought. He tried not to think about what else McGregor had said, afraid he might be right about that, too.

Carver told him what had happened in Fort Lauderdale at Frank Wesley's condo. Gave him a description of the two men with guns who'd been waiting in the dark when the door opened.

When he was finished, McGregor bowed his head. Rubbed his long chin with his thumb and said, "You mean you got no idea who those two guys were?"

"The Latin one might be Ralph Palmer, the man who hired Bert Renway. Why don't you check out the name, see if there's a sheet on him?"

"Don't tell me how to do my job, Carver. But do tell me why you said the body in the Caddie was Renway's. Way it looks here, everything you said the day of the bombing was bullshit. It was Frank Wesley came to hire you and then got himself killed in his car despite his seat belt being buckled."

"I thought you could tell me something about that," Carver said. "What happened in here just before the bombing went exactly the way I said. The man who hired me told me his name was Bert Renway."

"And gave you cash, but you weren't suspicious."

"You get cash often in this business," Carver said.

"I just bet."

"And I went by Renway's mobile home out west of town. Place called Beach Cove Court. Nobody was home. The grass needed cutting. His neighbor hasn't seen him in weeks and says his car hasn't moved."

"I went by there, too," McGregor said. "You see a beach or a cove out there?"

Carver said he hadn't.

The tall man thoughtfully picked at his nose for a moment. Examined his fingernail and decided there was nothing stuck under it. "Renway ain't been around, like you say. But then, apparently neither has Wesley."

"You see the autopsy report on Wesley?"

"No," McGregor said. "They carted what was left of the corpse down to Miami, where they got the lab facilities to make sense outa that kinda mess. But it was dental records proved the body was Wesley. Dental records don't lie. So Wesley must have lied to you."

"It looks that way," Carver admitted. "He came here and gave me a story about Renway impersonating him. But why? And where's Renway?"

"Maybe you forgot, those are the kinda things you're supposed to find out. You was even paid to find out. It'd look sorta funny if I went pokin' around in it, at least in areas where you can snoop. You and me are the only ones that know about the Renway story. That's not the kinda thing I'm expected to keep to myself. On the other hand, you got the permission of the law to investigate."

"Want to put that permission in writing?" Carver asked.

"No need," McGregor said, waving a long-fingered hand in a languid gesture of dismissal. "Old buddies like us, we trust each other, hey?"

"I don't have to trust you," Carver said. He absently laid a hand on his recently repaired answering machine–tape recorder. Patted cool plastic.

McGregor looked at the hand. Said, "What's that supposed to mean?"

Carver didn't answer. Let the bastard think about it. Let him wonder if Carver had recorded their initial conversation about the car bombing.

"Both our asses will be in a sling if you got anything on tape," McGregor said. "If I threatened you and tried to influence you, you shoulda reported it, not cooperated. Just remember that."

"And you remember cooperation works both ways. Get with Records and see what you can find out about Ralph Palmer, then pass it on to me."

McGregor stood up straight. Stretched his arms so his fingertips almost touched the ceiling. Then he exhaled loudly, hitched up his pants, and tucked in his shirt. Said, "Why is it I gotta get mixed up with shitbums like you?"

"What do you expect? You got no friends."

"You don't either, Carver, you only think so. If they see they can use you, comes time to shit or get off the pot, they'll shit—and all over you."

"You the exception?" Carver asked.

"There are no exceptions." McGregor smiled lewdly and sort of swung his weight across the small office to the door. Long legs covering the distance in two steps. Maybe flaunting his mobility in front of Carver. "Could be I'll get back to you, Carver."

He went out, still smiling, leaving a wake of cheap perfumy cologne polluting the thick air.

Carver sat for a minute thinking about how things were breaking. Realizing McGregor was right, it *was* hot in the office. Maybe the explosion had somehow screwed up the air-conditioning unit on the roof.

The lieutenant wasn't somebody to underestimate, Carver reminded himself. Nobody was, if they possessed the ambition of Napoleon and the scruples of Attila the Hun.

He stared at the rough blank surface of the plywood covering the window, remembering the noise and shock of the explosion. The spray of broken glass. The contorted black thing behind the burning Cadillac's steering wheel.

He sat forward in his chair and dragged the phone across the desk. Lifted a pencil and pecked out a number with the eraser.

It was time to confide in someone about his arrangement with McGregor.

Chapter 10

Edwina said, "I heard on the news it was actually Frank Wesley who got killed outside your office."

They were seated at the white metal table on the brick veranda. Carver was facing the ocean, looking beyond her at a cluster of colorful triangular sails out near the horizon. They were all banked at precisely the same angle into the wind and seemed to move only gradually. Big boats, maybe competing in some sort of regatta. He expected they were making their way across the wavering blue carpet of sea toward the Del Moray port, on the final leg of their course. North of them, closer to shore, a large trawler plowed its way out to sea. Commerce and play. A cloud of gulls circled gnatlike behind the trawler, no doubt feeding on jettisoned garbage.

"Fred, you hear me?"

"Yeah," Carver said. "Sorry."

"So it was really Wesley who hired you? Gave you a phony story?"

"Looks that way."

"Know why he did it?"

"Not yet."

He looked at her obliquely as he spoke, as if not wanting to acknowledge her presence. She'd come home for the afternoon but was going back out soon to meet a client. Something about helping to arrange a mortgage loan. Relaxing now, she sipped a gin-and-lemonade from a tall glass, the breeze toying with her long auburn hair. The same breeze that was propelling the sailboats, larger now, toward shore. One with a tall yellow sail had broken from the pack and was well in the lead. There was some sort of design on the sail, but he couldn't make it out. A skull and crossbones?

Edwina said, "I sense in you a certain reticence." She was smiling at him as she set down her glass in its ring of moisture on the table, causing ice cubes to clink faintly.

Carver was drinking beer out of the can. Budweiser. He lifted the can and said, "It's better you don't know anything else about this. It's more complicated than I thought."

"By that you mean more dangerous?"

"That, too." He took a swig of beer. Backhanded cold foam from his upper lip. *You'd think by now they'd have come up with a better design for openings in beer cans.* "Somebody oughta write a letter."

"About what?"

"Openings in beer cans. How to make them so they don't dribble beer when you tilt the can."

"You use a glass, that solves it."

"Yeah, I suppose. Or maybe the cans are okay and it's my lip that's the problem."

"Or maybe you're being evasive because you don't want to involve me beyond a certain point in this case."

"Best if you don't get involved."

"I don't mind. What you do for a living, you need somebody to talk to now and then. I want that somebody to be me."

He sighed. Smiled at her. Knew she was right about that part of it, but she still underestimated the danger.

"You glad you're working out of an office now and not the house?"

"If I'd still been using this place as my office," he told her, "Wesley would have been blown up over there in the driveway. Blast mighta taken down part of the house."

Her face got tight and pale. She hadn't thought of that. A trickle of perspiration ran down her cheek right in front of her ear, then down her neck, leaving a shimmering track. Beautiful women didn't sweat, they glistened.

"So, yeah," he said, "I'm glad I'm working out of the office. It's a shitty business sometimes. That's why the less you're connected with what I'm doing, the better off we both are."

She looked at him, her gray eyes serious and her smooth fighting chin jutting out at an almost jaunty angle. Sometimes she could look as strong-willed as she was. She'd exorcised some formidable internal demons, and not much that came at her from the outside scared her anymore. Tough lady. "When you feel like talking to me about it," she told him stubbornly, "you can."

"I know that. I appreciate it. I don't tell you enough how much I appreciate it."

Ice clinked again, musically this time, as she tossed back her head and finished her drink. Grinned with the wetness still on her lips. "Maybe you can show me instead of telling me."

He felt a tightening in the core of him, but he ignored it. Said, "Desoto's due to show up here any minute."

She said, "Good. I feel better if he's involved in whatever it is you're planning."

"I'm not planning anything," Carver said. "Just trying to puzzle out and muddle through. Keep McGregor off my ass and hang on to my investigator's license."

"Would McGregor really make that kind of trouble for you?"

"Sure. The way he gets his jollies."

"But you and he are in this together; it takes two to have an agreement."

"I can't prove he's involved. His word against mine."

"But if it really was Wesley in his car, and he lied to you about his identity, how can McGregor harm you? What's he got for leverage?"

"The fact that the man who was murdered right outside my office was my client, and I neglected to mention it to the police. Any way you turn it, it's still withholding evidence in a homicide investigation."

"Can he prove that?"

"Somebody can. Somebody else knows about it. Whoever saw Wesley enter and leave my office. That means McGregor might be able to prove it. So I've gotta keep going on this and get it puzzled out."

She ran her fingertips lightly down the side of her empty glass and said, "You couldn't stop picking at the case anyway, could you?"

"No," he admitted. She knew him too well. The way Laura had. Yet in ways Laura had never dreamed existed.

Tires crunched on gravel, faded to silence. A car door slammed.

"Desoto," Edwina said. She stood up, carrying her empty glass, and ambled over to the wooden gate. Arrived there the same time as Desoto and held the gate open for him. He gave her a peck on the cheek and they talked for a minute or two without looking over at Carver, then Edwina walked toward the house. Desoto watched the elegant sway of her hips with an appreciation so blatant there was an innocence about it. He simply loved women, did Desoto. They loved him back.

Orlando Police Lieutenant Alfonso Desoto strolled through sunlight and shadow toward where Carver was seated at the round white table. He was impeccably dressed as always.

Maybe even slept that way. Tailored cream-colored suit, lavender shirt, mauve tie, black shoes that looked made for dancing. Carver couldn't remember ever seeing him sweat. Gold glittered on his wrists, his fingers, his tie clasp. He was a tall, slim-waisted man with broad shoulders and a large, noble head. Half Mexican and half Italian, he was handsome in the classic Latin manner, with a sharp profile, gentle dark eyes, and sleek black hair the wind never dared to muss. Watching him approach, Carver wondered when he'd stop walking and break into a tango.

He smiled at Carver; perfect white teeth in a gold complexion. "Have I told you that yours is a beautiful woman, *amigo?*"

"Yeah, but you probably told her more often."

Desoto unbuttoned his suitcoat and sat down in the white metal chair opposite Carver's. As he adjusted the chair's position, steel legs scraped noisily over the bricks. He said, "I want to make sure you know you're lucky. That you appreciate her."

"We were just talking about that," Carver said. The scraping of the metal chair legs had started the steady ringing in his ears again. Like a distant tuning fork vibrating. He tried to ignore it, regard it as background noise, like the sound of the sea. "She's aware I appreciate her."

"As it should be," Desoto said. "Women are too often taken for granted. Even women like Edwina. The best things in life we take for granted, you notice?"

"That's because they're the steadiest."

The breeze got under the table's umbrella. Lifted it slightly and snapped the material taut. The umbrella shaft moved with the wind.

"Thanks for coming here," Carver said, changing the subject. "I'd have been glad to drive over to Orlando."

Desoto shrugged. "No trouble. I had police business in Vero Beach, so I was gonna be in the area. Planned on dropping in on you anyway."

Carver nudged his beer can with a knuckle. "Want one of these? Or anything else to drink?"

Desoto shook his head. "Edwina already asked and I told her no thanks." He rested his elbows on the table and folded his hands. Gold cuff links peeked out from beneath his suitcoat sleeves. "I didn't like the way you sounded on the phone. You in some kinda trouble, *amigo?*"

Carver said, "I stepped—or I guess I was pushed—into something nastier and deeper than I suspected." He told Desoto about Wesley-Renway coming to his office, the car bombing, the pressure-forged arrangement with McGregor, the two hard cases in Wesley's condo in Fort Lauderdale.

When he was finished he felt better. Noticed the ringing in his ears had stopped.

Desoto had listened quietly, with a calm, almost melancholy expression on his dark and dramatic features. Then he said, "That McGregor, he's some asshole, eh?"

"He hasn't changed," Carver said. "Still giving ambition a bad name."

"This Renway is still missing?"

"Far as I know. Though nobody's reported him as such. Nobody around who cares, really."

"That's kinda curious, eh? That Wesley would say he's this average-joe kinda guy Renway, living in a trailer here in Del Moray."

"There's a lot I'm curious about," Carver said. "Can you contact somebody in Miami without making ripples?"

"You know I can."

"Find out what there is to know about Wesley. And about a guy named Ralph Palmer. Hispanic, probably Cuban.

About six feet tall, speaks with a slight accent. Handles guns as casually as if they were cooking utensils. I asked Mc-Gregor to check, but you know how that'll go. If he does come up with something it won't reach me, especially if it's valuable information."

"True," Desoto said. "He sees information as currency. He isn't wrong about that, but he wants to hoard it and get rich, spend it only when he can get the most in return. Works for him, up to a point."

Carver grunted agreement. Watched a large egret over the water, sun winking off white wings. You didn't often see egrets around this part of the coast. They were usually farther south toward Lauderdale.

"I'll make the moves," Desoto said. "Call you later this afternoon, probably. Where you gonna be?"

"Most likely my office. I oughta be there when they put in the new window."

"You should ask for Plexiglas instead of regular glass," Desoto said. "It's stronger and doesn't shatter. They use it in the cockpits of military planes. Even machine-gun bullets bounce off the stuff."

"If I thought that was gonna be a factor," Carver said, "I'd order a sheet of steel."

Desoto grinned and leaned back, clasping his hands behind his head and gazing out to sea. The sailboats were nearer to shore and farther south now. Only a few of them were visible around the blue-misted curve of the coast. The trawler was a distant gray form in the haze. A couple of gulls soared and screeched, not flapping their wings at all. Desoto said, "A beautiful spot, here, *amigo*. Beautiful place, beautiful woman. Garden of Eden stuff, eh? You're lucky. You maybe don't wanna fuck around and get the serpent upset."

"McGregor doesn't leave me much choice."

"And you," Desoto said, no longer grinning, "you can't

leave it alone anyway. I know you, Carver; you get your teeth sunk in and can't turn loose. You don't mind my saying so, you're kinda screwy that way."

"Edwina agrees with you."

"Sure she does." Desoto leaned forward again, swinging his hands around from the back of his head. He said, "She's your lover. I'm your friend. We understand you."

There was more truth to that than Carver liked to admit. He glared at Desoto.

Unperturbed, Desoto stared again out at the sea with rapt brown eyes. Said, "You know, I think I'll take that drink now, *amigo*. Anything that's wet and isn't poison."

Carver hadn't gone back to the office. Instead he'd made love slowly and gently to Edwina. Appreciating her.

After she'd left to meet her client, he lay perfectly still on the mussed, sex-scented bed and enjoyed the cool breeze pressing in through the window. Listened to the secretive, repetitive whispers of the ocean. Gossip human ears couldn't sort out. What did the sea know? What had it known for ages?

At eight o'clock that evening Carver answered the phone. Desoto's Southern Bell–processed voice said, "Thought you were gonna be at your office, *amigo*. All I got was your answering machine when I called." There was very faint static on the line, like sandpaper being scraped lightly over wood.

"Changed my plans," Carver said, wishing at that moment that he hadn't gotten the answering machine repaired. "Find out anything?"

"There's no Ralph Palmer with any kind of record," Desoto said. "Guy doesn't exist. Not even as an alias."

"He exists," Carver said.

"The autopsy report on Wesley's very hush-hush for some reason. Probably because Wesley was an important fella. My Miami contact was scared shitless, and that's all he'd say. I found out a couple of things that didn't make the news, though. Wesley was a big-shot businessman from Atlanta, Georgia. Founder and chairman of the board of Wesley Slaughter and Rendering, Incorporated."

"Slaughter and Rendering?" Carver said. "What the hell's that mean?"

"Means they butcher hogs. Something to do with rendering fat from them, among other things. It's a damned big outfit. Gets pigs from all over the South, turns 'em into hams and little pork sausages, then sends 'em to various outlets."

Carver thought that described a slaughterhouse as well as he'd ever heard. A merging of meat and manufacturing.

"I was told Wesley Slaughter and Rendering's the largest and most successful company of its kind south of the Mason-Dixon line," Desoto said. "And that's saying something, 'cause it's a very competitive business."

"Ham-to-ham combat," Carver said.

"Whazzat, *amigo?*"

"Nothing."

"Here's the thing, though," Desoto said. "The condo in Fort Lauderdale's not Wesley's regular address. He lives in Atlanta. The condo's owned by his company. Corporate bigwigs are sent there for vacations from time to time. Executive privilege, eh? Don't it make you wanna run out and buy one of those leather briefcases?"

"What about the car?" Carver asked.

"Mine'd be a BMW."

"I mean Wesley's car."

"The Caddie was a rental leased by the company."

Carver sat quietly trying to digest what he'd been told, wondering what it all meant.

"Any of this help you, *amigo?*"

Carver said, "Hogs, huh?"

Chapter 11

Booking a resevation on a flight into Atlanta on short notice was no problem. Every commercial airline flight that went anywhere in the country seemed to be routed through Hartsfield-Atlanta International Airport. It was to planes what the hive was to bees.

Carver got up early and drove through slanted morning sunlight into Orlando. Left his car in a pay lot and rode a shuttle to the airport. Boarded his plane almost immediately. Sat on the motionless, stifling Boeing 747 for an hour reading the airline magazine over and over, until he was almost ready to send away for the wristwatch with a face for each time zone. Heard the ringing in his ears begin again as finally the engines fired up and the plane taxied out onto the runway and took off. Endured the screams of the infant in the seat in front of him, the boring conversation about industrial couplers from the salesman next to him. Ate some roasted peanuts from a cellophane wrapper. Dribbled coffee on his shirt. Stood in line at the Hertz car-rental counter in Atlanta until he thought his patience or his cane might snap. And by 11:00 A.M. he was checked into the Holiday Inn on Piedmont Road in downtown Atlanta. Simple.

The hotel was a large, sand-colored structure with a high-rise section. Carver was given a room on the fourteenth floor, a pleasant, airy one with a dark green carpet and green flower-print drapes and bedspread. There was a green velvet chair on gold casters. A small sofa. The light wood dresser, writing desk, and nightstands were of the sort that are stamped out at some factory that furnishes all hotels everywhere. The walls were pale beige, as was the spacious, tiled bathroom.

Carver had rented a big Ford Victoria that he could get in and out of easily with his cane. After changing into a clean white shirt, he shrugged into the conservative blue suitcoat that matched his slacks, then knotted a plain maroon tie around his neck. He smiled at his reflection in the mirror over the washbasin; smiling back at him was a bald, middle-aged executive type. Plain vanilla, but with a no-nonsense air about him. Might be midlevel in the company, or might be the guy who could and would fire you on a whim. A real asshole with a country-club membership. Just fine, he thought.

He looked up Wesley Slaughter and Rendering in the phone directory. Then he took the elevator down to the parking garage and drove the big blue Ford out onto Piedmont and away from the downtown area.

He soon found that Atlanta was encompassed by Interstate 285, and an unwary driver could travel in circles until the gas tank hit empty, all the time thinking he was going somewhere other than around.

Carver steered with one hand, held the Hertz road map flat against the seat with the other. Finally he managed to exit from the highway and drove about ten miles before turning onto a narrow road that snaked through Georgia red-clay country. There were low rolling hills here, soft and gentle as the curves of a gracefully lounging woman. In the bright blue sky, distant birds that looked a lot like vultures wheeled on the wind and soared in unpredictable lazy patterns, as if tracing messages in the air.

At the edge of a thick wood was a large metal sign lettered WESLEY SLAUGHTER AND RENDERING, with an arrow pointing up a side road. There were several bullet holes in the sign; the graffiti of high-spirited hunters.

Carver followed the arrow and was on a two-lane concrete road that skirted the woods for about half a mile, then abruptly cut through them. Angled up a slight grade. The sun was suddenly half as bright, as if light were absorbed and hoarded by the surrounding trees. It was quiet inside the car. Carver cracked the window a few inches. It was quiet outside, too. Something about this place; even the songbirds and crickets seemed to prefer elsewhere.

He smelled the slaughter and rendering plant long before he saw it. Up close, the odor must be overpowering.

A huge semi pulling a stake trailer used for hauling livestock loomed around a bend, roared and rattled past him going the other direction, and disappeared from his rearview mirror. The sign on its trailer read MANGLY BROS. PRIME HOGS. FEEDER PIGS.

Carver drove for another few minutes, then braked the Ford to a halt when he saw the sprawling complex on the wide plain below.

The buildings were gray and vast, with flat, corrugated steel roofs broken by chimneys and vent pipes. Behind the largest structure a line of at least twenty boxcars rested on a siding. Along the side of the same building was a row of parallel truck trailers backed to a dock. Here and there among the buildings were fenced rectangular areas crowded with hogs. Hundreds of hogs, milling about and so close together their motion created a wavelike effect. A truck was backed against the chain-link fence of one of the rectangles, and several men were offloading hogs, using what looked like electric prods to hurry the animals down a wooden ramp and through a gate.

Ominous dark smoke hung like a pall above the endless blacktop lot. The afternoon sun glanced off row after row of parked cars, providing the only brightness and color in the scene below. The stench that drifted up to Carver was of warm internal organs and fresh blood, cloying and stomach-jolting. A job was a job, he told himself. Still, he wondered how the employees ever got used to coming here day after day. But he knew that any job created mental calluses; in St. Louis, he'd known slaughterhouse workers who casually drank the blood of slain cattle for nourishment and antibodies to help them fend off colds.

His mouth was full of saliva that tasted bitter. He swallowed. *Yuk!* Licked the same vile taste from his lips.

He pressed the button that raised the car's power window, but as he drove toward what looked like the plant's office, the smell found its way into the car with increasing potency. Hertz would have to hose out the vehicle with disinfectant.

He drove down a narrow dirt road he probably wasn't supposed to be on. Saw dozens of hogs being prodded along through a slanted wooden chute. Workmen in blue denim joked and yelled for the livestock to keep moving toward a shadowy doorway. The wallowing hogs balked, bumping into each other in confusion something like panic, their tiny eyes glittering like diamonds set deep in flesh. Carver didn't like the noises they were making. And there was something different about the smell now that he was much closer, something subtle yet familiar. Then he recognized it; he'd been aware of it in the cramped backseats of police cruisers, in stark interrogation rooms. The undeniable scent of terror. For the first time, he considered becoming a vegetarian.

He circled beyond some new-looking truck trailers lettered with the company name, then parked the Ford in a visitor's slot along the front of a smaller brick building set well apart from the others.

When he climbed out of the car into the heat, the stench of slaughter was even thicker and more acrid. He was surprised to feel weakness in his good knee. This was nauseating. It was like being inside a castaway tire with something a week dead. He smoothed his pants, buttoned his suitcoat, and limped along the walk toward glass double doors that hinted at cool, pure air on the other side.

The smell wasn't nearly as strong in the reception area, but the grim charnel odor of mortality still clung. The crescent-shaped room *was* cool, however, and surprisingly plush. Behind a long desk that was curved to run parallel with the curving, richly paneled wall behind it, sat a slim, gray-haired woman who once must have been a beauty but who'd been assailed by time. She wore oblong glasses with thick dark rims, and Carver was sure that if she removed them and revealed the flesh around her eyes she'd look close to sixty. With the glasses on, a quick glance at her would lead to an estimate of forty. The desk she sat behind was covered in front with the same thick red carpeting that was on the floor, without a break or visible seam, as if the desk had sort of grown up out of the stuff like a mushroom. There were brass-framed modern prints on the unpaneled walls, and on the curved, paneled wall, large gold letters spelled out WESLEY SLAUGHTER AND RENDERING, INC., above three closed doors that Carver assumed led to offices.

As he approached the woman behind the receptionist's desk, she smiled at him and slammed a fist down on a stapler to attach some papers to a sheet of thin cardboard. Her smile and her abrupt action seemed incongruous.

She couldn't do anything about her hands; they were at least sixty. The brass plaque on her desk said her name was Maxine. No last name, just Maxine.

She gazed up at him through the lenses set in the thick frames. They magnified her blue eyes and gave her a fishlike expression that failed to diminish the impression that in her youth she'd been quite a number. But she'd either never learned to put her lipstick on straight or she'd lost the knack. Or perhaps she'd been in a hurry this morning. Her lips were the same violent red as the carpet.

Carver planted his cane in front of her desk, returned her smile, and said, "Boyd Emerson to see Mr. Wesley, Maxine." Nice name, Boyd Emerson. Substantial. The real Boyd Emerson was a con man who died of a heart attack in the patrol car when Carver was in the Orlando Police Department.

The woman's fish eyes didn't blink. The askew red lips said, "I'm not Maxine. She's the regular receptionist."

"Well, can you tell Mr. Wesley I'm here, please?" Carver stopped smiling and glanced at his watch. Busy and important man; no time to fuck with peons.

The woman who wasn't Maxine didn't seem impressed. She said, "I'm afraid that's impossible."

Carver put on a puzzled and annoyed expression. Getting into this acting thing. The Boyd Emerson executive persona. "We had a definite lunch date."

"I see. But—"

"Check his appointment book, can you? Emerson of Longbranch Feeder Pigs."

"I'm sorry, Mr. Emerson, but I don't have to check his appointment book. Mr. Wesley's . . . well, he's passed away."

76

Carver did a shocked expression. Then one of grave concern. Paul Newman, one of his favorites, never did it better. "My God, when was this? I saw him just two weeks ago. He didn't say anything about being ill."

"He wasn't ill," the woman said. "It was a car accident. In Florida."

"Christ, that's terrible. I mean, not that we knew one another all that well. Only met half a dozen times, actually, at this function or that. But he was such a healthy, vital man."

"We're all grieving," the woman said, "as you can well imagine."

"Of course," Carver said, "of course." He stroked his cheek thoughtfully. "Then the contract . . ."

"Pardon me?"

"Oh, nothing. Business, but it can wait till later. When you've adjusted to the change here." He bowed his head for a moment. "Something like this, so unexpected, has a way of jarring things into proper perspective."

"Yes, it does."

"Well, business should take a back seat at a time like this."

"Mr. Mackey is who you might want to talk to."

"Later's fine," Carver said, backing away. "Tell you the truth, I'd better consult with the board, anyway, before we move on this. Let them know what happened."

"It was in all the papers," the woman said. "All over the news media." An uncertain light entered her bulbous blue eyes. Everyone in big-business circles, especially in the South, should know of Wesley's demise. Suddenly Carver didn't seem quite genuine.

"And I apologize for not being aware of it," he said hastily. "I've been traveling. In Europe. I'm afraid the tragedy never made the news there."

"No," she said, "it wouldn't." She used a tiny gold pen

dangling from a chain around her neck to jot something on a note pad. "I'll mention to Mr. Mackey you were here, Mr. Emerson."

"Fine," Carver said. "You might tell him I'll be in touch. Probably next week."

"Of course."

He stopped halfway to the door. Said, "I don't want to pester you at a time like this, but could you tell me if there's going to be a service for Mr. Wesley? Longbranch will want to send flowers."

"That's quite all right, Mr. Emerson. The remains are being sent back from Florida. Mr. Wesley will be cremated, but there'll be a service tomorrow morning at the Norrison Funeral Home in Atlanta, then an interment where only the family will be present."

Carver, thinking Wesley had already been cremated in his company car, sighed and shook his head. "Well, my condolences to all of Wesley Slaughter and Rendering."

"Thank you."

He gave the woman a good-bye nod and limped across the deep red carpet and out the door. Back into the heat and thick stench. The oppressive smell seemed even stronger. Blood and death and lies. He wondered if he'd ever get it out of his clothes. Out of his pores.

He lowered himself into the Ford and drove away. Boyd Emerson of Longbranch Feeder Pigs.

Wondering what the hell was a feeder pig?

Chapter 12

Carver had a salad for lunch in the hotel restaurant. Iced tea and a roll to go with it. There were bacon bits in the salad. He nudged them aside with his fork.

After he paid the relentlessly cheerful cashier, he limped out to the gift shop and bought an *Atlanta Constitution*. Settled into one of a dozen identical, comfortable wing chairs in the lobby, and wrestled with the newspaper until it was turned to the obituaries.

Ah! There was a death notice on Frank Allan Wesley, and he was important enough to rate half a column. The praise was lavish: Wesley had been a businessman and civic leader in Atlanta since 1970, when he'd moved the main operation of Wesley Slaughter and Rendering from New Orleans to Atlanta. He'd given generously to charity, organized political fund-raisers, was a member of various lodges. Had been a major booster and financial supporter of the Atlanta Falcons football team. He was survived by a daughter, Michelle, now married and living in New Jersey, and a wife, Giselle, in Atlanta. A private memorial service, the paper said, and gave no time or location. *Private* was the operative word. It was fortunate that Boyd Emerson had paid his visit to Wesley Slaughter and Rendering.

Carver went up to his room, stopping on the way at an alcove where there were soda machines and an ice dispenser. He paid a clinking, clunking machine too much for a can of Diet Pepsi, got some of it back by reaching into the ice dispenser and getting a free ice cube to munch on as he limped down the hall. You had to make your own justice in this world.

His room was cooler than when he'd left it. Almost cold. But it felt good and he left the thermostat alone. The maid had been in and done a nifty job, left the drapes open wide enough to provide bright but subtle light, but not so wide as to inflict him with a view of the highway overpass construction going on outside. Most of downtown Atlanta seemed to be a construction site; the New South still being born.

He sat down on the bed and used the window light to search in the phone directory for Frank Wesley. Was mildly surprised to find a Frank A. Wesley listed. Things were seldom this easy, and people like Frank Wesley often had unlisted phone numbers. The address was 218 Cabin Lane.

Time for real detective work, Carver told himself. He reached over to the dresser and snatched the Atlanta street map he'd bought down in the lobby. Spread it out on the bed and found Cabin Lane in G-7, north of the downtown area and in a wealthy community known as Buckhead.

He scooted sideways on the mattress until he could reach the phone on the nightstand. Pressed 9 for an outside line, then punched out Wesley's phone number. Listened to the ringing at the other end of the connection.

It would be useful to know if the 218 Cabin Lane Wesley was the Wesley who'd been killed in Florida. Save Carver some driving if he wasn't.

But there was no answer at the Cabin Lane number.

So maybe things shouldn't be *too* easy; whence would come character? Carver hung up the phone, sighed, and scooped up the street map and folded it into a bulky rectangle. He crammed it into a pocket and limped from the room.

Half an hour later he was driving north on Peachtree Road. He turned on West Paces Ferry Road, then did some winding around on woods-flanked streets lined with palatial homes that were surrounded by acres of ground. He made a right turn on Cabin Lane, where the lots were so large the houses could only be glimpsed here and there through the trees.

Number 218 was a heavily wooded lot with a wide concrete driveway blocked by heavy black iron gates mounted to flanking stone columns. Beyond the columns, chain-link fence stretched into the dappled shade of the trees and disappeared.

Carver braked the Ford and nosed in to the gates, then peered through the windshield at the heavy chain and shiny brass padlock securing them. Chain and lock looked brand-new, and there were no nicks and scratches on the gates near where the chain was draped. On one of the stone columns was a gray metal intercom box with a fancy black handle that matched the curlicued design of the gates. Class, Carver supposed.

He got out of the Ford and limped over to the box. Opened it and pressed the button beneath a speaker and mike.

Waited a few minutes and pressed it again.

No reply from the house.

As he limped back to the car, he eyed the chain-link fence more carefully and saw that it was topped by a tangle of razor-sharp concertina wire. An improvement on barbed wire, if such a thing needed improvement. Barbed wire was primarily used for keeping livestock in. Concertina wire was for keeping humans out, and unlike barbed wire, its finely honed, widely spread gap-toothed surface would slice to the bone like a razor blade as long as the slightest pressure was applied. It didn't poke holes in trespassers; it shredded them. Even with two good legs, Carver wouldn't have tried to scale the fence.

He lowered himself back into the car and drove a few blocks down the road, studying the estates on either side. Finally he turned the car around and parked it almost out of sight in a copse of trees a few feet off the road. It was virtually invisible here to anyone driving past.

After making sure no cars were approaching, he crossed the road and limped up a blacktop driveway. Lettering on a rural mailbox said the family living here was named Vermeer. The only visible part of the house was a vast red-tiled roof with several dormers. There was a metal rooster weather vane on the peak of one of the dormers. It couldn't seem to make up its mind which way the wind was blowing. Pointed at Carver for a second, as if he might be responsible for shifting currents, then turned away.

Halfway up the drive, Carver cut to his right, into the woods, and began making his way among slender hickory saplings. The ground was deceptively uneven, and he was careful about where he planted the tip of his cane before bringing his weight down on it. It was shady in the woods, but hot. Birds were nattering all around him, objecting to his presence. If he'd figured right, he'd be approaching the south side of the Wesley estate. He could only hope the grounds weren't fenced all the way around the perimeter.

But they were.

After fifteen minutes of limping through low underbrush that grabbed at his ankles and cane and tried to trip him, Carver found himself face-to-face with more chain-link fence and spiraling concertina wire. Wesley had been nothing if not security-conscious. Lot of good it had done him.

From where he stood, Carver could see the side of the house. It was only one story, but it sprawled wide; a main entry with tall Greek columns and a circular drive, then vast, low wings built on each side of the soaring portico. It was constructed of beige brick and had dark brown trim and gold accents. Thick ivy twined with green lustiness up the side nearest Carver, almost reaching the roof. He wasn't sure what kind of architecture the house represented; would have guessed neo-Grecian Ranch Glitz.

The place looked quiet. Empty. Carver wished he had the means to get on the other side of the fence and go exploring. A little B and E never hurt anyone, as long as nothing was stolen and no one was caught. He toyed with the idea of driving back into Atlanta, buying a bolt-cutter to cope with the fence, and returning. But that would be time-consuming and risky. When he got back, the house might be teeming with mourning family and friends.

Shielded by trees on either side of the fence, he made his way along the chain-link until the rear of the Wesley house came into view.

There was a beautifully landscaped rock garden back there, and he could see one end of a swimming pool. A diving board told him it was the deep end. On the other side of the pool was a redwood table with an umbrella over it. Redwood chairs with bright yellow cushions. One of the chairs had a blue towel draped over its back, moving slightly in the breeze.

Carver decided there was nothing here for him. He'd

hoped to talk to an unsuspecting family member or be able to look the place over and possibly find something revealing. Neither of those things was going to happen. He turned away and had begun limping through the woods when he heard a splash.

Turned back just in time to see the diving board still vibrating and the blue, blue water in the pool rippling and playing tricks with the sunlight.

The ripples calmed, then got hectic and slapped noisily in irregular rhythm against the sides of the pool.

Someone was swimming just out of sight.

The dazzling, sun-reflecting water made his eyes ache. Carver crouched on his good leg behind the fence and waited, one hand on his cane, the other with fingers laced through the chain-link. He realized he was sweating heavily.

He was patient, but the gnats swarming around him weren't. They got in his eyes and tried to flit up his nostrils. He brushed them away now and then but it did little good. They weren't giving up any sooner than he was.

About five minutes passed.

Slower than root-canal treatment.

This was no fun. He was coated with perspiration and his leg was threatening to cramp up. The cane was slippery in his grip.

More splashing noises came from the pool. Silence for a minute, and then music. Though not very loud, it reached Carver clearly: the old Bobbie Gentry song "Ode to Billy Joe." Whoever was there had turned on a radio or stereo.

Carver's body tensed as he glimpsed a wavering shadow on the poolside concrete.

The woman who strolled into sight was blond and slender. Though it was difficult to be sure from this distance, she looked about average height. She was wearing only the bottom of a skimpy red bikini, and her small breasts bobbed energetically as she walked. Her hair was long and soaked, plastered to her naked tan back. There was no difference in the shade of her tan around her breasts; she frequented tanning salons or she was in the habit of topless sunbathing. At first, because of her slimness, Carver thought she was very young, but even from here a more careful appraisal put her at about forty-five. Middle-aged women weren't built like twenty-year-olds, and that was that, Cher not withstanding. Carver wondered if he was looking at Giselle Wesley.

Whoever the woman was, detective work had suddenly become voyeurism, and that made him uneasy.

The woman picked up the blue towel from the back of the redwood chair and dabbed at her eyes. Dropped the wadded towel into the chair, then smoothed back her wet hair with both hands. She tilted back her head and swayed gently from side to side in time with the tragic, hypnotic music, smiling slightly into the sun. The grieving widow? Maybe the maid at play.

Carver was glad when she stepped up onto the diving board, strutted gracefully to the end, and jumped into the water feet first, folding her arms across her chest, as if she were cold, to protect her breasts. After the splash that sent thousands of glittering fragments of water flying like spraying glass, he could hear her swimming toward the other end of the pool.

He moved away into the woods and started back the way he'd come, thinking no one had seen him but knowing he couldn't be positive. He still didn't feel right about spying on the solitary swimmer. Breaking and entering was one thing, but it wouldn't do to be arrested and charged with being a Peeping Tom. The worst part was, he wouldn't have minded watching the woman for a while, if she'd stayed in view.

That was perfectly natural, he told himself. Wasn't sure if he believed it. Finally thought, hell with it. People who analyzed themselves into paralysis got on his nerves and he didn't want to be one of them.

The Ford's air conditioner felt great. As he drove back toward the main highway, he adjusted the dashboard vents so the cold rush of air was aimed directly at him. Felt perspiration evaporating where his shirt was stuck to his flesh.

Gave only a glance at the dusty black BMW sedan that roared around him from behind and accelerated out of sight.

Chapter 13

Carver parked the Ford in the lot of the Norrison Funeral Home on Roswell Road the next morning and sat for a moment with the motor running and the air conditioner on, watching the people who parked nearby enter the side door of the long, white clapboard building. The men wore dark, well-cut suits, the women subdued dresses. A few of the women wore hats with black veils. Carver thought veils had gone out of style, even at funeral parlors, but he wasn't up on that kind of thing and might be wrong. Miniskirts had come back; why not veils?

The other cars in the lot were mostly luxury models or sports cars. Expensive iron. They were all gleaming with fresh wax jobs, looked new and probably were. Money, money.

After about ten minutes, he turned off the engine and climbed out of the Ford. Heat from the sun-softened blacktop penetrated the thin soles of his shoes. Radiated up his pants legs and warmed his ankles. He used a forefinger to pry the knot in his tie a little looser, then limped across the lot into the funeral home, thinking Atlanta summers could be just as punishing as Florida's.

He was in a small foyer, painted white over swirly plaster

and with deep brown carpeting. There was a dainty gold sofa against one wall, obviously more for decoration than for comfort. A table with a floral arrangement. Mounted on the wall above the sofa were three large wooden keys painted gold. Carver wondered what, if anything, they were supposed to signify. On what looked like a painter's easel was a directory. It said that Francis Allan Wesley was in Suite E. A suite, no less, as if he might still be alive and seeing callers.

Carver made his way down the hall to partly opened beige doors, the nearest of which displayed a gold *E* inside a circular floral design. Frank Wesley's suite, all right. The murmer of voices drifted out between the doors. Frank throwing a party?

He found the right angle for leverage and pulled the lettered door open wider with his cane. Stepped into the suite.

It was a large, paneled room lined with glossy dark furniture. About fifty small, padded chairs had been arranged in rows facing what looked like a genuine marble pedestal. On top of the pedestal rested the gleaming bronze urn that contained all that was left of Frank Wesley. The entire front of the room beyond the pedestal was heaped with funeral sprays and elaborate floral wreaths. A silent explosion of color. There was no photograph of the deceased. Thirty or forty people, most of them prosperous-looking middle-aged men, stood talking in low tones. A knot of men and two women stood or sat around a grouping of furniture near the pedestal and urn. Probably Wesley's daughter and widow. Maybe one of the men was the son-in-law, Michelle's husband. One of the women turned her head, and Carver saw that it was the swimmer from the previous afternoon. Her blond hair was combed back and piled up on her head now. A couple of stray curls had fallen onto her forehead, which gleamed with perspiration. Her eyes were red, and she dabbed delicately at one of them with a corner of a folded white handkerchief, as if trying to remove a cinder. Pluck it out and no more of death; her problems would be over.

No one paid much attention to Carver. He wandered over to the guest register book and signed it as Boyd Emerson. Across the room he glimpsed the woman he'd talked to earlier at the Wesley offices and nodded to her. She peered at him oddly for a second through her thick, dark-rimmed glasses, like a curious trout—*know you from somewhere*—then smiled and nodded back.

Carver milled around for a while, wearing an appropriately glum expression and eavesdropping, but he heard nothing of interest. Talk seemed to be focused more on the economy than on the deceased. But then, something could still be done about the economy.

When a severe-looking man in a black suit took up position near the urn, and people began sitting down in the rows of chairs and waiting for the service to begin, Carver decided to slip away. That was okay, he was sure. Boyd Emerson and Longbranch Feeder Pigs had paid their respects. And while Carver had overheard nothing of apparent use, he'd made mental note of the people at the funeral home and would recognize them if he saw them again. He'd also noticed how the widow's attitude contrasted sharply with what he'd seen when she was at home swimming.

The parking lot seemed even hotter, and there was a stickiness to the air that made it feel almost like a warm liquid that lent resistance to movement. He was glad to lower himself into the Ford and get the air conditioner cranked up.

They were waiting for him in his room at the Holiday Inn. A large man. A larger man. A woman. The merely large man was expensively and conservatively dressed in a gray business suit, white shirt, and paisley tie. Wore almost as much gold jewelry as Desoto. You had to look past the suit and glitter to notice what *he* looked like. Average. Smooth, symmetrical features. Sandy, thinning hair. He was about sixty but his eyes were ageless. They were the impersonal, avid eyes of millions of years of predators. When you looked into them it was like gazing into a deepening blue void, and then he didn't seem average at all.

The huge man, not much over six feet tall but probably two hundred and fifty solid pounds, had a round face, leering fat lips, tiny and tortured brown eyes set deep in tanned flesh, and a haircut that might have been administered with pruning shears. Mouse-brown hair stood up in short tufts all over his round head and well down on his neck. He was wearing white slacks and a loose-fitting, untucked white shirt. He looked as if he might be in his late thirties and had gotten there the hard way. What appeared to be knife or razor scars marked his meaty forearms and the backs of his hands.

The woman, sitting on the edge of the bed with her legs crossed, was wearing a gray blouse, black skirt, black high heels. She had a gold chain around her neck, another around her left ankle. She might have been Hispanic, but Carver couldn't be sure. She wasn't beautiful, but somewhere she'd learned how to dress and apply makeup. Her appeal was mostly the result of presentation. Take away the dark mascara and lipstick, the high heels and tight skirt, and she would have been an ordinary woman in her late twenties. Include them and she was something bright and shiny that grabbed attention. The sort of object that attracted predators. She was smoking a cigarette in a long black holder. Her large dark eyes gazed with something like amusement at Carver as she exhaled a thin vapor of smoke from deep in her lungs. She made smoking seem erotic.

Carver leaned motionless on his cane just inside the door. The other three didn't move, either. Didn't speak. A still-life study that took on weight and urgency.

Finally Carver said, "Got the wrong room?"

Gray suit said, "Wrong for you or for us?"

"Word games?" Carver asked. Trying to figure this. Thinking he could make it out the door and back into the hall. Wondering whether they'd come after him. Maybe not. He could raise hell out in the hall, possibly draw some help. Possibly. But he didn't move, only stood there listening to his heart. He was apprehensive about this, but his curiosity kept him glued where he was.

"No kinda game," said the wide man in white. His deep, phlegmy voice rolled like gravel through his leering lips. Carver looked into his tiny, pained eyes and wondered if there might be something seriously wrong with the mind behind them.

Gray suit said, "Come on in, Mr. Carver," as if it were his room. "Sit yourself down and we'll talk." He had a rich Southern accent and made "Carver" three sliding syllables.

Carver limped a few steps farther into the room. Stayed standing.

The man in the suit said, "I'm Walter Ogden." He motioned with an elegant gold-ringed hand toward the other man. "This is Butcher. Young lady here's Courtney Romano."

"Holiday Inn send you to check on towels?" Carver asked.

Butcher giggled. It sounded like a cat screeching beneath the phlegmy gravel. "Got him a sense of humor," he said. More Deep South accent. "Betcha he could lose it in about ten seconds, I decided to cut it outa him. Where's your sense of humor, Carver? Some people's is around their heart, others just 'neath their liver. Simple thing to pluck it right out no matter where 'tis, even if you gotta look a while." He used his leer again. Resembled an oversized gargoyle.

Ogden said, "Calm down now, Butcher. Maybe I'll throw you some meat."

"I'm countin' on it."

Courtney crossed her legs the other way with a loud swish of nylon and kept staring at Carver. Smoke from the cigarette holder trailed across her face but she didn't blink. Telling him she was a hard number and not to look in her direction for sympathy.

Butcher drew a bone-handled knife with a long, thin cutting blade from beneath his shirt. The kind used in slaughterhouses to strip meat from bone. Said, "Ever seen how livestock starts out on its trip to the dinner table, Carver?"

Carver knew this was all being done for effect. These three, laying it on thick. An act designed to intimidate, with Ogden, who seemed to have an agile mind behind his good-ol'-boy-sophisticate pose, the director. Still, it was working. Butcher's words, Butcher's baleful steady gaze, sent a tiny cold centipede scurrying up the nape of Carver's neck. He said to Ogden, "Spare me the scary part and get to the point. Then get outa my room."

Courtney said in a calm, Deep South voice that held a hint of Spanish, "He talks like a real rough man, don't he, though?"

"Not actually," Ogden said. "But I hope he's a sensible one. What I'd sure like to know, Mr. Carver, is why you went to Wesley Slaughter and Rendering and represented yourself as someone else. And why you just attended the memorial service for a man you never met."

"Didn't stay for the service, actually."

"Smart fucker," Butcher said. Then to Ogden: "Sometimes them kind's the most fun. Don't take 'em long to realize they ain't so smart, though, then they're like all the rest. People an' hogs; ain't none of 'em more'n just blood, guts, an' bone."

Carver thought he saw Courtney shiver. Genuine revulsion? Or more playing for effect?

Ogden, using a more reasonable tone of voice, said, "It's this way, Mr. Carver. Wesley Slaughter and Rendering's in a very competitive business, and there's some delicate negotiations going on that will continue despite Mr. Wesley's death. We don't want anything happening that might upset those negotiations." He smiled. "This all clear to you?"

"Sure. You think I'm an industrial spy."

"I think it'd be smart of you not to show your face around Wesley Slaughter and Rendering again. Not to ask any more questions about poor Mr. Wesley. Not to trespass on private property. Spy on grieving widows. That kinda thing."

"Or?"

Butcher smiled. Carver like him better leering.

Carver said, "Your buddies tried to scare me off this case down in Florida. They the ones aimed you at me?"

Butcher stiffened. Drew invisible little circles in the air with the point of the knife. Ogden seemed genuinely puzzled. "What buddies in Florida?"

"You know the two. Down in Fort Lauderdale. Black guy and a Hispanic."

Courtney drew in her breath sharply.

"Their act wasn't nearly as frightening as yours, though," Carver said. "Guns and tough talk was all. Gun can do more damage in a second, but there's something unsettling about a knife."

Butcher said, "Ain't there, though?"

Ogden said, "Well, you shoulda listened to those fellas,

Mr. Carver. Been best all around." He reached into his suitcoat and drew a fat white business envelope from an inside pocket. "Here's the way we can do it," he said. "There's a lotta money in this envelope, and I'm gonna leave it down at the desk for you. Come morning, you and that envelope be gone. You understand?"

Carver said, "People don't run other people out of town anymore. Not even very often in the movies."

"Ain't no movie," Butcher said.

"If I reclaim that envelope tomorrow, you'll wish you'd beat me to it," Ogden said. "We clear on that?"

Still looking at Ogden, Carver pointed with his cane at Butcher. "Didn't you just hear Butcher say this wasn't a movie?"

"Think on it," Ogden said. "Whatever it is, it's up to you whether it has a happy ending."

Courtney stood up from the bed. She was shorter than Carver had imagined. Nicely built but thick through the waist. She drawled, "You better listen and do, Mr. Carver."

"He's been given time to consider," Ogden said. He started toward the door. Butcher followed. Then Courtney. Like ducks in a row.

As he passed Carver, Butcher reached into his pants pocket and held up what looked like a rawhide necklace strung with about half a dozen tiny misshapen beads of leather. Said, "I carry this here for luck, Carver."

"They're earlobes," Ogden explained. "Real ones, you can be sure. He's got him a little eccentricity and sorta collects them."

Courtney looked bored but slightly ill.

Carver said, "They bring you luck, Butcher?"

"More luck than the folks I cut 'em from," Butcher said logically, grinning and slipping the leather loop back into his pocket. He smoothly inserted the long-bladed knife into its sheath beneath his shirt.

Ogden smiled and said, "Don't trust too much in *your* luck, Mr. Carver." He held the door open as Courtney and Butcher slid past him into the hall. Shook his head and said in an amused, boys-will-be-boys tone, "Earlobes. Ain't that something?"

"Something," Carver agreed.

But the door had already closed.

Chapter 14

The next morning, as he limped through the Holiday Inn lobby, Carver tried not to look at the envelope stuffed in the box beneath his room number. A lot of money, Ogden had said. And, to Ogden, a lot would indeed be a lot. There was no telling how much was in the bulging white envelope. Maybe even six figures. Possibilities endless and shining.

Better not think about that.

But his mind kept returning to the knowledge of the envelope the way the tip of a tongue keeps returning to an aching tooth. And finding decay.

He got the Ford from the hotel garage and drove through iridescent streets damp from a dawn rain to the Atlanta Public Library, only about six blocks away on the corner of Carnegie Way and Forsyth.

The library was a gray stone building with dark-tinted windows. There was a wide concrete area out front that seemed to be home to half a dozen street people. This was a teeming corner, with lots of traffic, both car and pedestrian. Busy Atlantans rushing here and there, conducting the business of the New South.

Inside, the library was cool and spacious, with beige carpet and cream-colored walls. Carver pushed through a turnstile, and a woman at an information desk told him newspaper back issues were kept on microfilm on the fourth floor, then with a darting glance at his cane directed him to an elevator.

Same beige carpet on the fourth floor. Same cream-colored walls. Microfilm records were stored in rows of multicolored file drawers, while current newspapers were kept in racks in their original form.

After removing the appropriately dated small cardboard boxes from one of many gray drawers, he sat at one of half a dozen blue-and-gray viewers and got busy.

He had to sift through several microfilm spools before he found what he wanted in a July 12, 1970, edition of the *Constitution*. The moving of Wesley Slaughter and Rendering's corporate headquarters to Atlanta from New Orleans, along with plans to construct a vast operation south of the city, was front-page news in the financial section. There was a separate item on Wesley himself, recounting how he'd been born in New Orleans into one of the city's oldest and most prestigious families. His father had been a local political kingmaker, *his* father a two-term congressman in the U.S. House of Representatives. Wesley had made a name for himself as a high-school halfback, but he hadn't played college football because of a knee injury. He'd attended Washington and Lee University, graduating *magna cum laude* within three years. In a surprising move, he'd used family money to buy into Clark Rendering with a college friend, Keith Adkins. The two of them soon had corporate control. Within five years Adkins left the company, whose name was changed to Wesley Slaughter and Rendering. Under Wesley's guidance, it soon became the largest operation of its kind in the South. Wesley was also a member of an organization called the Southern Christian Businessmen's League, as well as several other civic groups.

Next to the news item was a photoghraph of Frank Wesley in his forties, dark hair worn long over the ears, drooping dark mustache, the sort of smile people associate with daredevil pilots and heartbreakers. Nice-looking guy in a suit and tie, posed with his arms crossed, a freshly slaughtered hog dangling upside-down on a meat hook in the background. Today's carcass, tomorrow's bacon.

It was a striking photograph for several reasons, but the reason it struck Carver was that he was sure the man in the 1970 newspaper photograph and the man who'd died in the car bombing in Florida were two different people.

He turned the knob that made the lens zoom in on the section of the newspaper page containing the Wesley story. Figured out the instructions printed on the side of the microfilm machine, fed a quarter into its plastic and metal guts, and in a slanted plastic tray received a copy of what was on the screen. Wesley's photograph had reproduced beautifully.

Then he leaned back in his chair, holding the copy and the crook of his cane in the same hand, thinking.

The two gunmen in Wesley's condo in Fort Lauderdale hadn't seemed surprised when he'd walked in through the unlocked door. It was almost as if they'd been ahead of him in the game and were sitting there waiting for him. And if he was any judge, Ogden, Butcher, and Courtney had been genuinely surprised by his mention of the two in Florida. As if they actually had no connection with them. Maybe didn't even know who they might be. Then he remembered Courtney's sharp intake of breath at the mention of the Fort Lauderdale conversation. Wondered what, if anything, that might mean.

But the discussion of the two gunmen was the only even slight digression from their scare-Carver act. It was as if they'd talked over beforehand what might frighten him into leaving Atlanta, then gone through their routine in his room and sweetened fear with money. Powerful motivators, cold fear and cold cash.

Carver had been tempted, but he'd never considered asking the desk clerk for the envelope in his room slot. Not really. Not beyond toying with the idea. He knew better than to take the money. Knew what part of himself he'd be selling. Convinced himself of that, anyway.

But he couldn't shake the fear.

Even if he did keep seeing Butcher's tiny, intense eyes behind the thin-bladed boning knife, even if he did keep thinking about the photograph of a young Frank Wesley standing and smiling in front of a fresh-killed hog, Carver assured himself that he was leaving Atlanta because he had no more business here at the moment.

As he checked out of the hotel that afternoon, he saw that the envelope was no longer in his box. He asked the desk clerk, a tall, elderly man with gray hair and a crooked spine, if he knew what had happened to it.

"Gentleman that left it came by this morning and picked it up," the man said, regarding Carver as if peering around a corner.

"Remember what time?"

"I'd guess about ten, sir."

Carver felt a sinking, cool sensation. They hadn't given him much time to claim the money. As if they didn't really care how he played it and could handle him easily either way. Hadn't been bluffing an iota. This wasn't comforting.

"That's okay, I hope." The desk clerk's gray eyebrows

formed a sharp V of concern. "When he left the envelope, he said whoever was on the desk at the time was to give it to whichever of you two gentlemen asked for it."

"It's okay," Carver told him. "I just wanted to make sure he got it."

He put his room charges on his Visa card and said yes, he'd enjoyed his stay. *Especially the guy with the knife.*

Digging the cane hard into the lobby carpet, he refused to let a bellhop carry his suitcase as he limped toward the exit. Despised the man's pitying and patronizing smile.

An hour later, he'd turned the rental Ford in to Hertz at the hectic Atlanta airport and was on a plane heading back to Florida.

The air was calm; the flight was smooth. He sat quietly sipping beer from a plastic cup, watching shredded cotton clouds glide past. Wondering what and how big was the thing he'd become involved in, and where it was taking him.

And how much had been in the envelope he hadn't claimed.

Chapter 15

∼∼ On the veranda at Edwina's house, Carver was watching McGregor. McGregor was watching the ocean, thinking over what Carver had just told him about what had happened in Atlanta. A gull circled in, screamed, and swooped at something out of sight below on the beach, soared almost straight up and flapped back toward the sea. The flashing white undersides of its wings were visible for a long time against the blue sky. The ocean breeze ruffled McGregor's sparse blond hair, causing a lock of it to flop down Hitler-style above his left eye.

He aimed his close-set little eyes at Carver. Said, "It don't make fucking sense, you telling me Wesley's alive."

"Has Bert Renway surfaced?"

"No," McGregor said. "I've had his trailer watched and he ain't shown."

"Then it makes sense that far."

A trickle of sweat ran down McGregor's forehead, into the corner of his eye. Seemed not to bother him. " 'Cause nobody's seen a man in a while, that don't mean he's dead. Might be he's visiting his old mother in another state; that ain't quite like being dead. Or maybe he met up with a hot opportunity and he's balling some divorcée tourist or something in a motel down the coast. Having himself a fine time and let the rest of the world go squat. Dipshits like you always assume the worst."

"Renway's almost sixty-five years old."

"Hey, you think that means he can't get it up?"

Carver said, "Christ!"

McGregor said, "There's a name pops up all over Florida, crime capital of the country."

"Frank Wesley wasn't in my office," Carver said simply. "He wasn't in that car when it was blown up."

"Sorry donghead, but it had to be Wesley. Dental records don't lie. No two bicuspids are alike, that kinda shit."

"Uh-huh," Carver said. "Like snowflakes and fingerprints. What are you telling the news media?"

"That progress is being made. Bomb pieces are being analyzed, backgrounds are being checked, witnesses are being questioned. You know the routine—public servants in high gear."

Carver knew the routine, all right. The more public optimism and suits and ties and reassuring grins, the more uniforms speaking as if they were dictating a report, the less was actually happening in the background behind the bureaucratic front. And nobody was better at diddling the news media than McGregor. "The lab learned anything about the explosion?"

"There were a few charred pieces of what looked like an electronic detonator. The explosive itself might have been a plastique. Kinda stuff terrorists use." McGregor suddenly sat up straighter. The scent of his unbathed body crossed the table. "Hey, you don't think we're into political shit here, do you?" As if he'd just now considered the possibility.

"I'm not sure," Carver said. "See if you can get me some information on the charming trio of Ogden, Courtney, and Butcher. Maybe that'll tell us something. Wesley was— is—from a wealthy Southern family that was active in politics. And he did some fund-raising for local candidates."

"That ain't nothing," McGregor said. "It's a part of life for most anybody that successful. Every big fish has gotta keep the bigger sharks happy. Probably's got no connection at all with what's going on."

Carver said, "You never know."

"You're the one seems never to know, asshole. You go traipsing off to Atlanta, and all that happens is you come back and throw shit into the game."

"Didn't traipse, took a plane. And if the picture's no clearer, maybe that's because it's bigger than a pea-brain like you had it figured for from the beginning."

McGregor shrugged. "Guy walks into your office, walks out, gets blown up. I wanna find out why. Specifically, want you to find out. Should be simple for a hotshot private investigator even if he is a gimp. Got your own office and telephone now. You're supposed to be a pro. I mean, I seen your ad in the newspaper business personals, right under 'Spicy lingerie to perk up your partner.' "

"Should be simple for a police lieutenant, too. But it isn't. Sometimes one door only leads to another, and you gotta keep opening them. Problem with you is, they keep leading to places only tend to get you more frustrated."

McGregor stood up and put on his mean expression. Must have taken very little effort. "You just see you get me *un*frustrated, you know what's good for you. You'll be limping around selling pencils instead of living here with your real-estate cunt and playing Sam Spade."

Carver gripped his cane and actually raised it a few inches, preparing to lash out at McGregor. To smash that lascivious, gap-toothed grin down his throat. He took a deep breath instead, lowering the cane. His knuckles were white against the dark walnut.

McGregor knew he'd rattled Carver and was grinning wider, playing his tongue around the space between his front teeth. He said, "I'm going now, fuckface. You keep in touch."

Carver said, "Works both ways. You gonna do what I asked? Get with Atlanta law and find out about those three names?"

"Sure. Why not?"

Carver smiled. There was a reason he'd asked McGregor and not Desoto to check with Atlanta. He said, "Be careful one of those sharks you talked about doesn't develop a taste for rotten cop."

McGregor spat on the brick, then ground the wad of phlegm into a flat wet spot with the toe of his huge wing-tip shoe. "Tryin' to spook me, jerk-off?"

" 'Course not. We both know you'll always be more ambitious than scared. Sharks don't much care what their supper's thinking, though."

McGregor stretched his long body, swaying from side to side as if trying to separate his ribs. He spat again, then turned and walked away. He was smiling but not fooling even himself. Like Carver, he was swimming in unfamiliar water that was proving dangerous.

Carver sat for a while, staring at the ocean and sipping his Budweiser. There was a big ship way out on the horizon, so far away it didn't appear to be moving. A couple of pelicans fished in the distance, skimming the waves.

Behind him, Edwina said, "Good, he's gone." She'd been waiting in the house for McGregor to leave. She pulled back the metal chair opposite Carver's and sat down. "That man makes my skin creep six different directions at once."

"You oughta tell him that," Carver said. "Believe me, he's not sensitive enough to be insulted."

Edwina smiled. Behind her the sea rolled blue-green and deep toward the shore. A sudden stiff breeze lifted the collar of her silky white blouse and the point of a lapel touched her cheek lightly, as if caressing it. The few clouds in the sky had disappeared. Nature seemed to approve of her having taken McGregor's place on the veranda. Carver agreed with nature.

Edwina said, "I can tell by your expression he cheered you up as usual." A smile. "Time to share? Or are you going stoic on me?"

Carver told her about his conversation with McGregor.

When he was finished, she said, "You better tell all this to Desoto."

Carver said, "Desoto's a straight cop. In his position, there are things he can't know without passing them on."

"He wouldn't pass them on if you asked him not to; he's your friend first, a cop second."

"Don't be so sure."

"I am sure."

"Well, because he's my friend, I don't wanna put him in that kind of dilemma."

"He wouldn't see it as a dilemma. Not Desoto."

Carver wondered if any woman had ever thought ill of Desoto. Probably not. He looked out at the distant ship again; it still hadn't moved. Maybe it was anchored there. The pelicans were gone.

"Think about it," Edwina said.

"Sure," Carver told her. "About that and a lotta other things."

"What you need," Edwina said, "is to forget everything

for a while." She grinned as lasciviously as McGregor, but on her it looked fine. "I don't have to go back in to work today. Not a thing to do till I meet some clients tonight."

He said nothing as she got up, walked around the table, and bent down so her head wouldn't bump the umbrella. She kissed him on the mouth, letting it linger, using her tongue. She'd been drinking lemonade laced with gin; he could taste it.

Carver ran the backs of his knuckles lightly over her smooth cheek where the lapel had touched it. She was perspiring but cool to the touch. He felt himself responding to her. The buzzing in his ears was starting again, but it wasn't loud or unpleasant. It occurred to him that he hadn't heard it the past day or so except on the plane from Atlanta, and that might have been because of the change in air pressure.

Edwina kissed him gently on the forehead. Straightened up and moved away.

He said, "Me, I got no pressing business, either."

She said, "Oh, yes you do."

Later, in the cool and quiet bedroom she removed her mouth from him long enough to say, "I'm scared for you. Talk to Desoto. Please."

Carver said, "Ummm. Sure."

Promise them anything.

Chapter 16

〜 Desoto listened carefully as Carver talked. They were in Desoto's office on Hughey in Orlando. The window air conditioner, which supplemented the central air on particularly warm days, was humming and gurgling away, fighting the good fight against the relentless heat. There were three yellow ribbons tied to its grill, standing straight out and fluttering in the cool breeze to show the filter was clean and the blower was working fine. Reassurance that you were comfortable while you sweated.

On the sill of the window next to the one with the air conditioner sat Desoto's portable Sony radio. He'd turned the volume low enough so it could barely be heard above the noise of the air conditioner, and Latin music seeped from the speakers into the office. Music from *Evita*, Carver thought. Desoto seemed to like, even need, a Latin beat to help him through his days.

Patti LuPone was singing forlornly about Argentina when Carver finished talking and Desoto leaned back in his chair and looked thoughtful. Desoto had on a white-on-white shirt with French cuffs and a wine-colored tie today. Razor-creased slacks that were beige but so pale they were almost white. A dark brown sport jacket was draped on a wood hanger that was looped over a fancy brass hook near the office door. A tough cop and a dandy, Carver thought, was an odd combination that often caused Desoto to be underestimated. But Carver had seen Desoto with his back to the wall and no longer sold him short.

Desoto said, "You underestimated me, *amigo*, by thinking you maybe shouldn't have told me this. What you should do is listen more to Edwina. Should appreciate her more."

"Dammit, I appreciate her," Carver said. "I listen to her. That's why I'm here."

"She's a rare woman."

"She knows it and so do I. You don't have to keep telling both of us."

Desoto raised a dark eyebrow, looking like a matinee idol in a silent movie. The heroine had been rescued and now it was time to get down to business the censors demanded be conducted off camera. "Ah, you jealous?"

"No."

"You see? You should be. If I had Edwina I'd be jealous of every man she smiled at."

"Forget about Edwina. She advised me to come here and talk to you, put you on the pin. If you have to pass any of it along, I'll understand."

Desoto said, "Nothing you told me leaves this office."

"Thanks," Carver said, meaning it, hoping Desoto knew it.

"We're friends first," Desoto said, sounding like Edwina, "everything else second, eh?"

"Unless fingernails start getting peeled back. Then sometimes it's best not to know things."

"Hmm . . . I'll think about that next time I'm getting a manicure, but not now." Desoto idly played with the gold ring on his left hand, rotating it back and forth on his finger as if about to try slipping it over the knuckle. Light streaming through the blinds reflected off the ring and danced wildly across the desk. "You say Wesley isn't dead, I believe you."

"I didn't say he wasn't dead," Carver pointed out, "I said he wasn't the guy blown up outside my office."

"Point taken. And Bert Renway hasn't been seen since the bombing, according to McGregor. Also, you don't think the Atlanta goons know about the Florida goons."

"That's my guess."

"But you say maybe the girl knows. Courtney they called her?"

"Maybe Courtney. She's the only one who showed any reaction stronger than surprise when they learned about the Fort Lauderdale conversation."

"She strike you as Ogden or Butcher's girlfriend?"

"No. But I might be wrong about that. I'm not sure why she was there, unless she's in the same line of endeavor as Butcher. She came across as genuinely mean and tough, even through the melodrama they were putting on to scare me."

"From what you say, this Butcher should have some kinda record even if the other two are clean."

"If he doesn't, they should pass a law to convict somebody for suspicion and general nastiness."

"Those earlobes he showed you—think they were real?"

"Yeah," Carver said, "and he had both of his still on his ears."

Desoto stopped toying with his ring and abruptly folded his hands, as if he were a small boy in school told to stop fidgeting. "McGregor might tell you something about the three in Atlanta, but don't count on him sharing all his information with you. I'm on better terms with the law in Atlanta and elsewhere; I can find out things people won't tell him, figuring he's not to be trusted. Anybody knows him five minutes, he's an automatic loser in a popularity contest with a viper."

Carver said, "If the autopsy report out of Miami is phony, something heavy's happening."

"And somebody isn't playing by the rules, which is why I don't mind stepping outside them. There aren't that many people can swing their weight and get an autopsy report faked. What you've done, *amigo*, is you got me curious."

"You think we might be into some kind of political mess?" Carver asked. "I mean, a car bombing using a plastique, that smacks of folks with turbans and dark beards, or maybe the Irish Republican Army."

"Terrorists aren't the only people who stash bombs in cars," Desoto said. "Been a favorite mob method for decades. You ever watch that old TV series, 'The Untouchables'?"

"Jesus!" Carver said. "This is real life."

"Real death," Desoto corrected. "Rest easy, *amigo*. What I'll do is, I'll put out feelers so thin nobody'll notice them, but they'll reach the right places. I'll find out what the deal is. People owe me; I can collect. How police department politics work."

"I don't want to put you in a position where you're crossing McGregor," Carver said. "He bites."

Desoto grinned. No doubt his predatory bedroom grin. Strong teeth stark white against his handsome tan features. "Don't we all?"

Chapter 17

Carver hadn't brought his gun to the new office. After driving back to Del Moray from Orlando, the Olds's top down and the hot wind crashing in his ears, he headed up the coast highway to Edwina's house to arm himself. It was slightly cooler by the ocean; or maybe the endless rolling blue water and the gulls circling high against the vastness only made it seem cooler. Suffering in the tropics was subjective.

Edwina was out showing a beachfront condo she'd mentioned, in one of several newly constructed developments north of Del Moray. Carver wondered if Florida would soon reach the point where condos outnumbered people. Sometimes the condo market suggested that had already happened.

He parked the Olds alongside the garage and limped to the back door, hearing metal tick behind him as the car's big engine cooled.

The house was locked and quiet. After letting himself in, he made his way through the kitchen and down the hall to the bedroom. Even though cool air wafted from the vents near the ceiling, the window was slightly open and he could hear the repetitious breaking of the surf. Edwina liked to make love with the window open so she could lie motionless afterward and listen to the sea. Carver liked to listen with her.

He pulled the top drawer of the dresser all the way out and removed the Colt .38 automatic taped to the back of it. He thought about getting the leather shoulder holster from the back of the closet, but decided against it and untucked his shirt, then stuck the gun in his belt beneath it. The Colt lay heavy and ominous against his stomach.

Carver felt a brief wave of revulsion. He'd known what bullets could do, but the pain and the sight of his ruined knee were still raw in his mind. The personal violation. Some nights he'd dream about how casually the kid at the convenience store had aimed at his knee and squeezed the trigger. *Stopped by for a quart of milk and a holdup, shot this off-duty cop while I was there.* He'd feel again the disbelief and terror. Hear the blast. See the muzzle flash. His world changed in the incredibly brief time it had taken a bullet from a cheap handgun to rend flesh and bone. And now guns were even easier to get and to keep in Florida. Cops didn't like that. Not most cops. Not most people, if they really stopped to think about it, which they didn't. What the hell were the politicians thinking? Who and what did they owe?

Carver lifted his shirt and checked again to make sure the Colt's safety was on, then replaced the dresser drawer and limped from the bedroom.

Standing outside again in the heat, he'd shut the back door behind him and was keying the deadbolt when a voice said, "We might as well go back inside where it's cool."

Carver turned and saw the rough-hewn black guy from Fort Lauderdale. His smooth Latin sidekick, the probable Ralph Palmer, stood beside and a little behind him. They were both wearing conservative light gray suits, white shirts, red ties. Like a couple of menacing accountants.

Carver had the Colt out from beneath his shirt even before he'd turned and planted his cane, feet spread wide in a shooting stance.

He'd surprised them, all right. The black guy's eyes got round and he shuffled backward. Bumped into Ralph Palmer, who seemed perfectly calm but frightened and very alert, like a man about to work on disarming a bomb. Carver was the bomb. He'd shocked them. Folks didn't wander around with guns in such easy reach and with the decisiveness to draw and point them. Maybe on "The Untouchables," but not in real life. Not even in Florida.

Well, maybe in Florida. Which was why the two men in front of Carver were especially scared.

Carver let them stay scared. "I've got the gun this time," he said. "Not like in Fort Lauderdale. The conversation's gonna go a little different here."

The black guy said, "I'm about to get something out of my pocket, Carver, and I'd like for you not to blow a hole in my suit."

Carver said, "No deal. I don't wanna see pictures of your kids. And if they were here, they wouldn't want you to reach in that pocket."

"I got no kids, and you watch me real close, because I'm gonna show you you're dealing with the U.S. government here."

He had nerve, did the black one. Not moving his frightened eyes from the Colt, he shifted his hand toward the lapel of his suitcoat. Beneath the material and out of sight. Inching toward the inside pocket. Gave Carver his choice—squeeze the trigger, or hesitate and take the chance.

Carver took the chance. His heart hammering. Making a show of tensing his finger on the trigger.

What came out in the black guy's hand was a worn brown leather folder. The kind that usually contained a badge.

Holding it well away from his body, he let it flop open facing Carver.

Badge, all right. And Carver recognized what kind.

The black guy said, "I'm Ben Jefferson. Drug Enforcement Administration. This is agent Ralph Palma, also DEA." "Palma," not "Palmer," as he'd told Renway.

Not politics—drugs. Sure! What else, in Florida? Not knowing quite what to say, Carver said, "So?"

"So put down the fuckin' gun," Palma said.

Carver didn't move the gun. Not yet. But he knew this figured. The DEA could take precedence over the Miami police. Get the autopsy report faked so it looked as if Frank Wesley and not Bert Renway died in the car bombing. A federal agency had that kind of clout. Maybe only the weight of the federal govenment could do it. And it *had* been done.

"The ID's authentic," Jefferson said.

"I know." Carver lowered the gun. Tucked it back into his belt beneath his shirt. He'd never thumbed the safety off, but Jefferson and Palma hadn't noticed. Guns caused people not to think straight. People behind and in front of them. Guns didn't kill people, people with guns killed people.

"Why don't we go in the house?" Jefferson said. "Hot as the surface of the sun out here."

Palma was grinning confidently now. The gun was back where it didn't pose a danger and the balance of power had shifted again to where it belonged. These were all of a sudden very official dudes, with the intimidating force of the U.S. government behind them. Big Uncle Sam.

Carver said, "You wanna talk, we can sit at the table on the veranda."

Jefferson said, "You're a hard man."

Carver said, "Believe it."

When they'd crossed the brick veranda and were seated in

the shade of the table's wide umbrella, Jefferson, who seemed to be in charge, said, "What do you know, Carver?"

"Enough not to spill all of it to you."

Palma said, "You're fuckin' with a federal investigation here. Better tread light."

"But I don't think your superiors, or the news media, would like the way you used guns and bullshit to scare a U.S. taxpayer in Wesley's apartment in Fort Lauderdale."

"The taxpayer was where he didn't belong," Jefferson said.

"So were the DEA agents. And they didn't identify themselves."

"We go where we want," Palma said, "and we belong wherever that is."

Carver said to Jefferson, "He's kind of haughty."

Jefferson smiled and said, "Well, sometimes we need that in this job. We've identified ourselves now, so let's all three of us forget about that Fort Lauderdale thing. Start over and even."

Carver glimpsed another, unexpected side to the powerful and fierce-looking Jefferson; he could be, when he chose, a charming and persuasive man.

"What I know," Carver said, "is that Bert Renway came into my office and hired me to find out why *he* was hired by you to impersonate Frank Wesley. I took the job, Renway left the office, and got blown up in his—Wesley's—car before he had a chance to drive away. Only it turns out the autopsy report says the body was Wesley's. I expect you two had something to do with that."

Jefferson said, "Everything to do with it." Palma looked cool, but beads of sweat were tracking down Jefferson's broad dark face. The sun was getting to him today, making him suffer. But he made no move to take off his suitcoat or even loosen the knot on his tie. Man wouldn't make concessions even to God.

Carver was slightly outside the shadow cast by the tilted umbrella. His bald head was feeling the heat. The sun was no friend of the hairless. He said, "Let's go inside and talk."

Jefferson grinned. Palma made a languid, waving motion with his hand, as if he couldn't care less where they sat and made conversation.

Carver could feel the two men watching him as he limped ahead of them to the house.

In the living room, Palma sat on the sofa, legs crossed, hands folded in his lap. Jefferson remained standing, as did Carver. The sound of the surf was barely audible.

Jefferson mopped perspiration from his face with a wadded white handkerchief, looking for a moment like Louis Armstrong without a trumpet. He said, "Thanks for inviting us in. Nice and cool here." He stuffed the handkerchief back into a pocket and nodded toward Carver's cane. "You oughta sit down, take weight off that bad leg."

Carver said, "I'm fine standing."

"How'd you hurt the leg?" The good twin asking.

"Guy with a gun hurt it for me."

Jefferson stared at him, then shrugged almost imperceptibly, as if deciding not to pursue that line of conversation. He glanced instead at Palma.

Palma said, "We'd like to know what you were doing in Atlanta, Carver. Why you paid a visit to Wesley Slaughter and Rendering. Why you went to Frank Wesley's memorial service."

"And I'd like to know why you're asking."

Jefferson blew out a long breath and shook his head, the picture of exasperation. "It'd sure help if you'd stop being a smartass, Carver. You know how it works. We're government agents; we ask, you goddamned well better answer, or you'll wish you had." Bad twin again.

"I don't recall breaking any federal laws in Atlanta," Carver said.

Palma smiled almost sadly. "But you never know, the law being so complicated."

Jefferson slipped just his fingertips into the rear pockets of his suitpants, the coat folded back and bunched between his wrists. His powerful thigh muscles worked beneath the thin material as he paced a few steps away, then turned and came back.

Now that he'd turned around, he was a different man altogether. Like an impressionist who'd slipped into a new identity. The irritation on his face had been replaced by a peaceful, almost blank expression. Guy was changeable as a chameleon. Now he was oddly amiable. He said, "We know something about you, Carver. Know you're not some fool. We're DEA, so you must have figured out by now we're investigating a narcotics-related crime."

"I got that one pretty early," Carver said.

"There's this group of Southern businessmen," Jefferson said. "Some twenty-five years ago they formed an organization headquartered in Atlanta."

"The Southern Christian Businessmen's League?"

Jefferson pursed his lips and nodded. "That's the one. After 1973 it ceased to exist—at least publicly. But its core group of very wealthy Southerners remained banded together secretly for mutual profit. For a while it was good old white-collar crime on a high level. Stock manipulation, phantom collateral, political graft. Last year or so, though, they've moved to where the big money is. They're smuggling narcotics into this country. It's shipped or flown to Mexico, then brought by boat into Florida. A lot of it—we aren't sure how much—is then transported in various ways to Wesley Slaughter and Rendering. Shipments of animal products from Wesley to certain distributors are as much drugs as pork. Usually the stuff is hidden inside meat products— sausages, pork bellies, what have you."

Carver asked the obvious. "You know all this, why don't you stop them?"

"We were in the process of doing that," Palma said, "when you came along and fucked up the works."

Carver shifted his weight. Moved the cane and used the toe of his right shoe to scruff out the indentation made by its hard rubber tip in the soft carpet. Nothing Jefferson had said surprised him much, yet there was something about it that didn't rest level.

He said, "I didn't come along and do anything. You recall, it was Bert Renway who came along and hired me to find out what was going on. I was sitting there doing nothing when he was blown up outside my office after he paid me to do my job. Which is why I'm doing my job now. Where were you sitting when he was killed? What were you doing?"

For the first time, Palma looked uncomfortable on the sofa. He uncrossed his legs. Crossed them the other way. Adjusted a thin black sock that had slipped down on his ankle. He said, "Your client dies, doesn't that sorta release you from obligation?"

"Not necessarily."

"Come on, Carver," Jefferson said. "You must have a better reason than that to be making our lives difficult."

Carver considered telling them about McGregor. Serve the conniving bastard right to have the federals on his ass. But that one cut both ways, so he kept silent.

Jefferson said, "Carver?"

"How come you hired Bert Renway to impersonate Wesley?" Carver asked.

"You got this all backward," Palma said. "*We* ask, *you* answer."

Carver said, "Maybe if I talk to the right people, they'll ask. Then you'll have to answer."

"Threats are something we get a lot of," Palma said.

Carver placed both hands on the crook of his cane, leaned forward. "Some of them must be more than just threats."

Jefferson said, "Let's cool down here." He moved closer to Carver. Locked gazes with him. There was now something deep and dangerous in Jefferson's dark eyes. Something as implacable and relentless as time itself. Carver had seen that kind of look before but couldn't remember where. "About a month ago," Jefferson said, "Frank Wesley arrived at the condo in Fort Lauderdale. After a few days, he left on a boat that took him to Mexico. From there he was flown to Bogotá, Colombia. We had him watched in Bogotá, and we hired Renway to take his place in the condo while he was gone. Hired him because he was about Wesley's age and fit Wesley's general description amazingly well. Had him wear Wesley's clothes, drive Wesley's car. Then we kept him under surveillance to see who'd contact him."

"Used him as bait," Carver said in disgust.

Palma said, "We don't see it like that."

"Call it what you will," Jefferson said. "We're not dealing with Sunday-school teachers, and sometimes we have to use unconventional methods. The Justice Department understands that and gives us leeway."

"Christ! *That* much leeway? Methods *that* unconventional?"

"Sometimes. We're sorry about Bert Renway. You can believe that or not."

"So Wesley realized you were on to him, and he decided to stay dead after Renway was killed and mistakenly identified as him. You faked the Miami autopsy report to keep the deception alive."

"That's about it."

"But why do *you* want Wesley to stay dead?"

"We have our reasons."

"Such as not wanting anyone to find out you hired Renway?"

"That's only part of it."

"But Wesley has to realize somebody must have put Renway up to impersonating him. Somebody must know he isn't really dead."

"He knows we did it," Jefferson said. "He also knows we can't have that made public in light of our investigation. It was a rival drug faction that killed Renway, thinking he was Wesley. You heard about the drug wars in Central America?"

"Sure. Sometimes they make the papers."

"Well, Wesley wants to stay dead as far as the killers are concerned, so he'll be safe from another assassination attempt. I told you, Carver, these ain't Sunday-school teachers. As much money as there is involved here, it brings out the animal in people. They get to be hogs, just like the ones at Wesley Slaughter and Rendering. Sometimes they end up the same way. And the ones that aren't the victims are the killers."

"Even DEA agents."

"Don't lay that guilt bullshit on us," Palma said wearily. "Half the kids in this country got fried brains because of attitudes like yours. We're in a war, we gotta fight it any way necessary to win."

"I wouldn't call Bert Renway a winner. He didn't die for his country in wartime; he died because a couple of asshole drug agents got obsessed with their cause and became anything-goes zealots."

Palma stood up slowly from the sofa, the expression on his face unchanging but his eyes bright and alive.

Jefferson moved with his smooth little shuffle so his bulk was almost between Carver and Palma. Said, "Ralph, why don't you step outside for a while. Let me talk to Mr. Carver alone. Maybe convince him of a few things."

Palma relaxed enough for the whiteness at the corners of his compressed lips to go away. He said, "Okay. That seems like a sound idea." He buttoned his gray suitcoat, spun gracefully on his heel, and walked from the room. Carver heard his measured footsteps on the kitchen tiles. Heard the back door open and close.

Silence.

Jefferson looked at him almost pityingly. "We're alone now, Carver. That cane, that gun in your pants, they don't mean shit."

Carver tightened his grip on his cane and thought, Here come some more unconventional methods.

Chapter 18

Jefferson said, "You oughta know this about me, Carver. I'm straight serious about what I'm doing. Not dicking around in the slightest. You comprehend?"

"Sure. I'm the serious type myself."

"You think you're jiving me, but I happen to know about you. Know you're telling the truth about being serious. Least you're the kinda guy has to be taken seriously." Jefferson spread his feet wide and placed his fists on his hips, squarely facing Carver. "I wasn't always a DEA agent, Carver."

"I didn't figure you emerged from the womb with a badge and read the doctor his rights."

"I emerged from the womb in a shack down in Waycock, Georgia. Wasn't no doctor present, neither; which is maybe why my mother died givin' birth to me."

What was this? Jefferson's voice had changed subtly, taken on a hint of black street-talk tone. All of a sudden he seemed like a wealthy drug dealer jive turkey dressed as a Wall Street broker. This guy was a pip.

Carver said, "You gonna give me the poverty-stricken-black-who-made-good tale?"

"You *are* a hard sonuvabitch."

"I'll melt some. Go on with your story."

"Naw, that's been told too many times, and hasn't been a honky-ass like you ever really understood it. My daddy was a hard-rock Baptist preacher."

"Sounds like a song title."

"Ain't though. This was real, down in godforsaken Waycock. Full-time man of the cloth, part-time janitor at the county library. Back in 1968 when I was fourteen years old in a Deep South that wasn't much like the South we got now, though in some ways there ain't a bit of difference. Was a lot goin' on then with the civil rights movement, an' both blacks an' whites was all riled up mosta the time. Got especially so when certain things happened, like the riots after Martin Luther King got himself shot in Memphis. Hell to pay then. Lots of demonstrations in them days."

Carver was surprised to see Jefferson's large brown eyes shine with moisture. Either he was an Academy Award–class actor, or what he was saying was wrenched from down deep and dragging painful memories up with it. Hard to say for sure whether he was faking it or really going to the well.

"My daddy decided to lead one of them demonstrations," Jefferson went on. "Peace and equality and all that stuff it's s'pose to be naïve to believe in these days. Said it was his Christian duty and his mission on this earth."

Carver said, "Maybe he was right."

Jefferson's Adam's apple worked. He flexed his thick fingers, clenching and unclenching his hands into fists. "Could be. I've thought about that. But the thing is, the Klan figured *their* mission was to stop him."

"Klan as in Ku Klux?"

"The same."

"Did they stop him?"

"Yeah. Within an hour of word gettin' out about his plans.

They stopped him by hangin' him from the big willow tree next to his church. Willow branches are real flexible, Carver; Klan had to find a big one, high up, but even then Daddy's feet nearly touched the ground. I remember it. His big brown work shoes came to within a few inches of solid earth, but them inches made all the difference between here and eternity. I was hidin' in the church like my daddy told me the night they came, just before it got dark. There was over a dozen of 'em, all drunked up, drivin' their cars and pickups right up into the churchyard. Gunnin' engines and spinnin' tires till you could smell hot rubber. One of the bastards even parked his truck in the cemetery out back. Can you picture that? Knocked over a tombstone and didn't give a shit. Couple of 'em tromped into the church and found me where I was curled up in the rectory. Hee-hawed when I got scared enough to wet myself. Dragged me out so I could see what was goin' on. What they was gonna do. Few of 'em wanted to hang me alongside Daddy, but some of 'em said it wouldn't work, the willow branch'd bend and touch the ground. Couple of 'em wanted to shoot the young nigger dead, but that ain't their style so it didn't happen. What they did, they held me and made me watch while my daddy kicked and his eyes rolled back and his tongue got all purple and slithered outa his mouth farther'n you can imagine, like some foul thing that'd lived in him an' was seekin' light now that it was the end.

"Then his bowels emptied out and he stopped twitchin' an' that was that. Some of the Klansmen laughed and hooted. One of 'em threw a beer can so it bounced off Daddy's head, as if it made any difference by that time. I can still hear the sound it made, though. Don't ever open a beer can that I don't think about it. Then the ones holdin' me tossed me aside like somethin' used up and didn't matter, and they all climbed back in their cars an' trucks an' tore ass outa there.

"I sat in the dark and cried till the congregation members

with the guts to show themselves come an' got me. Everything goin' on around the country at the time, it was hardly noticed what happened that night in Waycock, Georgia, little shitpile of a place not even a flyspeck on the map. Not important."

Carver tried to speak. Found he had to clear his throat. Said, "Important to you, though."

"Uh-huh. Most important night of my life."

"Guess it would be."

Jefferson's breathing was loud. Even and deep.

"What's it got to do with now?" Carver asked. "You suspect Frank Wesley was one of the lynch-mob faces under those hoods?"

"Hoods shit!" Jefferson said. "They didn't bother wearin' sheets and hoods. Didn't care who saw their faces. You don't understand, killin' a dirt-poor nigger back in them days in the South wasn't much different from doin' away with a dumb animal. Same thing, in lotsa people's minds. Some people that part of the world still think that way. Last several years, things gone backward 'stead of forward."

"Then you know who the men were?"

"Just recognized two of 'em. Never saw the others again."

"What about the two you recognized?"

"They went to trial. Got acquitted. No surprise. Couple of weeks later, they both got killed when a train hit the car they were in. I know what you're thinking, but it ain't true; I had nothin' to do with the accident."

"You wouldn't be dumb enough to admit it if you had."

Jefferson smiled; there was nothing behind it but darkness. "True enough," he admitted.

"Why are you telling me this?" Carver asked.

" 'Cause I want you to know where I'm comin' from, as they used to say. I got somethin' personal against the scum of this world, and I fought my way out of an orphanage and through school just so I could do somethin' about 'em. What I do, it's more'n a way of turnin' a dollar. I got no family and few friends, so this occupation's who and what I am. You understand? Helluva lot more'n just a job."

"A mission?"

"Might call it that. Preacher blood in me, I suppose. Thing is, I want you to know this: You might be a hard-ass, but I'm harder."

Carver said, "I kinda sensed that from the beginning."

Jefferson smiled and nodded. The dark eyes that had softened and misted were unblinking and had a hard sheen on them now, revealing nothing. Even as the outwardly amiable smile revealed nothing of why the facial muscles had arranged themselves in that configuration.

Jefferson said, "Afternoon, then, Mr. Carver," almost in a mocking emulation of Southern black subservient dialect.

But he didn't bow before he left.

Carver didn't show Jefferson out. But as soon as he heard the DEA agents' car start and gravel crunch under tires, he was limping toward the door with his own car keys clutched in his perspiring hand.

He drove for only a few minutes along the coast highway before spotting the gray Dodge half a mile ahead.

Whichever of the two agents was driving held steady to the speed limit. The Olds, with its muscle-car V-8 engine, throbbed beneath Carver and wanted to take a big bite out of the highway. Carver restrained it.

About a mile outside Del Moray, sun glinted off the Dodge as it slowed and turned off the highway into the lot of a motel.

Carver knew the place: the Sundown Motel, a recently constructed two-story structure of pale brick and stucco, forming a U around a swimming pool and featuring its own wide, private beach. A well-appointed motel, but not one of the luxurious ones. It was nice to see that Jefferson and Palma weren't abusing their expense accounts, though no motel along the Florida Gold Coast was exactly cheap.

Carver slowed the Olds and coasted to a stop on the road shoulder where a grouping of date palms and tall red azaleas obscured the car from view. Beyond the tops of the azaleas that were swaying gently in the breeze, he could see Ralph Palma strolling along the catwalk to a middle, second-floor room. Just the top of Jefferson's head was visible as he walked to a first-floor corner room facing the beach. Then his entire body came into view. He managed to let himself into the room after a brief struggle with the lock.

The Sundown Motel was doing a good business. The sun was glancing off the roofs of fifteen or twenty cars in the parking lot. Beyond the flat-roofed, sharply angled structure, the sea lay blue and shimmering, the primal magnet that drew tourists even in the high heat of summer. Aside from a drifting, dissipating vapor trail from an airliner, there was nothing in the sky that resembled a cloud. It wasn't going to rain today.

Carver figured the Olds would be okay parked where it was for a while. He placed the Colt in the glove compartment. Then he climbed out of the car and locked it behind him. It wasn't exactly secure, but someone would have to slash the canvas top in order to get in.

He limped off the gravel shoulder, over soft and sandy ground toward the motel. Almost jabbed a small lizard with the tip of his cane. Didn't realize it was there, sunning itself, until it escaped in a sudden flash of green.

At the edge of the parking lot Carver stopped and peeled off his shirt, wadded it and carried it in his free hand as he continued toward the side of the motel where he'd seen Jefferson enter his room.

He'd learned long ago that if you acted as if you belonged somewhere, few people would question your presence. The veracity of the act sprang from inner conviction. Carver told himself he was one of the guests at the Sundown Motel, as he leaned into his cane and limped around the building to the beach.

The rooms that faced the ocean had the usual wide glass doors that allowed guests to walk directly out onto the beach. There were a lot of people sunbathing behind the Sundown Motel. Or sitting at the edge of the sea to let the surf foam around and over them and then withdraw. Two blond girls about seven, his Ann's age, were tossing a red Frisbee back and forth and never managing to catch it. Half a dozen people were in the water, laughing and shouting and riding the breakers as they rolled in. A couple of brave souls were far out at sea swimming parallel to the beach. A speedboat snarled past, skipping on the waves before they had a chance to break, farther out than the swimmers. The man at the wheel was wearing a yellow shirt and a crumpled white hat. As the boat bounced past, leaving a roostertail of spray, he turned his head toward the beach. Carver got the impression he was staring straight at him, but that had to be imagination. Nerves. Sometimes Carver's occupation played hell with the nervous system. Dried the mouth and shriveled the stomach. Yet— God help him—he knew there was a part of him that was enjoying this. For some people, adrenaline was a narcotic.

He glanced at the Frisbee-tossing girls again and thought of Ann. And Laura. Laura. When she and Carver were first married, it had seemed such a sure bet that it wasn't a bet at all. It was visceral. When they were in the same room, it was as if each of them had swallowed powerful magnets and were drawn to each other. Had to be together. To touch.

Then, when the magnetism had finally worn off, they'd discovered they hadn't much in common. Didn't really like each other's company. Mystified and helpless, they'd let the marriage drag on wounded until it died. How many people had that happened to?

Not the time to think about it, Carver told himself. Concentrate on the here and now.

The motel had furnished blue lawn chairs that were scattered about not far from the building. Most of them were occupied by sunbathers, but Carver found a free one and dragged it across the sand and positioned it carefully, as if seeking a precise angle of sunlight. What he was doing, actually, was arranging the chair at the desired angle to the wide glass door of Jefferson's room.

He settled down in the chair, resting the cane between his legs where it couldn't be seen if Jefferson glanced outside. He was facing three-quarters away from Jefferson's glass door, but by turning his head slightly he could see the vague shape of Jefferson moving around inside the dim room.

Carver felt safe enough here. Just another Sundown Motel guest and sunbather—as long as Jefferson or Palma didn't decide to log some beach time and happen to see his face. Should have brought my sunglasses, Carver told himself. Maybe a false nose, mustache, beard, and a toupee, some cotton wadding to puff out the cheeks. Newspaper with a peephole cut in it.

He knew his best protection was that Jefferson would never dream that he'd be here, lounging and soaking up rays not a hundred feet from his motel room.

Jefferson was moving around inside the room. He seemed restless. Too edgy to stay still. Peering through the plastic chair-webbing, Carver could see him pass in front of the pale corner of the bed. Bend over and open what looked like a suitcase near the bed. Not exactly a suitcase; a large duffel bag, probably. Jefferson withdrew something from the bag, a long object that appeared to be wrapped in cloth. No, not wrapped; in a case of its own. He unzipped it, and Carver knew: a gun case.

From the case Jefferson withdrew a rifle or shotgun. Guy came armed for anything.

What now? Was Jefferson going to clean the gun? Play agents and bad guys? What?

Nothing Carver could have guessed. Jefferson stood holding the long gun sideways before him in both hands, then slumped on the edge of the bed and laid it across his knees. Bowed his head and stared at it. After a while, his shoulders began to quake. Or was it the play of sunlight over the wide glass door?

No, Jefferson's shoulders were heaving, Carver was sure. The DEA agent was staring at the gun in his lap and weeping.

Made no sense.

Possibly it wasn't a gun. That could be it. But what then? Some sort of bizarre religious object that might prompt such emotion?

Carver waited.

Five minutes.

Ten.

Finally Jefferson straightened his back. He stood up slowly. Took a swipe at his eyes with the back of a hand. Looked as if he did that, anyway.

He placed the gun—plainly a rifle or shotgun now—back into its zippered case. Replaced it in the duffel bag. Stooped low and slid the bag beneath the bed. Walked almost out of sight into another room.

Carver saw a light wink on, for a second outlining Jefferson's broad body. Then Jefferson closed a door behind him, probably to the bathroom, and the world beyond the wide glass door was dark except for the pale rounded corner of the bed and the faint reflection of the sea.

Chapter 19

Carver waited all the rest of that day, eating supper in a Jack-in-the-Box across the highway, where he could keep an eye on the Sundown Motel parking lot. Neither Jefferson nor Palma had emerged from his room. Apparently they were sleeping through most of the afternoon, maybe resting up for whatever operation they had planned for that evening. Bad boys with badges.

At seven thirty, from where he was sitting in the parked Olds, Carver saw the gray, four-door Dodge pull from the parking lot with its amber directional signal blinking frantically. It turned to head south down the coast highway toward Del Moray.

He resisted the temptation to follow the car. Instead he forced himself to wait until nightfall. Darkness wasn't absolutely necessary for what he had in mind, but it would help.

Finally he peeled the back of his sweat-soaked shirt from the Olds's vinyl upholstery and dragged his stiff body out from behind the steering wheel. Stood leaning on the car and stretched the kinks out of his back and arms. Limped across the street to the Sundown Motel and to Jefferson's end room. Nodded to a fetchingly plump woman and her children splashing in the pool. Smiled at a young girl flouncing down the steps to meet someone waiting near the office. Carver belonged here. Every move he made said that he did. Stayed here every summer.

Even his brief struggle with the room lock shouldn't attract much attention. Motel locks. Wrong keys. Happened all the time. Only Carver was struggling not with a key but with his honed Visa card.

The lock slipped easily enough, like most motel locks. He pushed the door open and stepped inside, making it a point to switch on the light boldly, as if the room were his or he had some business there known to Jefferson.

It was like a lot of motel rooms. Done in shades of beige and with mass-produced wood-fiber furniture that was bolted to the walls or floor wherever possible. Never could tell when motel furniture thieves might strike. There was a faint, musty smell in the room; the scent of the sea had found its way in. Carver's heart was crashing in his ears; his blood was racing. He didn't mind.

To work.

He quickly crossed the room and pulled the drapes closed over the sliding door that led to the beach. Dragged a long canvas duffel bag from beneath the bed and opened it. Pulled out an old worn padded leather gun case and unzipped it.

This was what Jefferson had sat staring at with such wracking emotion. A Remington rifle.

Carver examined it closely. It was a Gamemaster pump-action model, a .30-06 caliber, old but in solid mechanical order. He worked the pump, listening to the precise metallic clicking of the action. Saw that the firing chamber was empty. The rifle wasn't loaded.

After deciding there was nothing special about the rifle, he slid it back in the gun case and arranged the case in the duffel bag as it had been, surrounded by faded Levi's and some sport shirts, none of which he could imagine Jefferson wearing. The impression was that the clothes were merely there to round out the long duffel bag and obscure the fact that it might contain the rifle. A DEA agent could travel with this setup, Carver realized. Even airport security checkpoints would pose no problem in the face of U.S. government credentials.

Carver checked the closet and found several suits, some slacks, and a sport coat, all on wooden motel hangers. Good-quality clothes. Stylish but not flashy. Drug agents had to be well dressed, Carver supposed. "Miami Vice" gone conservative.

He let himself out of Jefferson's room and returned to the Olds. Drove into Del Moray and had a dinner of salad and clams at the Happy Lobster with Edwina.

Afterward, he followed the red taillights of her Mercedes to her house and then made love to her, trying to forget for a while at least dead hogs and clients and backwoods preachers. People who carried knives designed specifically to separate flesh from bone. People who hanged other people and then bounced beer cans off their heads.

He succeeded.

He lay listening to the sea and his own ragged breathing, and felt contentment.

But later that night he dreamed he was swimming in a dark ocean of blood, and that his stiff leg was as unwieldy in liquid as on dry land and made it impossible to stay afloat.

And that his horror and the blackness he sank into were unending.

Chapter 20

McGregor had picked up Carver at the office in his unmarked police car, a pale blue Buick Skyhawk that looked like a family sedan but had a twelve-gauge riot gun mounted sideways out of sight below the dash. They'd headed west, away from the ocean, and now they were driving along Heron Street, through the poorer section of the generally wealthy community of Del Moray. Despite what the travelogues said, Florida wasn't all Disney World with beaches. Even Mickey Mouse had his dark side. Ask Minnie.

Small, dingy shops lined both sides of Heron, and down the cross streets Carver could see rows of almost identical clapboard houses whose state of disrepair was emphasized by the brilliant morning sun. Though it wasn't quite eight o'clock, most of the shops were already open. In front of a liquor store, a fat Hispanic man wearing baggy khaki shorts and what looked like a wildly colorful pajama top had tossed a pail of soapy water on the sidewalk and was methodically sweeping the suds toward the gutter. Behind him a sign in the window proclaimed that paychecks could be cashed at the store with a purchase. Quite a contrast, Carver thought, between this neighborhood and the creamy pastel stucco, clean wide streets, white belts, gold chains, and green money of the east side of Del Moray. The nearer the ocean, the higher the net worth.

McGregor slowed the Buick and cruised slowly, baring his long yellow teeth and glaring at a mangy, collarless dog rooting in a ripped plastic trash bag at the curb. Waxed paper and what looked like chicken bones were spread all over the sidewalk. The dog stopped what it was doing and glared back at him. Maybe something passed between them; McGregor shrugged and, if he'd thought about shooing away the dog, changed his mind and drove on. Said, "I checked on your three friends in Atlanta. Walter Ogden's an officer of Wesley Slaughter and Rendering. Been with the company since the mid-sixties. What exactly he does nobody's sure, but he wields clout with the company brass. He's got no police record at all, not even traffic violations, which ain't surprising for a guy like that. Got him the drag to fix it when he's pulled over for speeding or DWI."

Carver said, "It was clear in Atlanta Ogden was the executive type. What about the other two?"

"There's no sheet at all on the woman, Courtney Romano. Probably not her real name, and nothing in the alias file. Butcher's Vincent Butcher. That's right, his *real* name. From New Orleans originally. He's got enough of a sheet on him to make up for the other two being clean. Got in trouble when he was a teenager for killing neighborhood dogs and cats with a knife. Didn't just kill them, though. Tortured them first. The courts decided he was mentally ill. Ain't that a surprise? They arranged treatment, and after six months, when he was seventeen, he went into the Marines. He wasn't one of the few good men, so they bounced him out within another six months on a medical discharge. Marines were right to do that. Two years later he tortured and killed a prostitute in Shreveport who tried to up her price on him. Did creative carving on the greedy bitch with a knife. For that one he did five years in prison, then he was paroled and put under the care of a psychiatrist. Get this—after a year the psychiatrist disappeared." McGregor turned his head and gave Carver his lewd, gap-toothed grin. "The shrink was never found. Authorities finally figured he ran away with his receptionist, who he seemed to be balling after hours, since she disappeared a few days later. Nothing was ever proved, though. Red tape ensued, and the Louisiana parole board decided Butcher had seen enough of doctors and got him a job with Wesley Slaughter and Rendering in their slaughterhouse outside New Orleans. Just the occupation for a fella fascinated by sharp steel, hey? When the company moved to Georgia, Butcher went along. Never had any contact with the Georgia law. So he either underwent a personality transplant or he's got powerful friends that clean up his messes soon as he makes them."

"Has to be friends," Carver said. "I don't see any change in his personality. And there's no way he could put together a human-earlobe collection without attracting at least some attention from the law."

"If what you saw were real earlobes. Those kinda guys like to puff up tough. Mighta been nothing but chunks of cured beef or pork he showed you, not earlobes at all. You said him and his pals were putting on an act for you, trying to scare you shitless so you'd back away from the investigation."

Carver said, "Think of it in light of his past."

"Real earlobes," McGregor said, after only a moment's hesitation.

He turned the Buick off Heron, onto West Belt Road, and they began driving north to the highway that would take them back to the coast. There was something dead on the pavement, a cat or small dog, directly in the path of the car. McGregor ignored it. Carver winced as a tire made soft impact.

McGregor said, "You had breakfast?"

"Yeah."

"I was gonna suggest we stop, but I'll get you back soon as possible instead so I can get at some sausage and eggs. There's this place on Magellan serves me free in exchange for a little added police protection." He nudged a few miles per hour more out of the Buick and concentrated on his driving.

Watching McGregor carefully from the corner of his vision, Carver said, "I found out the two guys that were in Wesley's Fort Lauderdale condo are DEA agents."

McGregor's long face didn't change, but his grip tightened on the steering wheel. "You shittin' me, Carver?"

"No. They're the ones set up the impersonation deal. Wesley's a big-time drug dealer, they say. He was out of the country, probably on a buying expedition, so they hired Bert Renway and went fishing."

McGregor said, "Some bait."

"That was my reaction. They took offense."

McGregor said, "The DEA don't usually work that way, though these days I wouldn't put anything past them. Do anything to get credit and publicity; fuckin' war-on-drugs glory hounds, stomp on people's rights so kids can grow up to be solid citizens and buy cars and deodorant instead of dope. Keep everybody employed. The U.S. Constitution means nothing to them."

"I didn't realize you were a patriot."

"Me? Hell, yeah. Even got towels look like flags." He drummed his dirty fingernails on the vinyl-covered wheel. "DEA, huh? Goddammit, I don't like this even a little bit, Carver!"

Carver said, "Well, there's nothing to like."

"This means we been screwing around with a federal investigation. Shit, shit, shit. That kinda thing can get your ass in a sling in a hurry."

"Ruin a career," Carver said. "Maybe when this is over we can get on somewhere as night watchmen."

McGregor glanced over at him. Shot him the same look he'd given the stray dog rooting through the trash. "You actually dumb enough to be enjoying this?"

"Only one aspect of it. The one that puts you behind the eight ball."

"Well, unless you shot off your mouth, far as the DEA knows, I thought from the beginning and still think the body in the car bombing was Frank Wesley. They don't know I know, and besides, they're the ones faked the autopsy report outa Miami. Lawless pricks." He shook his long head and frowned. "Damn! I shoulda guessed it'd have to be federal agency to put that kinda pressure on and phony up a victim identification. Fuckin' dental records!" The frown disappeared suddenly; the old gray matter was buzzing. "You know, there has to be something big in the works for the DEA to pull that kinda stunt to preserve their investigation. The attempt on Welsey's life has gotta be part of a much bigger picture."

Carver had to admire how McGregor had zeroed in on the one feature of the horrendous situation that might be worked to his benefit. Big pictures might mean big opportunities. The man was a survivor for reasons other than that he was an unprincipled carnivore.

"Thing is," McGregor said, "if either of us goes down he pulls the other one with him. Both of us been scratching around where we shouldn't. Been withholding evidence in a homicide."

"Your idea," Carver said.

"You can't prove it, though, asshole."

But Carver knew McGregor remembered the multipurpose answering machine with its tape recorder in the blast-littered office. No way for him to know for sure whether it was working and turned on when he'd arm-twisted Carver into cooperating with him.

Let him wonder, Carver thought, not answering.

When he got back to his office there was a message on his machine to call Desoto. The only message.

Carver settled down behind his desk and propped his cane against the wall. Phoned the Orlando Police Department and asked to be put through to Lieutenant Desoto.

Desoto had to put him on hold for a minute, then came back on the line and apologized. "Sorry, *amigo*, looks like a homicide over by Clear Lake. I'm gonna have to hang up and get out there pretty soon. Crime marches on. McGregor get back to you on your three visitors in Atlanta?"

"I just left him." Carver told Desoto what McGregor had said about Ogden, Butcher, and Courtney Romano.

"That's all straight stuff," Desoto said. "Jives with my information. This Butcher looks like the kinda psycho you gotta be awful careful around."

Carver said, "That came shining through."

"So you don't take chances with this one, eh?"

"Not me," Carver assured him.

Desoto said, "Bullshit. You never knew when to let go of something since I've known you. Kinda psycho yourself."

Carver knew he might be right. "Nice of you to say so."

"Well, at least I warned you, so I won't feel so bad if someday you're found sliced and ground." Desoto waited for a reaction from Carver. Got none. Said, "There was a reason McGregor got no feedback on the Romano woman. Something he doesn't know or isn't sharing."

Carver waited, actually still thinking about Butcher and

that "sliced and ground" remark. He was in Atlanta at the Holiday Inn, seeing Butcher staring intently at him over the blade of the boning knife.

Desoto brought him back, though, when he said, "Courtney Romano's a DEA agent, too."

Carver sat thinking about that one. Remembering Romano's reaction in Atlanta when he'd described the two men he'd talked to in Wesley's Fort Lauderdale condo. She'd been momentarily shaken. There was no way for her to be sure how the Fort Lauderdale conversation had gone. She was undercover and didn't like complications that might reveal what she was doing. Not with Butcher in the same room. Carver couldn't blame her for that. He remembered Butcher's eyes. Beyond cruel. Psychotic eyes.

Desoto said, "*Amigo*, you there?"

Carver said, "Me a psycho, huh?"

Desoto said, "I don't think that's too strong. Hey, crime calls. I gotta run."

Carver said, "Run."

Chapter 21

At just past ten o'clock, Walter Ogden walked into Carver's office, bringing with him a push of outside heat. He was wearing a pale gray suit, blue shirt, yellow tie. Glossy black slip-on shoes with tassels that had brass on them. His sandy hair was neatly combed except for a clump above his right ear that the ocean breeze had gotten under and caused to stick out at an angle like a crooked wing. He was smiling. Carver knew that meant nothing. Cobras smiled before striking.

As soon as he'd stepped into the office and nodded to Carver, he moved aside. Butcher and Courtney Romano entered, Butcher standing off to one side like a gentleman to let Courtney in first. She was wearing stylish, tight-fitting jeans, heels high enough to be stilts, a low-cut blouse that fit tight around her middle and showed off her breasts. Lots of wild dark hair and mascara. Carver thought she looked a lot like that singer, Gloria Estefan.

Butcher looked like nobody in show business. He was his unique, quietly sadistic self. Features showing no emotion but for his tiny glittering eyes, made to seem even smaller by the pads of flesh around them. He had on white slacks, a silky white shirt open almost all the way to his navel. He was wearing a silver chain around his neck with what looked like a polished white fragment of bone dangling from it. Animal bone, Carver hoped. Other than the bone fragment, Butcher was dressed relatively normally today.

Other than that.

Ogden said, "Well now, I suppose you didn't expect to see us again so soon."

"I took you at your word," Carver said, wondering if he could get to the Colt in the file drawer next to Ogden. "After all, I didn't pick up the envelope you left for me at the Holiday Inn desk."

Ogden surprised him. "Forget about the money, Mr. Carver. Apparently you're a man possessed by ethics." He spoke of ethics as if they were demons. "Now, that isn't necessarily all bad."

Butcher was gazing balefully at Carver, as if he didn't like the way the conversation was going and wished he could get busy with the blade. Courtney Romano was perspiring just enough to put a soft sheen on her bronze flesh. She was leaning with her hands behind her on the back of the chair near the desk, her arms braced with the elbows in. The pose made her breasts jut aggressively beneath the tight blue blouse. She belonged on the cover of one of those true-crime magazines. Probably knew it. She was rocking back and forth on her very high heels, glancing over at Carver now and then deadpan. Gun moll of the month.

Ogden said pleasantly, "Butcher's got something for you, Mr. Carver."

As Butcher advanced, reaching for a pocket, Carver grabbed his cane and levered himself up behind the desk, ready to drive the cane's tip into Butcher's gut if he had the chance.

Ogden chewed the inside of his cheek and nodded thoughtfully, obviously impressed by the lame man's surprising quickness. Carver had to be reassessed again. My, my. Ethics, and now unsuspected physical ability.

Butcher didn't pull a knife from the pocket. Instead he grinned and withdrew a handful of photographs. They were color shots of the sort taken with an instant camera. Butcher dropped them on the desk and Carver saw that the top photo was of Edwina in her blue bathing suit, standing at the side of the pool behind her house, her arms extended in front of her as if she were poised to dive. She'd already been in the water; her hair was wet and lay flat against the back of her head and neck and shoulders. She was squinting the way people do when they've just had an eyeful of pool chemicals.

Butcher said, "Clear shots, huh? Had to get damn near close enough to touch her to get pictures like this." He gave his grating giggle. "Wouldn't mind touchin' her."

Ogden said, "They were taken just this morning. Less than an hour after you left Miss Talbot."

Something in Carver drew tight. He knew what this was going to be. He hadn't snapped at the money in Atlanta, now they were ready to apply another kind of pressure to get him to drop the investigation.

He was right, and then again he was wrong.

Butcher said, "She's a nice piece, your Edwina Talbot. Great legs and ass."

"Too pretty a woman to let her get messed up," Courtney Romano said.

Ogden patted at his hair. Discovered the wayward wing above his right ear and tucked it back deftly with a crooked forefinger. He said, "Butcher told you the truth; we were close enough to touch the young lady this morning. The point is, you don't want her touched. Neither do I. Now Butcher, here, he's another story."

"Another species," Carver said.

Butcher said, "There goes that sense of humor again. Dangerous."

"Someday he might die laughing," Courtney said.

Carver thought, Jesus, don't egg him on!

Ogden crossed over to the desk so he was standing close to Carver. He was still smiling, but not with a single thermal unit of warmth. He used a manicured finger to spread out the photographs on the desk. There were about a dozen of them, all of Edwina. Edwina in her suit and rubber thongs, walking across the veranda toward the pool, her hair not yet wet. Edwina in the water, head and shoulders visible, right arm slung forward, hand cupped, stroking toward the pool's edge. Edwina pulling herself up out of the pool, her suit wet and plastered to her body, her buttocks straining against the thin and flexible material. Butcher tapped that photo with his knuckle. "That'n there's my favorite."

"We took these photographs," Ogden said, "to show you how accessible your Miss Talbot is to us. The camera might just as well have been a . . . well, something else."

Carver said, "I could make sure she wasn't so accessible."

"Could you really?" Ogden seemed remotely amused. "For how long? One thing we've got is patience. Another is time."

"He thinks he could move her to another state," Butcher said, gloating about Carver's predicament. "Just give her another name and make believe she's somebody else."

Courtney said, "We'd find her." She looked at Carver and he thought he saw something, a momentary soft earnestness, in her eyes. "I mean that. We'd find her."

"That I promise you," Ogden said. "And we always keep our promises."

Carver knew they were right. It wasn't necessary to

kidnap Edwina in order to use her continued well-being for leverage. And they knew she wouldn't simply give up her life in Del Moray, even if Carver asked her to leave for her own safety. Besides, leaving was no guarantee of a long and untroubled existence. Always there'd be the apprehension, the imagined movement in the corner of vision, the shock of the late-night phone call or doorbell. Not a way for Edwina and Carver to live, holding their breath in Oskaloosa, Iowa, or some such place where they might pretend to be distant and secure, knowing all the time they *were* pretending.

"You're telling me to drop my investigation," Carver said, "or you do something to Edwina."

"No, no," Ogden said, shaking his head. "Things have changed."

"What changed them?"

"Some thoughts we had after our little get-together in your hotel room in Atlanta."

Carver glanced at Courtney. She was staring straight ahead, nervously kneading the chair back behind her with her square, strong hands.

"Main thing is," Ogden said, "we know the two men you talked to in Frank Wesley's condo were federal narcotics agents. They don't like you mucking around in this investigation any more than we do, but there you are, mucking around, and I think it's safe to say you plan to continue."

"Safe to say," Carver agreed. "Mucking is in my blood."

"What we want," Ogden said, "is for you to talk to those two agents whenever either of them suggests. From time to time you'll get a phone call, and you'll report what those conversations with the DEA were about. You'll report anything else that might interest us. I making myself clear?"

"You want me to spy on the government for you."

Courtney said, "I think he's got it."

Ogden picked up three or four of the photographs and let them slide from his hand, back onto the desk. "I think *you* want to spy on the government, Mr. Carver, considering that if you don't, Butcher gets Edwina Talbot for as long as he wants her."

Butcher beamed and said, "For me it's a win-win situation."

Ogden said, "Tough choice for any man, but I'm afraid we don't have much time to wait for your answer. What's it gonna be, Mr. Carver, love or patriotism?"

Carver stared down at the photographs. The shutter had been slow, catching splashed water in midair but making it look milky. Slightly blurring but lending grace to the arm Edwina was using to stroke.

"Mr. Carver?"

"Love's harder to come by," Carver said. "I'll be your informer."

Courtney pushed away from where she was propped against the chair. Shoved up the three-quarters-length sleeves of her blouse so they were wadded above her elbows. "That's a sensible response."

"I think so, too," Carver told her. But they both knew that now he posed a danger for her.

Ogden said they'd contact him soon. Walked out of the office and was followed a second later by Courtney, then Butcher. Might have been a sneer on Butcher's round face. Might have been a smile. Might have been gas.

A few minutes later, when they drove away from the office in a rented white Lincoln, Carver followed them. Ogden had mentioned love and patriotism. Forgotten about ethics.

Chapter 22

They drove inland fast, due west directly away from the sea. Carver stayed well back in the Olds, watching the distant white form of the big Lincoln shimmer in the heat like an illusion.

But it was real enough. The big car, the people in it, the problems they'd brought with them.

Within an hour they were in central Florida's orange-grove country. Fields of citrus trees, their lush green dotted with oranges or grapefruits that somehow didn't seem to belong, as if a child had dabbed repeatedly and randomly at a landscape scene with a soft crayon. The land stretched level on both sides of the highway. The trees were in neat rows whose receding parallels made their march to the horizon seem even longer than it was. Here and there awkward iron pipework loomed among the trees like a child's erector set, irrigation equipment jetting rainbowed sprays of water into brilliant sunlight, lending a waxlike gloss to the leaves.

A semi roared around the Olds, and for a short while its boxy trailer blocked Carver's view of the Lincoln. Then the truck drifted into the passing lane again, and he was surprised to see that the Lincoln was only about half a mile ahead, brakelights flaring, turning onto a side road. The speeding truck snaked around it and belched dark smoke, making time toward its destination.

The road the Lincoln had turned onto was unpaved as well as unmarked. Carver jockeyed the Olds past it and parked on the gravel shoulder, trying to decide what to do.

There was no telling how far the road ran through the fields of citrus trees. Narrow as it was, turning a car around on it would be difficult; he'd be taking a chance tailing the Lincoln along it in the mammoth Olds. Might find himself with no way to go except forward toward something unpleasant.

He drove down the highway to a spot where he could turn the Olds around, then parked out of sight on the other side of the road.

He got out and stood alongside the car, peering westward. The Lincoln must be traveling fast; dust from its passage hung in a low haze over the bright tops of the orange trees. Heat rolled out from under the Olds and over Carver's feet and ankles. Damned uncomfortable.

He set the tip of his cane, crossed the highway at an angle, and began walking up the dirt road.

Carver stayed to one side and limped along one of the Lincoln's tire tracks, where the powdery earth was packed flat and firm. There was no sound but the soft drag of his feet and cane in the dust, and the faint rustle of leaves in the breeze that played over the orange trees. He figured he could duck into the thick rows of trees if he heard a car coming. Make himself reasonably invisible.

The trees were all about the same size, not large enough to provide shade on the road. Now and then the breeze kicked up, and the insistent rustling of the leaves, all around him, was like urgent whispering. The sun was a hot weight on his shoulders, burdening him and slowing him down.

He'd gone only a few hundred feet when, through the trees, he saw the dust-coated white trunk and chrome rear bumper of the Lincoln.

It was parked in front of a small and decrepit white clapboard farmhouse. Not much more than a cabin, with slanted wood front steps and a wide screened-in porch.

Carver crouched motionless in the cover of the orange trees and watched. There was movement behind the rusty screen. The indecipherable murmur of voices.

Then Ogden, Butcher, and Courtney Romano came out of the house. The screen door was on a spring, and Courtney let it slam behind her. The slap of wood on wood reverberated over the fields like a rifle shot.

Butcher was carrying two small red-and-white TWA flight bags. Courtney had a black garment bag slung over her shoulder. The three of them stepped down off the porch and walked out of sight around to the back of the house. Courtney was walking with a kind of rolling, cautious strut, the way women do in high heels on soft ground. The heels of the two men were kicking up powdery clouds of dust.

Carver moved closer to the house, then off to the side so he could see behind the low clapboard structure.

There was a large rectangular clearing behind the house, green and level. A small, new-looking, single-engine airplane sat at the edge of the clearing. It was a high-winged plane, white with a red propeller. Had red stripes down the sides of the fuselage. Carver thought it was a Cessna but he wasn't sure. As with boats, types of aircraft had proliferated.

Butcher swung open a door and loaded in the flight bags. Took Courtney's garment bag and carefully laid it inside. Ogden and Courtney climbed up into the plane. Butcher raised a beefy arm in a casual wave.

There was a grinding sound and the engine coughed and turned over; the red propeller danced and then became a shimmering blur in the sun. Butcher dashed around the plane and yanked chocks from in front of the wheels.

The engine snarled louder and a hurricane of dust rose and drifted toward Carver. Through the haze he saw the plane's flaps and vertical stabilizer wriggle back and forth in a test of the controls. Then the plane, perfect for short takeoffs and landings, bounced over the field and out of sight behind the house.

A huge form was moving through the dust haze. Butcher. Head down, swinging his arms. Like prehistoric man lost in time. Which maybe he was.

Carver braced with his cane and shuffled back into the trees. Bumped his head on an orange or grapefruit.

But Butcher was in a hurry and didn't notice him. Climbed into the Lincoln and was pulling away even as the plane's motor changed pitch and roared in takeoff.

Butcher and the Lincoln were gone, leaving only tire tracks and settling dust. Carver didn't think Butcher would notice his footprints inside the car's previous tire tracks, or the Olds concealed on the other side of the highway.

He glanced up through the branches and caught a glimpse of the plane. It was climbing steeply, heading north.

After a few minutes the drone of its engine faded and died. Carver was alone in the heat and silence.

He straightened up and limped toward the house.

The closer he got, the more it struck him that there was an air of desolation about the clapboard structure. Paint was faded and peeling. A section of gutter over the porch sagged wearily. Up close, the front-porch screen appeared even rustier and there were gaping holes in it.

Moving quietly, he made his way to the shade side of the house and peered in through a dusty window.

Nothing.

Not even furniture visible through the dimness.

Carver limped around to the front of the house, up the slanted wooden steps, and through the screen door onto the porch. The porch floor wood was rotted. A dusky palmetto bug at least an inch long crawled sluggishly into a shadowy gap near the front wall. At first Carver thought the door to the cabin was open, then he saw that there was no door. It was leaning against the opposite wall and draped with cobwebs.

He went inside, his cane making hollow thumps on the plank floor. Wiped his forehead. Stood in muted light and stifling heat and listened to the steady drone of flies. What was drawing them were several crumpled white McDonald's bags in a corner. An open foam container that held traces of a hamburger. Lettuce, something gooey—maybe cheese. A few curved strands of onion stuck to the Styrofoam. There were footprints in the dust on the floor. Two sets of men's. One of a woman's high heels. Against a wall was an old oak table, a couple of wooden chairs. A chair lay on its side like something dead near the table. Sunlight lanced through a hole in the roof and spread a bright puddle of light near the upended chair. Dust motes swam where the sun penetrated.

Obviously the cabin itself was unimportant, and the citrus trees primarily cover for a landing site.

As he limped back outside into brighter air and lesser heat, Carver asked himself what he'd expected to find. Bales of marijuana? Kilos of cocaine? The Southern Christian Businessmen's League would run a narcotics operation that was too efficient and sophisticated to play so loosely with its product.

He used his tongue to work grit from his teeth and then spat. Moved down the narrow, dusty road toward the highway. Limping in the same tire track he'd used to guide him to the parked Lincoln and the desolate house.

Laboring with his cane, he remembered the hulking, primal form of Butcher loping effortlessly through the haze, and he shivered in the heat.

Chapter 23

Carver drove toward Orlando, stopping once at a roadside restaurant to wash the dust from his throat with iced tea and eat a club sandwich for lunch. The restaurant was called Citrus Charlie's and featured orange juice drinks with every meal, some of them innovative. Fancied itself a family establishment, according to scrawled lettering on the orange-colored menu. Below "Desserts," right under "Orange Dip Delite," was written "Jesus Saves," as if He were a regular customer and always ordered the special.

There were orange THANK YOU FOR NOT SMOKING signs all over the place, so after eating, Carver paid his check and limped outside. Glared up at the orange sun, and then stood in the shade of the souvenir shop built onto the side of the rough-cedar building and smoked a Swisher Sweet cigar. Watched the traffic on the highway. Lots of campers and motor homes out today. Northerners dumb enough to come to Florida in the summer.

Even in the shade, the sun got to be too much after about five minutes, so he flicked the cigar butt away and got back in the Olds.

It wasn't much cooler in there. Carver started the car and

got back on the sun-blanched highway. The Olds's prehistoric engine didn't mind the heat. Not like a little four-cylinder, flailing away at peak efficiency just to hold the speed limit.

He set the air conditioner on high, and after about twenty minutes he could touch the vinyl upholstery without burning himself.

Today it was marimba music. A syncopated song of lament throbbing like a strong but irregular heartbeat from the portable radio on the sill behind Desoto's desk. Next to it the yellow ribbons tied to the air conditioner grill whipped from side to side like pennants in a sea breeze. Made the office look cool, anyway.

Desoto sat behind the desk thinking about what Carver had just told him. He had his white shirtsleeves rolled up in concession to the heat, but his ice-blue silk tie remained tightly knotted. He was even wearing a thin gold tie bar to keep the knot at a stylish angle.

When Carver was done talking, Desoto said, "Sometimes they're like wolves, *amigo*. They just lie back and watch. Nothing happens till you run, then they give chase."

"You saying I should leave Edwina in Del Moray?"

"Might be the best thing. You gonna tell her she's been photographed and is being watched?"

"I don't know yet how to play it," Carver said, "I'm not sure I *should* tell her."

"She'll be pissed off if you don't."

"Pissed off if I do. And she might try something stupid, like confronting Butcher." *Jesus, earlobes!*

Desoto leaned back in his chair. Laced his fingers behind his head carefully and lightly, so as not to muss his sleek dark hair. More a pose than a relaxed attitude. As if there might be some photographer sneaking around *here*, snapping shots for a most-eligible-bachelor calendar. He said, "I think you should bring McGregor into this. Let him assign somebody undercover to protect her."

"I thought of that. Don't like it but I might do it."

"As it is, you got no choice but to play along with the Atlanta crowd. You'll be spying on the DEA while the government knows about it. Spying on the Wesley operation all the time you're doing that." He shot Carver his matinee-idol smile. Handsome matador out of place and costume. "What's that mean, I wonder; you're a double agent? Triple?"

Carver said, "Means I'm in the middle."

Desoto brought his arms around in front of him and sat forward. Folded his hands on the desk. The breeze from the air conditioner stirred the dark hair on his right forearm. The marimba band harmonized softly and earnestly in Spanish. "This citrus ranch with the deserted house," Desoto said, "you think it's nothing but a drug drop?"

"I don't know. Seems to me it's too dangerous to be used as that. More likely a place for small aircraft to land so they can shuttle people in and out of Florida without drawing attention. Speaking of which . . ."

"I checked as soon as you phoned from the restaurant," Desoto said. "Vincent Butcher took a twelve-thirty commercial flight back to Atlanta. Looks like his job was to fly down early and set up a rental car, so Ogden and Courtney Romano could get here at their convenience and he could pick them up when they landed. Play the chauffeur."

"These people," Carver said, "they've got clout and balls. They know the DEA's watching them and still they plan on operating."

"Not balls," Desoto said, "it's the money. So much money they don't have the balls to turn away from it. So they chance almost anything. Do almost anything to anybody.

The profit's the thing, so fuck the risk. It clouds their thinking, *amigo*. Gives the good guys the advantage in the war on drugs and creates the impression it's a war that can be won."

"You don't think it can be?"

Desoto shook his head sadly. "Ever see the monthly statistics on drugs confiscated? Arrests made? Compare them to estimates of what's flowing into the country from every place else in the world? Hell, it doesn't even have to come from outside the country; people grow the shit in their basements under ultraviolet lights."

"The DEA's headache," Carver said. "I don't look at the stats or read about the drug epidemic. Enough bad news without that. Let the DEA do their thing. I only wish they could do it without me."

"Yeah. Problem is, you can't really trust the DEA. Not after the Renway deal."

"There's something wrong about all of it," Carver said. "Jefferson. He doesn't seem quite level. Not your usual DEA operative."

"Seems not. Guy sounds like a zealot."

"He is. And the dangerous kind that's hard to recognize because he doesn't foam at the mouth."

"So he's a rogue agent. It happens. Who's gonna stop him?"

"I don't know."

"What about Palma?"

"I think he's afraid of Jefferson."

"Are you?"

"No. But I probably should be."

Desoto said, "I can't think of anybody involved in this who *shouldn't* scare you. No—hey, wait. Except for your client. Because he's dead."

The marimba band swung into "La Cucaracha." Made Carver wish he were Spanish. Wish he could dance.

He snatched up his cane and got out of there.

Chapter 24

McGregor said, "I don't like it. You tell me the three black hats from Atlanta turn up here in Del Moray, then you drop by my office. Case you haven't caught on, I'm not supposed to be involved in this investigation of yours."

"Of ours," Carver corrected.

McGregor ignored him. Swiveled in his chair to gaze out his office window, stirring the air just enough to send the cloying scent of his cheap cologne Carver's way. Smelled like furniture wax and stale sweat. He'd been on the Del Moray police force long enough now that his fellow officers knew him and despised him. Knew him and were afraid of him. Not because he possessed greater talent or resolve, but because he'd resort to anything, no matter how unethical, to get what he wanted. What he wanted was advancement. Power. He was getting it. Using what he had to get more. That was McGregor's life.

He'd connived his way into one of the better offices, though still not the best in the converted home that was Del Moray police headquarters. But it did have a much-coveted window, even if the view was of the pale gravel parking lot.

Officers' private cars. A few angled, dusty patrol cars, one with COPS SUCK boldly scrawled with a fingertip on a dirty front fender.

Carver said, "Stop worrying; I told you, they flew back to Atlanta. They've got no way of knowing I came here to see you." He didn't like being in McGregor's office. Liked even less that he'd come here to ask a favor. To McGregor, favors were currency as real as folding money. Debts to be collected with interest.

McGregor swiveled back around to face him again. "They like homing pigeons? They only fly one direction, so eager they just gotta get back to Atlanta? They so careless they didn't leave a man behind to watch you? See what kinda fuck-up you're gonna pull next?"

"They didn't need to leave anyone behind."

"How 'bout those DEA assholes. Think they might not be keeping an eye on you?"

"What if they are? What if anybody is? I'm a private investigator, and this is police headquarters. You might not have noticed it, but we're in more or less the same business. Florida's got more crime than sand. I might be here on a matter unrelated to narcotics or Renway's death."

"We both know that's bullshit. Either of your sets of friends knew you came here, they'd sure as hell lean on you to find out why. Cut off selected body parts till they found out."

Carver figured McGregor was right, but why give him satisfaction by admitting it?

"What makes you think the Atlanta faction didn't leave somebody behind to keep watch on you?" McGregor asked. The possibility was clearly worrying him.

"They worked it out so they don't need to watch me; they tied a string to me. That's why I came to see you."

A wary look drifted into McGregor's pale blue eyes. He brushed his lank blond hair back from his long forehead. Darted the tip of his tongue out between his widely spaced front teeth. He said, "String? What's that s'pose to mean, you're a yo-yo? You think you're a hip guy talking street slang like the rest of the shitheads out there? What kinda string?"

"Edwina." Carver explained about the photographs, the threat to Edwina if he didn't keep Ogden informed about the DEA investigation. Then he hit McGregor with his request. He didn't tell McGregor about Courtney Romano being DEA. That would put Courtney in worse, if not immediate, danger. She was surrounded by people hungry for money and power. If it suited his purpose, McGregor would toss her like meat to trailing wolves.

McGregor stood up, stretched his elongated body languidly, and walked out from behind the desk. Lanky and looming, hollow-chested but with a rangy, tireless look about him. He paced slowly, his fingertips caressing his jutting chin. Posing. Showing Carver he was carefully considering. He had his suitcoat off and perspiration stains formed dark crescents beneath the arms of his wrinkled white shirt. The narrow end of his tie dangled down an inch below the wide. His pants looked as if they'd been ironed with a hammer, and he'd missed a belt loop so the material bunched up in back as if his diaper needed changing. He was a tower of bad taste.

After a while he said, "Uh-uh, Carver, I ain't gonna assign someone to guard her."

Anger dug spurs into Carver's stomach. He told himself he shouldn't be surprised by McGregor's refusal. "Why not?" he asked.

"Whaddaya mean, why not? It oughta be obvious, even to an airbrain like you. We all got our personal and intimate responsibilities."

"Which means?"

"Means you're the one runnin' cock through Edwina Talbot, you take care of her."

Carver sank the tip of his cane into the soft carpet and hauled himself to his feet. Took an awkward half-step. He mentally measured the distance between himself and McGregor. The length of his arm and the cane?

McGregor grinned at Carver's rage; he enjoyed getting under people's skin. "Also, there's lotsa crime happening around here. I can't spare the manpower."

Carver said, "I don't like your explanation."

"Really? Which one?"

"Neither."

"No shit? Well, it's this way: I can't take the chance. Can't afford to have the DEA or your Atlanta buddies or the department here make any connection between me and what you're doing. You're a detective, fuckhead, you shoulda been able to figure that one out. So I can't give your cunt protection. No way, José. For*get* it!"

"You're the one who set all this in motion," Carver hissed through clenched teeth. "*You've* got a responsibility. For Christ's sake, you're a cop. If nothing else, it's your *job* to protect a citizen if you know her life's in danger."

McGregor spread his plate-size hands and pretended to be puzzled. "Whadda we got here, the Judeo-Christian work ethic or something?"

"It's your job," Carver repeated evenly. Thinking, despite himself, maybe McGregor had something with that "work ethic" remark. Cynical prick! But if his work—this kind of work—wasn't important, what was?

"I can't know shit about a job," McGregor said, "since we never had this conversation. And it's a fact we never had this conversation, 'cause I don't know a thing about what you been doing this past week or so. That's why you should realize I got no choice but to tell you no. So send your lady friend outa town. Outa the state. If that ain't safe, it's at least safer than in Del Moray. Sleep alone for a while and jerk yourself off. Just don't involve me in your problem."

Carver had to fight the impulse to club him with the cane. "Don't involve you in my problem? You *are* my problem, you kink-brained bastard! You're why all this is happening."

"If I'm your problem," McGregor said, "then you got a problem ain't humanly possible to solve."

"That's because the only thing human about you," Carver said, "is that you walk upright."

"I'm no different from you, except I'm smarter and keep two moves ahead. I don't do dumb things and get myself in trouble because of some fucked-up sense of morality that don't mean a thing unless I got the luxury of being able to practice it. You say I ain't human, but you're wrong; I'm what human beings are all about. Looking out for ourselves, that's us. Boil it down, that's what it's about for all of us in this shitty world. And that's what the world is—fermenting shit. I at least got the sense to learn to live in it. Learn to kinda like it, even. More sense than a John Wayne jack-off like you, with your box-top code of honor. Tell you, Carver, the only difference between you and me is I *know* there ain't a difference between us. That's why you're the one caught in the middle and getting the juice squeezed outa you."

"Oh? You think we're not in this together? What are you gonna say if somebody asks you what we talked about here in your office?"

McGregor smiled confidently. "I got a cover story all worked out. It didn't surprise me, you being rammy enough to come here big as a hard-on despite our agreement. I didn't get where I am by forgetting to cover my ass."

Carver believed him. Covering his tracks, covering his ass,

that was McGregor's game and he was the best at it. Still, there was the possibility of that tape recording when he'd put his proposition—his ultimatum—to Carver in the littered office after the car bombing.

Carver said, "What if I told you our conversation in my office the day of Renway's death was taped?"

"I'd tell you that I don't believe it. 'Cause I phoned your office that same day and didn't even get a ring outa that piece of Japanese junk on your desk. So I'm willing to chance it, if it comes to push and shove. Willing to bet that you can't prove I put you up to whatever it is you been doing. I figure it's the word of a has-been gimp keyhole-peeper against that of a respected police lieutenant."

"Who respects you?" Carver asked.

McGregor shrugged. "Legalese," he explained. "That's what I'll be in court, a respected police lieutenant. The guy they'll *have* to believe before they believe you. Otherwise where would the law and order come from in this pea-brained society, they start doubting the word of the law in court? That's what you'll hear, you fuck with me. The law talking."

"Some law," Carver said, glaring at him.

"Right now," McGregor said, "the law says get the fuck outa my office. It's not that I ain't got compassion, but I also got work to do."

"That's your final word?"

"My final word is, if you're afraid she'll get photographed to death, take care of the bitch yourself."

"Compassion," Carver said in disgust, "is something you know nothing about."

McGregor grinned, absently scratching his testicles like a major-league batter on TV, and said, "Nothing or everything."

Chapter 25

~~~ Carver decided he had to go see Lloyd Van Meter. The man was bizarre, but he had resources and he'd help. And he was a friend, which was a good reason both to confide in him and to leave him out of the action. McGregor had left Carver little choice but to bring Van Meter into the game. That could be like inviting Howard Hughes to sit in on Monopoly.

Carver had first met Van Meter when, as an Orlando patrolman, he'd arrested a burglary suspect who happened to be the wayward lover of Van Meter's client, a wealthy New York society woman who ran an exclusive call-girl operation. Van Meter had been small-time back then, but he'd gotten the help of a local high-powered lawyer and created enough smoke and confusion to get the suspect returned to New York in a tangle of red tape. Carver had never seen the burglar again. The unconventional but effective Van Meter, with the money-laden gratitude of his wealthy New York client, had soon become head of one of the largest private-investigation agencies in Florida. Within five years he had offices in Miami and Tampa, as well as new and impressive offices in Orlando. Crime paid, even if indirectly.

He sat now in his main office on Orange Avenue in Orlando and listened to Carver. The office was furnished in Danish modern, no doubt by a decorator who'd never seen Van Meter. He was the only thing in the plush office that didn't fit the decor. His bulk seemed to threaten to break everything. Especially the spindly straight legs of his desk chair. The desk itself was a pale oak creation that sort of resembled the state of Florida painted by Picasso. It was as sharply angled as the obese Van Meter was rounded. On one of its many corners was an ornate walnut pipe rack containing only one curve-stemmed pipe with a huge blackened bowl. A comfortable-looking accessory that also seemed foreign to the room but not to its occupant.

Van Meter, who claimed to be the illegitimate son of famous Prohibition-era gangster Homer Van Meter, was more massive than when Carver had last seen him. His features were sharply defined despite his fleshiness, and his thick white hair and flowing white beard gave him a Biblical look that inspired certain clients with confidence, especially in central Florida. He dressed as if he'd had all his clothes made from fabric bought at an awning-factory sale of material that wouldn't move. He was wearing a yellow-and-white-striped suit. White shirt with yellow flecks in the material. Brown tie with what appeared to be a yellow mermaid painted on it. Perched in his dainty little chair, he looked like a huge scoop of lemon-vanilla ice cream about to melt over the sides of a dish.

After listening to Carver, he waved a hand bearing a massive silver-and-turquoise ring and said, "Sounds like you're in deep and sinking toward the bottom to join the whale shit."

Carver said, "I came here to see if I could borrow some buoyancy."

Van Meter grinned and patted his huge, protruding

stomach. "Came to the right man, old buddy." He leaned forward; the frail little chair squealed in fright. Van Meter glanced around the office. "I wish somebody'd come in here one night and break all this crap into sticks. I paid a fortune to have it decorated last year; put it all in the hands of my secretary, Marge. It'd hurt her feelings if I told her I didn't like it and was afraid someday it'd break under me and give me splinters."

"Must be some secretary, that Marge."

Van Meter shrugged beneath the yards of yellow material. It was like watching a sail billow. "Well, she's an old man's pleasure, you might say."

Carver figured Van Meter was only about fifty, not much older than Carver, but he let it go. He wondered if Marge was the one who'd ushered him into the office, a tall, noble-looking gray-haired woman, probably older than Van Meter. The sort of woman who'd be attractive all her life. Good bones. Good everything.

Something hissed like a snake in the corner. Carver turned his head and saw one of those automatic scent dispensers timed to emit periodic sprays of fragrance into the air. He sniffed and recognized the scent of cinnamon.

"Another one of Marge's ideas," Van Meter said. "She don't like it when I smoke my pipe in here. Says it smells up the place for a month."

Carver said, "Maybe you oughta try some cinnamon-scented tobacco."

"They make that kinda crap?"

"Sure."

"Hmm."

The little square scent-dispenser clicked and whirred. Something in it had rewound.

"Women and money," Van Meter said, shaking his head, "they cause us to do things we wouldn't ordinarily."

Carver said, "That's what keeps you and me in business."

Van Meter stroked his long beard. Looked wise as Moses behind his peculiar angled desk. "Why you're here, in fact, would be my guess."

"That's right," Carver said, "Edwina. I want to hire you to put an operative on her for protection, but it'll have to be without her, or anybody else who might be shadowing her, knowing about it."

"Okay. Just leave me a can of that powder makes people invisible."

"C'mon, Lloyd."

"What you're asking won't be easy."

"Possible, though. And the only way I have to go."

"You could tell her about this," Van Meter suggested. "See what she wants to do."

But Carver knew what Edwina would want. What she'd do. She'd stay in Del Moray. And if she knew she was under surveillance she'd act as if she knew. Might even confront whoever was watching her. She'd lost herself during a disastrous marriage. Became even more lost after her divorce when she'd rebounded into a crippling love affair with a con man. Found herself only after the death of the con man and the help of Carver. Would never run from herself or anything else again. Carver had taught her that and he couldn't argue now that she should run. She'd stick despite anything he might say; she'd developed the territorial possessiveness of a bull terrier. He thought that was fine—usually.

But he had to protect her from Vincent Butcher. Christ, Butcher with his string of human earlobes.

"Carver?"

"I can't tell her," Carver said. "I know her, and that'd only make things worse."

Van Meter lifted his wide shoulders again. Held them

raised for a few seconds and then let them fall. "Like I said, things we wouldn't ordinarily do. I can put Hans on this. He's a damn good operative and sneaky as a cat burglar. 'Tween you and me, I think he *can* make himself invisible."

"I hope so," Carver said. "I wouldn't want to understate the danger."

"Hans can manage. He has before. But I gotta tell you, there can't be a guarantee in anything like this. I mean, Edwina might be on melting ice, judging by what you say. And you're playing in the big leagues of drugs. The worst people on earth. The camera that took those photographs could just as easily have been a gun. If something should happen to her despite Hans . . ."

"I'll understand," Carver said. *Will I?*

Van Meter picked up a ballpoint pen from the desk. Clicked the spring-loaded mechanism. "Where you gonna be so I can get in touch?"

"I better not tell you."

The scent dispenser hissed again. Cinnamon rode the air. Van Meter set the pen back down and studied Carver. "If you're about to try something cute with the characters you just described to me, I hope it works."

"Me too."

The office door opened and an attractive young blonde with a trim figure, a short leather skirt, and a beauty-pageant smile sashayed in. Said, "Hi, sweetballs." Stopped cold when she noticed Carver. Blushed and said, "Sorry, Lloyd, I though you were alone."

"S'okay, babe," Van Meter said. "This is an old friend. Carver, meet Marge." He beamed possessively. "My very private secretary."

Carver stood up, leaned on his cane, and shook Marge's small hot hand. She was sporting a gold cocktail ring with a pea-size diamond.

Marge said, "Listen, I'll get outa here and let the two of you talk."

Carver told her to stay, he was leaving anyway. At the door, he planted the cane and twisted his upper body so he was looking back at Van Meter. "I appreciate this, Lloyd."

"Ah, we don't do each other favors, who else is gonna help us? Our profession don't inspire trust among outsiders. Even our clients usually don't trust us."

"Maybe they're right," Carver said. "My last client trusted me, and look what happened. Bye, Marge."

Limping through the outer office, he heard her call, "Nice meetin' ya!"

The gray-haired duchess behind the receptionist's desk glanced at Carver and rolled her eyes.

Carver thought, What did she know? Marge seemed happy with Van Meter, and Van Meter deserved his perks. Sometimes the world worked just right.

Chapter 26

It was obvious Jefferson didn't like being awakened at one A.M. Especially by Carver.

He stood in the doorway of his room at the Sundown Motel, squinting out at Carver, his right arm hung at an angle so the hand rested out of sight behind him. He was wearing only pants; suspenders were still attached to them and draped down around his hips and thighs. Even in the faint and wavering light from the illuminated pool, Carver could see the ridged muscle of Jefferson's upper body. One time or another, Jefferson must have done considerable work with weights.

The hand came out from behind his back. There was a revolver in it. Jefferson said, "Fuck you want, this time of night?" He stepped back to let Carver inside, keeping the gun low but with his finger still curled around the trigger.

Carver planted his cane and entered the dark motel room. It was too warm in there and smelled of sweat. "You always answer the door with the lights out?"

"Yeah. With a gun, too." Jefferson reached over and switched on a table lamp. Blinked at the sudden glare. Never stopped looking at Carver, though. "Heard the knocking, thought at first it was a fuckin' dream. Still have hopes."

"Not a dream," Carver said, "me."

"So I see. Nightmare, more like it; too much pasta coming back to haunt. Now, why would you wake me up at"—he glanced at his watch—"oh, God, one o'friggin'-clock in the morning?"

"I thought it was the safest time to come here without being seen."

"By your Atlanta friends?"

"Right. You must have been in contact with Courtney Romano."

"We are frequently," Jefferson said. He revealed no surprise that Carver knew about Courtney. Used his free hand to scratch lazily beneath his rib cage. "She likes it that way."

"Don't blame her, having met Vincent Butcher. You ever had the pleasure?"

"No, but I know a great deal about him. More than you know. None of it's nice. So maybe I don't blame you for sneaking over here in the wee hours. But how the hell did you know where to find me?"

"Called the main DEA office in Washington and they told me."

"I'll ignore that, but I don't wanna hear any more smartass remarks."

"Courtney tell you the arrangement I'm supposed to have with the Wesley people?"

" 'Course she did. That's her job. A useful arrangement, you ask me. You're gonna be a double agent, my man. No, wait a minute, triple agent. Working for us, but they think you're working for them, only we know about it and you're working for us. A three-cushion shot."

Carver remembered Desoto mentioning that.

Jefferson sat down in a small wing chair. He let his powerful arms drop limply to the sides, let the gun dangle. The lamp highlighted his washboard stomach; the kind of guy who could drive himself to do hundreds of sit-ups each and every day. Or who was driven to do them. "No time at all you've gone from keyhole-peeker to goddamn triple agent," he said. "Something, huh?"

"Only in America."

Jefferson's eyes, yellowish in the lamplight, got hard. "When we got something we want Wesley to know, we'll get in touch with you. Tell you what to pass on."

"And if they find out I'm passing on stacked information, what about me?"

Jefferson barked something somewhere between a snort and a laugh. "You're the one wanted into this game, Carver. Now you're in and you got no choice."

"Maybe. But I want something from you."

"I gathered that, considering you were knocking at my door at one A.M. and we never got together much socially."

"The woman I live with, Edwina Talbot; if I get outa line they'll sic Butcher on her. That's the string they tied on me."

Jefferson nodded, staring at Carver. "Courtney told us. So you stay in line, only what you tell Ogden and Butcher is what we want them to know."

"That's not staying in line," Carver said. "It's dangerous for Edwina."

"Not to mention the intrepid private eye. You guys tinker around with serious matters, get in our way. Well, this time you poked your pecker in a steel trap. Nothing you can do but play along with Ogden and Butcher. Which means there's nothing you can do but play along with us."

"Maybe," Carver said. "But you got no choice other than

170

to make sure nothing happens to Edwina Talbot. You're not exactly running your own investigation by official procedure."

"I can't afford to be a bureaucrat," Jefferson said. "I'm out here in the field with my ass on the line."

"You know a private citizen's in danger, and you want to place her in even greater jeopardy by forcing me to lie to Ogden and Butcher."

"If that's the way you see it. Thing is, though, there's a kinda time limit on all this. There's supposed to be a Southern Christian Businessmen's League strategy meeting down here in the next few days. All the movers and shakers, discussing new routes for drug shipments from Central America. That's the reason Palma and I came to Florida in the first place."

"Time limit or not, the way I see it, you better do what you can to shield Edwina."

"You seem to have it backward about who's between the rock and the block, Carver. You gotta tell the Wesley people something, and if you pass on information we haven't okayed, you're guilty of complicity. It's gotta be one or the other. Them or us. No real choice there, the way it looks to me. How you see it I'm not sure. But it's down to the short strokes in this game, baby."

"Any way I move I lose."

Jefferson nodded. "Might."

"What if I tell Ogden you know about the SCBL get-together?"

"Then you're federal pen bound, Carver. But the SCBL knows we're onto this anyway. The meeting will come off, as long as they think we don't know where it's gonna be held. Florida's a big state, the size of some European countries, and big money makes for big egos and overconfidence.

Now if you were to find out the exact location of the meeting, it'd be smart to pass it on to me or Palma."

"Can't Courtney tell you?"

"They don't completely trust her." Jefferson swallowed hard. "And she's around because Ogden wants her."

"I didn't see any sign of that," Carver said. "I mean, of anything between them."

Jefferson said, "It's not a relationship based on love." He made a face as if he'd like to spit out something vile.

"She still figures to learn the meeting place before I would."

"Could be."

Carver made an effort not to look in the direction of the rifle in the duffel bag beneath the bed. He said, "There's something else operating here, isn't there?"

Jefferson said, "Huh? I don't follow."

"Something more than a drug-smuggling ring you're trying to break."

"Well, you never know what else some of these drug kings are into until you subpoena the books. Even then, they're so good at cooking the numbers you still might not know."

"That's not what I mean."

"Oh? What *do* you mean?"

"I'm not sure. Maybe you can tell me."

Jefferson's face twitched and the muscles in his neck and chest corded. For a moment he seemed about to say something. But only for a moment. Carver got a brief look at something inside Jefferson, writhing and agonized and dangerous. It scared him; a glimpse of a demon.

A wind kicked up off the sea. Something light bounced with force off the glass door beyond the bed. Outside, in the distance, a woman laughed loudly and maniacally.

"I came here to tell you to make sure Edwina has protection," Carver said.

"Why don't you simply get her out of town on the sly?"

"That'd only work for a while. Even if she'd leave, which she won't. Besides, there's always the possibility she'd be trailed to wherever she went. There'd be no way to know for sure. These people are pros. It'd be hard for her to go anywhere now without them knowing."

Jefferson yawned, his deep chest heaving. He ran a hand over his hair, as if to make sure it hadn't fallen out in the night. Studied his palm for a few seconds. "Yeah, you're right. So you're using what you perceive as leverage to get us to protect Miss Talbot."

"That's it," Carver said.

"Might surprise you to know we already got somebody watching over her. That was decided five minutes after our contact with Courtney. You're right, Carver, Miss Talbot's a U.S. citizen and has protection owed her."

"That's what I needed to hear," Carver said. He shifted position with the cane and limped toward the door.

"You mean I can go back to sleep now?"

"Or wake up. Maybe this *is* a bad dream."

"Yours, not mine. But wait'll I turn out the light before you open the door. Wouldn't want some fool to take a shot at you and hit me." Jefferson reached out a muscular arm and switched off the lamp. "We'll give you a call soon about what information to pass on to Atlanta."

"Sure. Thanks."

"Carver, something else."

Carver waited in the faint light.

"The way you'd feel if something happened to Edwina Talbot, that's how I'll feel if you screw up and something happens to Courtney Romano."

Carver looked at him, surprised. "So it's that way between you and Courtney."

Jefferson nodded slowly, his serious dark eyes shining in the dim room. "That way."

Carver stood quietly for a moment, thinking about Courtney and Ogden. About the rifle under the bed. A hunting tool. An assassination weapon. But what was the deal here? Jefferson could take out Ogden almost anytime he wanted. And he had to know Courtney was willingly doing her job. Jefferson of all people would understand that. "But there's more, isn't there?" Carver said. "Only you're not telling me. Something about you. Something keeping you wound tight."

Smiling, Jefferson said, "Get off that bullshit. You wanna play psychiatrist, go back to school."

Carver said, "You worry me."

"Least you got that much sense. Night, Carver."

"Night."

"So walk. I gotta get some sleep."

Carver limped out into the greater darkness of the night. He was satisfied now that Edwina would have the best protection possible. She'd be safer home and unaware in Del Moray than in a strange city, unfamiliar territory where she might have been followed or could soon be discovered.

From the shadowy room behind Carver, Jefferson said, "Remember, Carver, you're the one between the rock and the hard place."

Carefully skirting the edge of the gently lapping pool, Carver thought: That means it's time to move.

Chapter 27

Driving through the warm night, Carver wished he could return home to bed and Edwina, tell her what he was doing. But he knew it would be a possibly fatal mistake. The odds were good that Ogden—rather, the enigmatic Frank Wesley—had someone watching Edwina. Carver they didn't have to watch; he was attached to the end of a leash in the grasp of Walter Ogden. If he did something wrong he'd be punished by Edwina's horrendous rendezvous with Vincent Butcher.

If he did something wrong.

But if he did nothing, and if he slipped the leash, that would be different. If no one knew where he was. Or why. Then the result would be uncertainty. Edwina would be safe because Ogden wouldn't want to eliminate Carver's possible remaining value by harming her. Also, Van Meter's man Hans and the DEA would be watching over her. Jefferson and Palma would think Courtney Romano might be able to tell them where Carver had gone, but they'd be wrong.

Carver was going to move completely off the game board. Suddenly he'd no longer be a factor except by his absence, which could be interpreted a number of ways, but not with the certainty that would prompt action.

The Olds's canvas top was up but all the windows were cranked down. Wind boomed and swirled through the car's interior. Taut canvas slapped against the steel struts as Carver pushed the car hard along the Orange Blossom Trail toward Orlando. Flying night insects met hard and instant death against the windshield; Carver had to use the squirts and wipers now and then in order to see clearly.

At the Orlando airport he parked the Olds in an inconspicuous slot in a park-and-fly lot, then rolled up the windows, climbed out, and locked the doors. He limped around to the trunk and removed his scuffed leather suitcase. Lugged the suitcase over to the next row of cars and down about a hundred feet, where he'd left the green Ford he'd rented earlier.

He placed the suitcase on the passenger-side front seat of the Ford, then limped around to the driver's side and lowered himself in behind the steering wheel. Experienced that new-car smell everyone with big payments bragged about.

He'd asked for a Ford with the biggest motor they had, and Hertz had accommodated. The car's engine turned over on the first try and throbbed with quiet power. He backed out of the parking slot, slipped the automatic gearshift lever into drive, and the Ford jerked forward and wanted to fly. Carver smiled.

It was just past three A.M. when he drove from the lot.

The sun was only a faint and uneven red smear on the eastern horizon, like a novice painter's mistake, when Carver killed the Ford's headlights, tapped the brake pedal, and turned off the highway. He was jouncing over the narrow road that led through the rows of citrus trees to the small airstrip and abandoned house.

Carver braked gently and then parked about a hundred yards from the house, which he could barely see as a squat, dark form beyond the trees. Then he climbed out from behind the wheel and hobbled over uneven ground toward the decrepit structure, feeling ahead of him with the cane like a blind man. The only sound was the screaming of crickets in the field behind the house. If they were aware of Carver's presence, they didn't seem to mind enough to lapse into wary silence.

He kept to the side of the road, tasting the grit of powdery dust he couldn't see. The Colt in its belt holster was gouging the top of his right thigh with each step. He adjusted the holster. Didn't help. Hell with it. Sweat trickled down his rib cage. Some ran down his forehead and into his eyes. Stung. He wiped his face with his hand, wiped his hands on his pants leg, and kept limping through the velvet darkness toward the house.

It took him a few minutes to assure himself the house was unoccupied. Then he let himself in through the unlocked porch screen door and stood very still, peering around at the blackness.

It was even darker in the house than outside, and the screams of the crickets were muted. The place smelled musty, and the faint scent of greasy beef and onion lingered from the McDonald's debris he'd seen on his last visit. But now it had about it the cloying sweetness of garbage, and it almost turned his stomach. He swallowed saliva that tasted metallic, but he felt the nausea recede.

After a few minutes his eyes adjusted to the dark and he could make out objects. He limped over to the table, leaned on it, and used the crook of his cane to lift the nearby upended chair. Then he sat down in the chair. It creaked loudly, like Van Meter's delicate desk chair, and for a moment he was afraid it might splinter beneath him. But it held.

He placed the Colt automatic before him on the table. Waited for sunrise.

When the crickets had quieted and shafts of daylight lanced through the dirt-smeared windows, Carver left the house and returned to the Ford. It was parked beneath some of the older and larger orange trees that had thick foliage. The trees were dotted with oranges, probably Valencias, but they were too small for picking.

He opened the car's trunk and removed the suitcase. Opened the suitcase and removed a ball of thin but strong twine and a pocketknife. He placed the twine and knife on the Ford's grained vinyl roof and then limped around and slid the key in the ignition. Twisted it to the accessory position, then lowered the front left power window so he'd have a handhold to help him climb onto the car.

With the aid of the cane, he managed to pull himself up onto the hood. The thin steel gave and sprang back, pinging loudly beneath his weight. Thanks, Detroit. Careful not to step on the wipers, he clambered up onto the car's roof. Hertz wouldn't approve, but what the hell, he had more at stake than they did.

It took him about twenty minutes to bend the trees' lower and smaller branches and tie them so they were interwoven over the Ford. Crude but effective camouflage.

Sweating as if he'd been digging ditches, he slid back down to the ground, satisfied that the car couldn't be seen from the air or the road.

He raised the window, removed the key from the ignition

switch, and locked the car. Then he trudged back to the house, lugging the scuffed leather suitcase.

Seated again at the table, he got a thermos of hot coffee from the suitcase, poured some into the metal cap, then calmly sipped it. The steamy aroma whetted his appetite, but he decided not to eat anything until lunch. He knew he'd have to wait here a long time. Maybe days. Maybe a week. And maybe his waiting would be useless and he'd simply have to give up and try a different approach. He'd come prepared to wait. In the suitcase were a few changes of clothes, a small portable radio, some bottled drinking water, a box of granola bars, and some canned soup and packaged junk food. Also a large thermos of soup, some of which he was prepared to drink cold after the first day. Lunch.

Like most cops and former cops, Carver possessed a smoldering kind of patience that was almost infinite. Waiting was something he did very well. He could retreat into himself and block out everything else, but simultaneously retain an automatic alertness. Cops learned to do that instead of going mad with boredom.

He finished the coffee and then leaned back in the old wood chair and sat quietly, his eyes half closed. Not awake, not asleep. Not watching, yet aware. If the slightest change occurred anywhere around him, he'd know.

Nothing moved in the dim, ruined house. The day grew brighter, and the occasional moan of a passing truck on the distant highway drifted lazily to Carver. He didn't seem to notice. Last night had been long and exhausting, but he knew he couldn't afford to fall completely asleep. Not here. Not now.

He didn't mind. In a way, he'd gone on the offensive. Made moves that would confuse. He liked that.

Something small and frantic scampered lightly across the roof. In a four-footed hurry. Most likely a squirrel.

Carver ignored it. Probably it was on its way to feast on an orange. Maybe later Carver would follow the squirrel's example. Go out and try to find an orange ripe enough to eat. Have that with his soup.

He sat in the increasing heat and waited, his heart ticking out measured beats like the timer on a bomb.

Chapter 28

Just before sundown of the second day, they came. Carver saw the rising cloud of dust over the shimmering tops of the orange trees, then heard the faint but unmistakable revving of a car engine.

He turned away from the window, limped to the table, and scooped everything that was his into the leather suitcase that was unlatched and ready. Laid the chair on the floor where it had been when he'd first entered the cabin, then lugged the suitcase toward the back door, his cane banging out a hasty thumping on the plank floor.

Outside, he moved with his deceptively speedy hobble across open ground and into the cover of the trees. Crouched low and supported himself with his grip halfway up the firmly planted cane, his stiff leg jutting out awkwardly in front of him. He watched through the leaves.

The car's engine grew louder, then he could hear the rhythmic bumping of its suspension as it jounced along the narrow rutted road. A black Cadillac stretch limo with darkly tinted windows pulled into view. It was waxed to mirror finish except where the dust had powdered it behind the wheel wells. It came to a stop about a hundred feet in front and slightly to the side of the cabin. Sat there with its motor idling. The sleek limo reminded Carver of a monstrous and mutated black roach, filled him with vague dread.

Carver's portable radio had said the temperature topped a hundred degrees that afternoon. It was probably still over ninety, and cloudless. The lowering sun slanted in bright shafts beneath the branches, causing him to sweat so his shirt was plastered to him. He was sure he was well out of sight of the car unless someone inside happened to stare directly at him, but he tried to stay as motionless as possible. Some kind of flying insect he'd never seen before, long slender body, translucent green wings, droned around him curiously, occasionally darting in for a better view. He wondered if it stung; it looked like the sort of little bastard that would.

The limo's driver-side door opened soundlessly and a tall, thin man in a blue suit got out and stretched his arms. Peered up at the sky. He had dark hair growing in a sharp widow's peak above a narrow, hawk-nosed face. Even beneath the well-tailored suit, it was obvious he was very round-shouldered. His shirt was white, his tie was red, and his black shoes were shined. Carver had never seen him before.

After a few minutes the man cupped a hand over his eyes like an Indian scout and turned in a slow circle. His glance slid past Carver, who stayed motionless and held his breath, hoping his leg muscles wouldn't cramp and make him shift position, or that the flying insect wouldn't decide to swoop in and go for blood.

Then, shaking his head as if he suddenly realized he was miserably hot, the man lowered himself back in behind the steering wheel of the air-conditioned limo and slammed the door. Exhaust fumes rising from the car's tailpipe wavered and danced like a chimera in the hot air.

Carver glanced at his Seiko watch. Saw that ten minutes had elapsed since the arrival of the limo. Saw a rivulet of perspiration trickle down his forearm and puddle against the black leather watchband. Leather bands didn't last long in the Florida heat and humidity; like so many other things—and like people—they tended to come unglued.

Another ten minutes passed, and the sun was kissing the horizon, when he heard the drone of an aircraft engine. He gazed up through the tree limbs at patches of dimming sky. Saw nothing.

Then he caught movement and focused on a small twin-engined plane closing distance from the northwest and losing altitude fast. The guy in the limo must have finally heard it, too, because he climbed out again and stood leaning with both hands on the car's roof, head tilted back and eyes fixed on the approaching plane.

Carver recognized the plane as a Beechcraft. It could carry maybe four passengers and luggage. This one was blue and white. As it circled the field behind the house, he pulled a pen and a folded envelope from his shirt pocket and wrote down its registration number. Then he tried to get a look at the limo's license plate, but the big car was parked at the wrong angle.

He returned his attention to the plane. Its motors roared as it came in even lower, swooping down swiftly until it was out of sight beyond the house.

After a minute or so, he heard the engines snarl and then even out and drone steadily. Grow gradually louder. The plane had landed and was taxiing over the field. Carver caught a glimpse of it through the trees, then it rolled beyond his vision.

He took advantage of the limo driver's attention to the plane and moved off to the side until he had a view of a spinning propeller and a graceful thrust of blue-and-white wing.

The aircraft stopped and the engines fell almost silent, but the props kept ticking over.

The limo driver walked toward the plane. He'd taken only a few steps when a door in the plane opened and a hefty man in a gray suit climbed down to the ground. The wind from the idling propeller snatched at his long gray hair and whipped it around. He jogged away from the plane and smoothed the hair back flat against his head. In his left hand was a dark attaché case. Slung by a strap over his right shoulder was a leather carry-on garment bag, folded and buckled. He was in his sixties and had a broad face with a pug nose. Bushy gray eyebrows. Narrow slash of a mouth. Carver had never seen this one, either.

The limo driver ran up to the man and they shook hands. Then the driver took the garment bag and attaché case, which appeared to be heavy, and the two men trudged toward the limo. Behind them the propellers whirled faster and the Beechcraft's engines growled.

There was a burst of noise as one prop spun especially fast, kicking up clouds of dust, and the plane did a nifty tight turn and taxied out into the field. Turned again and picked up speed into the wind. The roar of the engines took on urgency. The plane was airborne and flying low into the closing darkness by the time the two men reached the black limo.

Carver backed away into the trees, then straightened up and limped toward where the Ford was parked.

He watched the dust rising against the purple sky. And when he figured the limo had about reached the highway, he started the Ford and drove it out from beneath its canopy of branches. Gunned it along in the limo's cloud of dust.

Reached the intersecting road and highway and tried to make out which direction the limo had turned. That was no problem. The big car had trailed its roostertail of dust a few hundred feet along the highway, until the wind had flushed it all from the wheel wells. Dust still drifted low over the pavement.

As soon as he caught sight of the limo up ahead, Carver let the Ford's speed decrease to the limit.

He stayed well back of the limo, letting cars get between them sometimes. The driver kept to a steady, legal speed and obeyed all the traffic laws. Following him was easy.

The limo picked up the Bee Line Expressway and glided east, then got on southbound Interstate 95 and headed toward Melbourne. Past Melbourne and south through darkness now, until the driver jogged east over to A1A near Jupiter. Then south again. At a slower speed, the limo skirted the ocean and rolled royally through wealthy Palm Beach, Boca Raton, Deerfield Beach. An automotive queen cruising her domain.

In Hillsboro Beach, just north of Fort Lauderdale, the long car slowed and then turned off the narrow highway into a driveway locked by tall chain-link gates. The foliage beyond the gates was so thick it was impossible to see where the driveway led. The property on this stretch of coast was among the most expensive in Florida, and privacy was part of what the owners had bought.

Carver passed the driveway and parked on the other side of the road. Adjusted the Ford's outside mirror and watched in it as the limo's driver got out and walked stiffly toward the gates. The driver leaned forward and said something into what must have been an intercom, then returned to the limo.

Within a few seconds the gates swung open automatically. The limo oozed through them and they shut smoothly behind it. Carver twisted in the seat and watched the limo's red taillights flicker and disappear in the night.

Great. All this way just to get locked out. Some slick detective.

You're doing okay, he reassured himself. Doing okay. Nothing's been easy since the divorce, then the shooting. Why should this be? *Self-pity, huh?*

Carver reached under the Ford's front seat and found the Colt automatic. He pulled it out and tucked it in his belt beneath his shirt.

Knowing what he had to do, he was afraid. But he climbed out of the Ford and crossed to the other side of the road, feeling like the chicken in the joke. Limped toward the tall gates.

He was ten feet away when a dark shape exploded out of the night and hit the gates so hard they rattled against their hinges. Carver leaped back and almost dropped his cane.

The Doberman pinscher barking and snarling at him on the other side of the gates was the largest he'd ever seen. It was immediately joined by three more Dobes almost as big. Fierce and yearning eyes, glittering white fangs. Made Carver feel like a nugget of Alpo.

Afraid the din would soon alert someone at the other end of the long driveway, he backed away and hobbled quickly into the shadows of some palm trees.

As he made his way down the road, keeping to darkness, the noise of the dogs subsided. Only one dog continued barking. Steadily, insistently, as if trying to relay information. Finally a man's voice shouted something and the dog was quiet.

Carver slumped behind the Ford's steering wheel, catching his breath and wondering what to do next. Obviously the security behind the gates was more than he could cope with; his presence would be detected within minutes after he set foot on the property. And within minutes after that, the dogs would be at his throat or a security guard would be holding a gun on him. Carver thought a security guard might look good at that point, considering the size and temperament of the Dobermans.

After about ten minutes, he drove the Ford another few hundred feet up the road and parked it in the shadows. Slid the gun back beneath the seat. Got out and again crossed the highway. This time he limped along until he found a driveway that was blocked only by a chain.

He made his way around the chain and started up the driveway, which was bordered by some sort of tall shrubbery with dark and aromatic flowers. Tried to place the scent. Lilacs? Like the perfume of someone he'd once known.

When he saw the lights of a huge house in front of him, he veered off the driveway and cut through trees and more dense shrubbery. This shrubbery bore no blossoms, but it had sharp thorns that scratched his bare arms and occasionally came dangerously close to an eye.

Past the house, the ground fell away and the rhythmic sighing of the surf, until now only part of the background noise, became louder. Carver stumbled several times when his cane sank too far into the sandy earth as he forged through tall sea grass toward the beach.

On his right he saw some wooden steps leading down to the beach, illuminated by dim lights recessed in a thick railing. He was tempted to use the steps, but he opted instead for the cover of darkness. There was only a tilted sliver of moon, and he was sure he could make it down the sandy slope to the smooth beach without being seen.

He sat down and scooted on his rear end down the steep slope, digging in the cane now and then, using it as a brake. The technique worked well, and he reached the level sand

and the ghostly rushing surf in good shape. Not counting bruised buttocks.

Quickly he stripped to his jockey shorts. Glanced around to get his bearings, then limped toward the water. Speared his cane into the sand and then tied his shirt to its crook like a flag. Felt for a moment like an explorer staking a claim.

He sat down in the soaked, firm sand, just beyond where he'd planted the cane, and waited for a large enough breaker to roar in. Wished one would hurry. He didn't want to be seen sitting here in his underwear on some rich bastard's private property. Aside from everything else, it would be damned embarrassing. Probably only designer-label trunks were worn on this beach.

Finally there was an express-train roar. A looming dark shape rising monstrously from the sea. The oncoming swell curled in on itself in the faint moonlight and broke into boiling whitecaps as it neared the shore. Crashed onto the beach and spread. Surrounded Carver, first with grasping fingers of white foam, then with cold water. Worked beneath him and gave him buoyancy. Lifted him gently and made it possible for him to do an awkward backward scoot seaward until the wave's receding force got well under him and carried him out into deeper water with its powerful back-wash.

He pushed against the water with both cupped hands as he struggled out farther into the ocean, feeling shifting sand and sharp pebbles beneath his bare feet. Drawing a deep breath, he ducked under another incoming wave, smaller than the one that had carried him out. Let the ponderous force of it break over him, then came back up and continued pushing himself away from shore until the bottom fell away and he was floating free. And even through his fear and hyper-alertness, he experienced the elation of having complete control of his body again. In deep water, he was as physically competent as any man and much stronger than most.

He swam out several hundred feet, beyond the breakers, then treaded water and looked back at the beach. He could see the faintly illuminated flight of steps. Farther up the rise, a vast house with several lighted windows. Down the beach a slight distance was a dock, and a large cabin cruiser bobbed at it in rhythm with the waves.

Carver stroked north parallel to the shore, toward the guarded property where the black limo and its passenger had disappeared. The dark water was cool and felt good. He moved through it as if he'd been born in it; since the leg injury and the countless therapeutic swims, it had become his element.

As he swam in his smooth Australian crawl, he watched the beach. The elegant estates and docked pleasure boats. At one house a party was in progress. Music drifted out over the water like signals from another world. There were bright lights. Carver could make out people dancing in a pavilion. He remembered the Latin music in Desoto's office. He hadn't danced in years, and now he wouldn't again. He kept stroking.

When he saw the wire fence extending into the sea, he was sure he'd reached his destination. Something would have to keep the dogs from roaming the beach and bringing back pieces of sunbathers.

He floated on his back for a while until his breathing evened out, rising and falling, gazing up at the crescent of moon. Then he swam to a point between the sections of wire fence and surveyed the area.

What looked like barbed wire curled along the top of the fence. The beach was flat and empty. Beyond it was an impressive house, only one story but with low wings that stretched on opposite sides of a larger main structure. Most of the windows were illuminated.

Carver stroked in closer. Palm fronds shook themselves in the warm breeze, sometimes waving between him and a lighted window and giving the impression that someone was moving around inside the house. There was a narrow pier built out from the beach. A large pleasure craft was docked there. Its graceful hull had to be fifty feet long. Light glowed behind three portholes and, faintly, higher up on the bridge.

Carver swam closer to the boat and could make out a name lettered near its bow: *Bold Entrepreneur*. That figured, on a boat that had to cost at least half a million.

As he stroked in nearer to the beach, he caught sight of a racing dark figure on the sand. Another trailing it. Like swift animated shadow. The dogs. Romping and kicking up sand. Damned things were even on the alert for someone coming in from the sea. One of them barked twice, but Carver was sure it wasn't because of him. Too playful. And he was still several hundred feet from the beach.

He swam farther out, then angled in so the graceful shape of the boat was between him and the direction the dogs had taken.

Breaststroking easily and almost silently, he moved up very close to the boat. Could have touched its hull. He was sure someone was on board, and he was hoping he'd hear something useful. But the only sound other than the sea lapping at the hull was music wafting out through one of the open portholes. Bach maybe? Beethoven? Elton John? Carver might not know the difference.

He swam alongside the hull until he could gaze around the stern at the house. The boat rose and fell gently, shoved a wave at him and he tasted saltwater. He breathed in instinctively, gagged and almost coughed. He had to be careful; if he choked, someone on board might hear him.

The house and grounds were quiet. Now and then Carver glimpsed one of the dogs trotting through its rounds. Once he thought he saw someone in uniform, probably a security guard, swagger along the beach wearing a nightstick and holstered gun like a cop.

Maybe it was a cop, Carver thought. Bent cop, moonlighting with drug kingpins. This must be where the strategy confab of the SCBL drug smugglers was going to take place. The private plane, and then the limo, had delivered one of those attending. Did Jefferson know about this location? Was Courtney Romano able to contact him and tell him? Did *she* know?

Carver decided to swim back to where he'd entered the water. He'd crawl back on land, get dressed, and then drive to a phone so he could get in touch with Jefferson and let him know what was happening and where.

Careful again to keep the boat between him and the beach and house, he stroked seaward. Glancing back now and then to make sure there was no one on deck who might notice him.

When he was far enough out on the dark sea, he swam south, angling gradually toward shore. Passed the dancers again. Watched until he spotted the illuminated steps leading up to the lighted house.

He swam toward a point just north of the steps, and ten minutes later he hauled himself onto the beach less than a hundred feet from his cane. Quite the navigator.

After retrieving the cane, he limped to where he'd left his clothes. Brushed water out of his thick fringe of hair and quickly got dressed.

He found that scaling the slope back up to level ground

was easier than going down. He could plant the cane like a mountain climber's piton and use it to lever himself along. Still, by the time he'd gained the top his breathing was deep and ragged. The ocean swim had been less of a strain.

He made his way back to the road, then limped along its shoulder, sure that he wasn't attracting undue attention. The sea breeze had almost dried his clothes and hair; what remained might have been perspiration.

He saw the dark shape of the Ford and hurried toward it.

As he settled in behind the steering wheel, he let out a loud sigh and smoothed back his damp fringe of hair again. Attack dogs, armed guards, fences with barbed wire. Like a luxury command post in a state of war. Hell of a thing to contend with. He was glad the night was over. That he was back in the cocoonlike safety of the car and could get away from here.

As he leaned forward to fit the key in the ignition, a motion in the rearview mirror caught his attention. He glanced at the mirror and his gaze froze on it. A pair of eyes was staring back at him.

Eyes he recognized.

Eyes that paralyzed him with surprise and fright.

Before he could move he felt a cold blade on the side of his neck. Vincent Butcher in the backseat, leaned close to him and smiled in an oddly amused and tender way. Carver could still see him in the mirror. Smelled his fetid breath. Their gazes were still locked. Horror became hypnotic.

Butcher said, "Where you been, sweetmeat, nosin' around?"

Gravel crunched outside the car. Footsteps.

The passenger-side door opened and Walter Ogden slid in and sat down. He was dressed impeccably in a window-pane-checked gray suit with a blue handkerchief in the pocket. Handkerchief matched his tie. He smiled at Carver. "Well, you seem to have dropped from sight," he said in an amiable tone. "Time you filled us in on where you been and why."

Carver said, "You didn't get my postcard?"

Butcher probed with the knife point. Might have drawn blood. "There's your funny bone actin' up again," he said. "Cut it out, huh, Carver? Or maybe I will."

Ogden, with less flair for melodrama, simply said, "Talk."

Seemed to mean it.

Chapter 29

Carver made up most of it as he talked. And it was good. Afraid as he was, he had to admire his skill. Almost believed it himself. Verbal dexterity came easy when inspired by a knife at the throat.

All the while he talked he could smell Butcher's sour breath. Feel the knife blade vibrate with his own heartbeat. Then he realized the blade was steady, it was his carotid artery that was pulsing against unyielding steel. Life against death.

"I laid low in Miami," Carver said, not wanting them to know he was aware of the citrus farm and the deserted house with the landing field behind it. "Kept moving and staying at cheap motels. Knew you or the DEA or both'd be looking for me."

"Why would a smart ol' boy like you do such a thing?" Ogden asked. Didn't quite believe Carver; sounded puzzled.

Carver shrugged. Felt the knife burn in and sat still again. "I was in a box. Right where you put me. Didn't know what to do, so I decided to do nothing."

"Don't sound like you," Ogden said musingly. "Not judging by what we know about you."

"Which is?"

"That you're an asshole," Butcher said softly.

Ogden ignored Butcher. He said, "You don't have a history of sulling up like a possum when trouble comes your way. If you're nothing else you're a determined asshole"—a nod to Butcher—"who keeps scrambling no matter what. No, more than determined. Obsessed."

Carver was tired of hearing himself described that way. "It's hard to be obsessed with something when you have no choice. When you've been forced into it."

Butcher said, "Speakin' of forcin' somethin' into somethin' else," and pressed with the knife point hard enough to make Carver gasp and draw back his head, arching his back as if sitting at military attention. What Butcher wanted to see.

Ogden sat quietly for a while with his head bowed, thumb and forefinger toying with the crease in his pants. Headlights from passing cars now and then illuminated his thoughtful features. "Know what I think?" he said, after a truck had passed and rocked the parked Ford with a brief turmoil of wind. He kept his head lowered thoughtfully, staring at the glove compartment. "I think you didn't short-circuit and go to Miami at all. I think you calculated we wouldn't know what to do if you simply dropped from sight, so we'd do nothing. Wouldn't that be just like you, to find a move we hadn't thought of? One all the way off the table?"

"Just like," Carver said.

"But to make sure your lady friend'd be safe, you kept an eye on us. Probably me in particular. That's what you've been doing the last several days, not jerking around down in Miami, but watching us. You followed us here, didn't you?"

"Think so?"

"How else could you show up here?"

Carver said, "You're the one dreaming up the story. I already told you the truth."

"No," Ogden said, "you're not to be trusted."

"Well, I'm not as upright as you two guys and Courtney."

"We spotted this car parked here," Butcher said. "Wondered why. Thought it was too much of a coincidence. Then we seen it was a rental so we waited to find out what happened. What happened was you limped outa the dark and climbed in. I wasn't surprised, Carver."

"That's because you're so good at thinking ahead."

"You bein' sarcastic?"

"Don't you know?"

Butcher said to Ogden, "He's pretty feisty, ain't he?"

"That doesn't matter," Ogden said. "Question is, did he manage to get on the property and see or hear anything?"

"With the fence and them dogs and security guys? Not hardly. Asshole here's probably been limpin' around tryin' to figure a way in without gettin' chewed and buried like a bone. Besides, ain't there an alarm system, too?"

"There's that," Ogden said, sounding annoyed that Butcher had mentioned it. Dumb to show a hole card when it wasn't necessary.

Carver knew they didn't realize he'd gone for his nighttime swim; they attributed his remaining dampness to perspiration. It figured. Butcher was used to making people sweat.

"Well, your lady's still okay," Ogden said, "though Butcher here was hard to hold back at times. He was awfully angry at you for disappearing."

"I wanted to skin some choice parts of her," Butcher said in a low monotone. "I can do that so it takes hours afore a person dies. Works on 'em just like it does on hogs."

Carver wondered if he could whip his elbow around fast enough to mash Butcher's nose and still avoid the blade. Decided he couldn't; Butcher knew his business. Knew knives. How much bluff he was, Carver couldn't be sure. None, probably.

Carver said to Ogden, "Your friend's a psychopath."

Ogden said, "Sure. That's why he's good at what he does. Only problem is, sometimes we run into someone like you who doesn't realize the gravity of the situation. That irritates me, but Butcher doesn't mind."

"That's because Butcher has no mind."

Butcher gave his deep phlegmy chuckle. There was no anger in it, only an amused patience with an edge of anticipation. Carver didn't like that.

Ogden said, "I gotta admire you, sitting there with a blade at your neck, smarting off all the same. But then, maybe it's because you know we still need you and won't open your throat. That it?"

Carver said, "I guess that's part of it."

"You can be wrong," Butcher said.

"Sure can. That's why I'm sitting here with you."

"Okay," Ogden said, his tone suddenly softer and serious. "Here's where all this leaves us. You don't stray again, or we'll consider your usefulness ended and your lady will meet Butcher. You stand by our original agreement and relay the content of any and all conversations you have with the DEA, in particular with Jefferson or Palma. If you don't stand by our agreement, or you drop outa sight one more time, sooner or later Edwina Talbot dances with Butcher. Maybe you can hold things off and make it later instead of sooner, but believe me, they've got a date." He took a deep breath and swiveled in the seat to face Carver. "Now, we finally got an understanding? Know each other's hearts and minds?"

Carver said, "Sure. You made it all clear."

"Well, I thought I had the first time."

Ogden nodded to Butcher, then opened the door and slid

out of the car. Fresh outside air moved in to take his place. A pleasant interlude that didn't last long.

As soon as the car door slammed, Carver felt Butcher's arm close on his throat. Somehow he still held the knife so it's point was digging into the side of Carver's neck. "Let's get outa the car, sweetmeat."

Carver opened the door and heard the rear door open at the same time. The blade was away from his neck for only an instant as Butcher moved with so much quickness he seemed to be standing outside the car even as the door opened. He laid the edge of the blade against Carver's neck again, then used his other hand to summon Carver out with a little scooping motion of his thick fingers. All the time with a sadistic grin that would have looked silly if Carver hadn't known the twisted drive behind it was real.

Ogden was standing in the shadows near the front of the Ford. "You wanted to see what was behind the gates," he said, "so we'll show you."

Butcher withdrew the knife. Said, "You wouldn't try to limp away on that cane, would you?" He laughed like a schoolkid who'd heard a dirty joke.

Ogden said, "Mr. Carver'll accompany us without any trouble. After all, we're taking him where he was trying to go. Actually he should thank us."

"Hear that, Carver?" Butcher said in a gloating whisper. "You oughta say thanks."

Carver limped along silently, setting the tip of his cane firmly with each step. He wasn't going to thank these bastards.

Butcher said, "Okay if you don't say it this time. You'll tend to get more agreeable as the night wears on."

They crossed the highway and walked back along the slanted shoulder to the driveway with the closed gates.

Chapter 30

~~~~ It was a long way up the driveway. Carver couldn't make out much about the house except that it was large, as it had appeared from the ocean. Only a few windows were lighted in the front part of the house. Oddly enough, he saw or heard no sign of the dogs or any other security measure. Apparently, when Ogden had used the intercom outside the gates, the way had been cleared immediately for them to set foot on the grounds.

Carver was led through a side door. Then, flanked by Ogden and Butcher, he was ushered down a long hall. The walls were sand-colored and rough. The floor appeared to be real marble, a pink-veined gray that reminded Carver of flesh struck lifeless. There was no furniture other than a long, uncomfortable-looking wood bench along one wall, and a potted miniature fruit tree near the far end where the hall either ended or made a right-angle turn. Sparse but stylish.

Ogden stepped ahead and opened a tall door with oversized hinges and knob. Butcher shoved the back of Carver's head to indicate he should follow Ogden into the room. Carver stumbled forward and almost fell, but he managed to remain upright. Knew he must look like a drunk lurching in a swaying world.

It was a large room, carpeted in deep maroon and with matching floor-to-ceiling drapes of some kind of velvet material. The walls were darkly paneled and covered with arrangements of fox-hunting prints. Red-coated riders on sleek horses leaping hedges and fences. Hounds streaming through fields in frantic chase. Carver noticed that the fox didn't appear in any of the prints. On a sort of pedestal near a massive stone fireplace was a stuffed fox, head turned, one front paw raised delicately, looking alert and ready to bolt for safety. The taxidermist had done a good job; the stuffed creature probably seemed more alive and aware than had the fox itself when blood coursed through its veins. Almost worth shooting again.

Butcher noticed Carver looking at the fox and said, "You and your furry friend'll have a lot in common you try any more bullshit."

Ogden said, "Sit down, Mr. Carver," and motioned with his hand toward a blue leather sofa.

Carver limped to the sofa and lowered his body into a corner of it. The leather was incredibly soft and he sank deeper than he'd anticipated. It wouldn't be easy to get up in a hurry if he had to; he propped his cane against the cushion, within easy reach, giving himself another second or two if it became necessary to act.

The door they'd come through opened with a faint brushing sound as it skimmed the carpet, and Carver turned his head to see a tall silver-haired man in his mid-sixties enter. He was long-limbed but thick through the middle, with a pronounced stomach paunch; it made him slightly resemble a spider. He had on pin-striped gray pants, a white shirt, red suspenders. Without speaking, he came around to stand facing Carver. Looked down at him sitting on the sofa and smiled with large yellow teeth. His eyes were pale blue and they weren't smiling. Something about him. He did look a lot like Bert Renway. The late Bert Renway.

Still smiling, he said, "Mr. Carver, I'm Frank Wesley."

There was an air of certainty and authority about him that Renway hadn't had. And a hard quality to the eyes. He filled his space in the world and was very much whatever he was. One look at him and people knew it instantly. Sensed his energy. Wesley was the sort of man who had his private concept of reality and could sell it to others by virtue of his belief in himself. People like him achieved fame or fortune marketing used cars or leading nations into wars. With Wesley it had been hogs. But now it was drugs. More money in drugs. More power.

Carver said, "You're supposed to be dead."

Wesley shrugged. "We're all supposed to be lotsa things we aren't." He had a thick Southern accent only hinted at when he'd first spoken. Maybe he could control it. Used it only when he wanted to, for effect. He said, "While I had the chance, I figured I oughta talk to you, explain there's big things in the wind and you're not one of 'em. You're a small thing might just get blown away if you're not careful."

"I try to be careful," Carver said.

"No, sir, I disagree. That's not your track record. But you are reputed to be a man of good sense, so I'm going to state to you the simple fact that there's a deal working that involves so much money it'd just be a meaningless figure to you if I said it. You understand, that much money 'bout to flow, we'll kill you in a minute if it don't look like you're of much use to us anymore. You follow that logic?"

"Perfectly. The more money the cheaper the lives."

Wesley had never stopped smiling, but now the yellowed

smile stretched wider. "That's a fine answer, Mr. Carver. 'Cause it's true. And that makes your life very cheap indeed."

Carver noticed Butcher had moved. Was out of sight somewhere behind the sofa. Flesh bunched on the back of Carver's neck, as if something were crawling there.

Wesley said, "I made my money the hard way, Mr. Carver, and I'll keep it the hard way if need be."

Carver said, "Need be. The DEA doesn't want your drug deal to happen."

"Well, that's natural enough, and surely nothing new. They're sort of an occupational hazard we long ago learned to cope with." He shook his head in mock concern. "The things 'n' people money buys. It might surprise you."

"No," Carver said, "it wouldn't."

"You might not see it from down where you live, Mr. Carver, but the truth is I'm neither more nor less than a businessman. Doin' what you'd do under the circumstances, granted you had the grit, know-how, and capital."

"What about Bert Renway? Was he part of your business?"

"Thing to remember there," Wesley said, "is it was the DEA and not me who put Renway in that car. Not to mention Renway himself volunteering."

Carver couldn't argue with that one. *The things and people money buys.*

"You're part of this team now," Wesley said, "whether you like it or not. Best you don't stray again. You truly realize that?"

"More or less."

"Gonna be more," Wesley said.

He abruptly stopped smiling and turned away. Walked back out the door. Carver had been dismissed from the minds of the self-important that way before. Wesley was finished talking to Carver; on to genuinely important matters.

Ogden was standing motionless with his head slightly cocked to the side, cupping right elbow in left palm, touching his chin lightly with two fingers. Made him look a little like Jack Benny. He was staring oddly at Carver.

That was when Carver detected an acrid medicinal scent. Something familiar, yet he was unable to place it.

Until Butcher, from behind, clamped a rough cloth over his mouth. Yanked back on his head so Carver gave an involuntary gasp. Carver recognized in that instant the stench of chloroform. Then Butcher's other hand grasped the back of his neck and applied hard pressure so Carver's head might as well have been locked in a vise.

Carver couldn't breathe. Gasped the dizzying fumes but couldn't exhale. He panicked and lashed back with his arms, but strength was draining from them and feeling was leaving his hands. Some of the chloroform dripped onto his chest, chilling him through his shirt. He heard Butcher laugh from a great distance. Felt his heart expand and pound against his rib cage. Saw pinpoints of light. Thrashed mindlessly with his arms and legs, thumping them against the floor and the sofa's arm and back.

Saw red.

Saw black.

Regained consciousness and didn't know where he was.

Slouched. Cramped. Leaning with his left shoulder against a hard surface.

He opened his eyes and saw gray vastness. Something dreamlike swaying in the corner of his vision. Recognized the something as a palm frond. He realized he was gazing out through a windshield.

What was the deal here?

He tried to move but his muscles were too stiff to respond. His bad leg was extended over to the passenger side of the car and he was half-sitting, half-leaning against the door. He blinked. Peered again through the windshield and saw that the sky was overcast and dim. Low gray ceiling of lead. It couldn't be much past dawn.

Something, a car or truck, swished past on the nearby road. He swiveled his head slightly to look. Pain! Stiff neck. He was parked far enough off the road, and among some trees, so that the car must be barely visible to passing motorists. And if anyone did happen to notice a parked car with the driver slumped behind the wheel, they'd probably figure Carver was wisely taking a short nap before traveling on.

Another car flashed past, and the whining retreat of its tires on warming pavement pulled Carver closer to full consciousness. The entire left side of his head was throbbing with pain. Nothing a couple of dozen Tylenols wouldn't help. More cars passed, and off in the distance a dog barked. The kind of frantic yipping a small dog makes, but it brought last night back to Carver in its entirety.

Rather, up to the time he'd been chloroformed.

He tried to scoot his body up straighter. Didn't work. The pain in his head flared. It was an odd, numbing kind of pain; Butcher must have pressed a nerve at the side of his neck. He rested his palm on the edge of the vinyl seat to push himself back and up. The heel of his hand encountered something sticky and slipped off the vinyl.

And Carver became aware of the smell in the car. Familiar, atavistic. Frightening and sickening.

Blood.

He felt around on the seat. There was quite a bit of the sticky substance. With a bolt of terror, he wondered if Butcher had gone ahead and cut his throat.

What was this? Was he dead? *What was this?*

Unable to look, clenching his eyes shut, Carver felt slowly and found that his pants were wet and sticky. His shirt. *Oh, God!* He felt the same disgusting stickiness on his stomach and chest, gradually and tentatively working his hand upward.

He finally groped at his throat. Felt more coagulating blood. Slid his fingertips through blood.

His blood.

But beneath the slime of it his flesh felt smooth and unbroken. He almost shouted with relief.

Then he remembered his peculiar throbbing headache.

Darted his hand to his left ear. Felt a fierce burning and almost fainted with pain and rage as he yanked the hand away.

Was afraid to touch again where his earlobe had been.

Chapter 31

The bleeding, profuse at first, wasn't bad now as long as he kept a wad of Kleenex pressed to his ear.

In Pompano Beach he found a medical clinic and walked into the emergency room.

He didn't attract undue attention there, alongside a twelve-year-old boy who'd had both legs broken when a car struck him on his bike, and a middle-aged man, balder than Carver, who'd suffered a heart attack. Carver heard somebody say the heart-attack victim was the driver of the car that had struck the kid. So what was an earlobe more or less?

Carver sat for a while in a red plastic chair and smelled Pine-Sol and watched white-coated professionals bustle in and out through wide swinging doors.

There were five other people in the waiting room, two men and three women. Relatives and friends of patients. They sat looking worried, or paced looking worried, or leafed through tattered old *Newsweek*s looking worried.

Finally a young redheaded woman he assumed was a nurse ushered him into a small green room where he was told to sit on top of a vinyl-padded table that had what looked like butcher paper spread over it. She said Emergency was busy but someone would get to him as soon as possible. As she was leaving she knocked his cane over from where he'd leaned it against the table. She scooped it up as it was still rattling on the tile floor, apologized, handed it to him, and hurried out. He sat quietly. Felt the white paper on the table and found that it was cool. The room was cool.

After a while an attractive young doctor who looked like an Indian woman who should have a jewel pasted on her forehead came into the room. She examined his ear and shook her head. Said, "That is a very bad cut. Almost the entire lobe of the ear is missing."

"An accident," Carver said.

"Accident?" She didn't believe him.

He smiled at her. She smiled back. Then she shrugged elegantly. He had a feeling she did everything with a kind of understated elegance. "If you insist," she said, "an accident and not a knife wound." She was busy with patients hurt more seriously and didn't have time to argue.

She dabbed something on the ear, then injected local anesthetic and stitched the lobe. There was some pain, but she had a very gentle and soothing touch. A talent beyond medicine.

"There was hardly enough left to suture," she told him, standing back and staring at her handiwork.

He said, "When it heals, will I be able to play the piano?"

She merely looked at him somberly. Said, "Medicine is practiced here, not comedy."

She quickly and skillfully covered the lobe, or what was left of it, with a pad of medicated gauze, laying on lots of white adhesive tape. "You need to be careful and not put strain on the stitches. Try to sleep on your back or right side."

He said, "If I'm asleep, it'll be difficult to decide which side to lie on."

She said, "I see you have Blue Cross. There'll be some forms for you to fill out. And the girl at the desk will give you a prescription for pain pills. Follow the directions on the label. Have a good day."

Carver thought it was already too late for that.

The ear didn't hurt much at all until the anesthetic began to wear off. Then Carver pulled the Ford off the highway and into the parking lot of a truck stop, restaurant, gas station, and souvenir shop. He swallowed two of the pain pills and then read on the label that they were to be taken after meals.

Meals. He decided to go inside and try to get down some lunch; he wasn't all that hungry but he needed fuel in his body for whatever else might be coming at him today. Besides, he was only twenty miles outside Del Moray; it was time to make a phone call.

He limped through the glitzy souvenir shop and sat in a booth by a window, where he could keep an eye on the rented Ford. Wondered what Hertz would think of all the blood on the front seat.

A young blond waitress who was beautiful despite the fact that she was overweight came over and said hello, said her name was Mandy, said would he like a menu. He said no menu, a club sandwich and black coffee would be fine. She scribbled on her order pad, did a double take when he moved and she saw the wad of white gauze and tape clinging to the left side of his head, but was too well trained or polite to ask him about it. "Be just a minute," she said, and hurried away. She had about her the same air of efficiency as the people in Emergency.

While he was waiting for the sandwich to be assembled,

Carver got up and limped to the pay phone he'd noticed just inside the door. On the wall next to the phone someone had scrawled in pencil *For a hot time call Dotty*, and then printed a number.

He got the number of the Sundown Motel near Del Moray from Information, then called the motel and asked for Jefferson.

The phone at the other end of the line rang ten times. Jefferson wasn't in his room. Or if he was, he wasn't answering his calls.

Beyond a revolving rack of sunglasses, Carver could see Mandy setting his cup of coffee on the table. She glanced around to see where he'd gone. Spotted him and smiled. Great smile; the kid could lose weight and be a stunner.

He decided he'd eat his club sandwich, hope the pills stopped the painful throbbing of his ear despite the reversed order of medicine and food, and then call Jefferson again. If he couldn't get Jefferson, he'd try Ralph Palma's room, though the two of them were probably off somewhere together playing catch-the-bad-guys and not having much luck.

The club sandwich was delicious, and it made Carver realize he was hungrier than he'd thought. He had Mandy bring him a wedge of apple pie and a second cup of coffee. Then a third cup. The coffee was revitalizing him, wiring him on caffeine.

When he was finished he left a tip, paid his check to a relentlessly cheerful cashier, then called the Sundown Motel again. Jefferson's room. Carver figured the room phone wouldn't be tapped; DEA agents had technology on their side. Little gizmos to detect that kind of thing. Carver usually treated high-tech gadgetry with disdain, but not this time. *Vive la* microchip. And the public phone Carver was on was surely safe.

He hooked the crook of his cane into the phone's coin return, leaned his weight against the wall, and waited, the receiver pressed to his good ear.

On the fifth ring Jefferson picked up his phone. Said only a flat hello, as if he'd been pestered all day by salesmen and this was probably another one.

"This is Carver."

Jefferson said, "Ah!" Not with real enthusiasm.

"I know where the SCBL strategy meeting's gonna be held. Only it's not just a strategy meeting; there was mention of some kind of major drug deal about to go down."

After a few seconds' silence, Jefferson said, "Talk to me, Carver."

"Phone safe?"

"You wouldn't have called here if you didn't think it was safe. You were right, it is. What about the phone you're on?"

"Safe enough for Dotty, safe enough for me."

"Huh?"

"Never mind." Carver told him about last night at the estate in Hillsboro Beach.

"Then you actually saw Wesley?"

"Talked to him. Or I'd say he talked to me. Did it to convince me I had no choice but to stay on a tight leash."

"But here you are chatting with me."

"Here I am," Carver said.

Jefferson said, "The man you described who flew in and was picked up in the Caddie is Jeb Garrity from North Carolina. He's a founding member of the SCBL. The rest of them are probably already in Florida, although I wouldn't think they'd all congregate at the Willoughby place."

"Willoughby?"

"Jack Willoughby. He's the owner of the home you were

taken to last night. Owns a chain of fried-chicken restaurants throughout the South, Willoughby's Wings."

"I ate at one of them a few months ago," Carver said. "It gave me indigestion, but nothing like this."

"It doesn't figure they'd meet like that, at the home of one member. Appalachian bullshit. More likely they'd choose neutral ground. Decrease the likelihood of being watched or listened in on."

"Why?" Carver asked. "On the surface, they're just an ordinary businessmen's organization. Chamber of Commerce South."

"On the surface."

"Courtney get any of this information to you?"

"She hasn't been heard from for a while," Jefferson said. "Courtney's gotta be careful these days, with somethin' blowin' in the wind."

"That was an old Bob Dylan song," Carver said, "from the sixties."

" 'Courtney's Gotta Be Careful'?"

"No, that was the Beatles."

"How come you waited so long to get this information to me?"

"How come you're so grateful?"

"Come off it, Carver, you ain't playing PTA politics here. I should think you realized that last night."

"I was gonna talk to you in person, then I figured you might be under surveillance—this not being PTA stuff. I decided the safest way was to use the phone, only you weren't there until after I finished my club sandwich."

"Despite what you been through, you're still a smartass."

"In the genes, I guess."

Jefferson seemed to snort in disgust, but Carver couldn't be sure. "Okay, Carver, you talked and I listened. Thanks."

Carver said, "Hold on. I want something in return."

"Oh? What would that be?"

"Vincent Butcher."

"What'd he do, talk nasty to you?"

"He cut off my earlobe. That's another reason I didn't get in touch with you right away; I had to get it stitched up."

Jefferson said, "Christ!"

"I want him," Carver repeated.

"This thing that's going on has got nothing to do with machismo, Carver. No time here for vendettas. 'Sides, Van Gogh had his *whole* ear cut off and did okay afterward."

"He cut off his own ear. Sent it to a woman."

"Yeah. She wasn't much moved by it, either."

"I didn't ask for pity, I asked for Butcher."

"I can't deliver; I'm not Revenge Is Us down at your local shopping mall."

"You can deliver."

"Well, if I can, I won't."

Carver said, "Fuck you, then, you and your assassination rifle."

"What?"

Carver hung up.

He sidestepped a display of caps lettered FISHERMEN DO IT DEEPER above the bills, pushed through the restaurant, and limped out onto the sun-tortured parking lot.

Old Sol was laying it on again today; during the brief time Carver had been in the restaurant, the Ford had gotten almost too hot to touch. When he lowered himself in behind the steering wheel and started the engine, he turned the air conditioner on high and then opened all the windows so the heat that had built up would be replaced by fresh and cooler air. Kept the windows down for almost a mile before sealing himself in again.

He was driving the rest of the way into Del Moray, passing the marina, when he saw a familiar cabin cruiser docked there. He slowed the Ford and peered through the space between two other docked boats, making sure he hadn't been mistaken when he'd read the name on the bow.

He hadn't. The flowing black script read exactly the way he'd first seen it driving past. The way he'd seen it last night from the dark ocean.

Bold Entrepreneur.

Willoughby's boat.

Chapter 32

Carver drove more slowly toward his office, his mind turning over. There were surely other boats christened *Bold Entrepreneur;* maybe one of those was the craft he'd seen in the slip at the Del Moray Marina. Not Willoughby's boat at all.

But he doubted it. The boat had struck a chord of familiarity even without the name lettered on the bow. The same sweeping white hull, the red stripe just above the waterline. The raked angle of the marine navigation antenna above the flying bridge. It had to be the same boat.

When he saw a public phone Carver pulled the Ford over. Limped into the sun-heated aluminum booth, and touch-toned out the number of the Sundown Motel. Asked for Jefferson and gave the room number.

Jefferson didn't answer. Neither did Ralph Palma when Carver rang his room.

Terrific. They were probably on their way to Willough-by's place in Hillsboro Beach, acting on Carver's information. And here was the *Bold Entrepreneur*. Docked the one place Wesley knew the DEA *wasn't*, if Carver had informed them about what had happened last night at the Willoughby estate.

He stood in the sun, wiping sweat from his forehead with his palm and maybe wising up. Wondering if he'd gotten into something beyond his capability. Had Wesley *known* he'd contact Jefferson? Had he, Carver, been used to misdirect the DEA while the *Bold Entrepreneur* roamed north along the coast to Del Moray? Carver sensed there was a complicated game going on that he didn't understand—and he was an essential, yet expendable, part of it. That made him uncomfortable.

A spate of cars passed doing close to seventy. Followed by a silver tour bus that rocked Carver with a crashing blast of wind that reeked of diesel exhaust.

He limped back toward the parked Ford, trying to figure out what to do.

The docked *Bold Entrepreneur* was probably waiting to be boarded by whatever SCBL members hadn't yet arrived. The meeting, and whatever other drug business was going to transpire, would happen out at sea on the boat, where there was no concern for security. What more logical and unpredictable location?

Carver lowered himself into the car, sat for a moment in the heat, then started the engine. Gunned it.

He drove fast. Cut west, then north again on Magellan to his office. Ran traffic lights; a wonder he hadn't picked up a cop.

He had in his desk drawer one of the tiny tracking gadgets known as bumper beepers. Van Meter had given it to him a few months ago. It was a simple and almost foolproof device, a small radio transmitter, about the size and shape of a quarter only thicker, with a magnetic base. It could be attached to almost any metal part of a car, where it would emit electronic signals until its battery ran down. Usually it was stuck on a car bumper, where it sent intermittent signals to a receiver tuned to the same frequency. In a car carrying a receiver, homing in on the electronic beeps made it relatively easy to follow or locate a car carrying a bumper beeper.

There was no reason the beeper wouldn't work on a boat, once it was attached. The problem was, the *Bold Entrepreneur*'s hull appeared to be fiberglass. The magnetic base of the tiny transmitter wouldn't stick.

Carver rooted through his bottom desk drawer until he found the beeper. Then he got a change of clothes from the office storage closet. Jeans, a clean black T-shirt.

With the scissors from a desk drawer, he hacked off the jeans' legs above the knees. Hadn't realized denim was so tough. He struggled into his just-made cutoffs, the T-shirt, and brown moccasins with no socks. Thought he might have torn off the rest of his injured ear when he pulled the T-shirt over his head. Hoped it wouldn't start bleeding again. *Butcher. Damn Butcher!*

He glanced at his watch; he'd been in the office less than ten minutes. Time didn't fly when you weren't having fun. He slid the tiny beeper into his pocket.

Carver limped from the office and drove to a nearby hardware store, where he bought a tube of model-boat-and-airplane glue whose label boasted that on fiberglass and plastic it formed a secure bond that was impervious to water. Nearby was a poster featuring a smiling man standing casually beneath a fiberglass sports car that was supposedly suspended from a steel beam with only some of the glue keeping it from crashing to the ground to claim a fatality. Carver thought that if the miracle gunk in the little tube held up a Chevy Corvette, it would suit his purpose just fine.

Assuming, of course, that there was at least some truth in advertising. Mustn't be too cynical; he'd promised Edwina he'd try to improve in that department.

Before leaving the hardware store, he phoned Jefferson and Palma again, but again got no answer.

Carver left the phone, paid the cashier in the front of the store for the glue, and went out into the heat. He got in the Ford and drove back toward the marina.

The *Bold Entrepreneur*, looking clean and neat and sleek, looking like money, was still bobbing gently in its slip. There was no sign of anyone on board, but Carver knew that meant nothing. Curtains were pulled over the portholes and bridge windows. And a boat this size was practically a ship, with plenty of room below deck.

Carver turned the small screw that activated the tiny transmitter's battery, then slipped the beeper back into his jeans pocket. He got out of the car and crossed the road. Made his way along the dock to where an old and apparently deserted Chris-Craft cruiser was tied up.

Because of the crushing heat, there were only a few people on the dock. An elderly man carrying a casting rod gave Carver a curious stare, then seemed to dismiss him from his mind. Put him down as maybe a beach bum who'd gotten in a fight.

On the other side of the Chris-Craft, out of everyone's sight other than two young boys fishing far down the dock, Carver sat down on the rough wood and removed his moccasins and T-shirt. Paused while a sailboat with its canvas down put-putted past on the power of its motor. A guy wearing only swimming trunks and a blue yachting cap was at the stern wheel. Stared straight ahead and didn't glance at Carver as the boat glided past. The boat left very little wake and looked graceful even with the sail down.

Carver wrapped the T-shirt around his wallet and keys, then weighted it down on the sun-warmed, splintered planks with his moccasins and cane.

With a quick glance around, he lowered himself into the water, holding the beeper high in his left hand to keep it as dry as possible. The little transmitters were supposed to be waterproof, but why take chances?

Carver stayed in the shadows below the dock as he swam slowly toward the *Bold Entrepreneur*. Even with only one arm, he was a powerful enough swimmer to keep his head well up so the dressing over his ear stayed dry. Bits of paper and garbage floated in the brackish water, and the darting shapes of small fish could be seen inches below the surface. An orange peel, curved like a tiny canoe, was tossed about on the ripples Carver was stirring up, and drifted away. Moved by stronger forces, the hulls of boats swayed and bumped against the tires lashed to the pilings to prevent damage, causing rhythmic hollow thumping noises that were magnified in the silence beneath the dock.

The *Bold Entrepreneur* was berthed in one of the larger slips, its bow at a right angle to the main dock. Carver had to be careful as he swam alongside it. The rough-hewn plank walkway above him was narrower than the dock itself and provided less shadow. He might be visible from the shore if he wasn't careful.

He lessened the strength and reach of his sidestroke, hoping no one aboard would hear him splashing around. Sometimes sound carried over water with unexpected volume.

Because of the way the boat was docked, the safest place to plant the beeper would be near the bow and well above the waterline. Keep the supposedly waterproof glue and transmitter dry and away from the force of the waves when the boat was under way. Dry as possible, anyway.

Carver held the beeper gently in his teeth. Treaded water

in the shadow of the slip as he wrestled the tube of glue from his jeans pocket. He removed the cap, then, treading briefly with only his legs, took the beeper from his mouth and squeezed out a generous glob of glue onto the magnetic base.

Gripping the beeper firmly and just so, he stroked out into sunlight, reached high above the red stripe near the waterline, and with a twisting motion fixed the beeper on the *Bold Entrepreneur*'s smooth hull.

He slowly withdrew into the cooler, shadowed water, satisfied. The beeper seemed firmly attached, and while it was well above the waterline, it was still below the curve of the hull where it wouldn't be noticeable from the dock. And probably no one other than Willoughby himself would think anything of the beeper if it *was* noticed. Anyone else would assume it was simply part of the boat. A ballast plug or capped vent, or some other mysterious piece of boating paraphernalia.

Carver backstroked until he was beneath the dock. Then, faster now with both arms, breaststroked parallel to the shore, back toward the paint-chipped wood hull of the aged Chris-Craft.

For the first time he noticed a sleek Cigarette speedboat tied at the dock. The elegant, dip-nosed Cigarette was designed by famous boatbuilder Don Aronow and was not so called because of its long low silhouette, as many believed, but was named after a Prohibition-era booze smuggler. The sexy and streamlined V-hulled craft, with its twin 450-horsepower turbocharged engines, could do over seventy miles per hour on open ocean. For its speed and not for its namesake, it was the favorite of drug runners. Carver wondered briefly if the presence of this one had anything to do with whatever was in the planning stages aboard the *Bold Entrepreneur*.

Within a few minutes he was back up on the dock, pulling

his T-shirt over his head with one hand, holding the material away from his injured ear with the other. Wriggling bare wet feet into his moccasins and then using the cane to lever himself to a standing position. He was breathing hard. Felt good. Great, in fact. The lump of gauze and tape over his ear was barely damp.

He limped back to the Ford and climbed in. Didn't notice the car parked a hundred feet in front of him until the doors opened simultaneously and two men got out slowly. Shut the doors also simultaneously and walked toward him. Their actions seemed choreographed; the two had gotten out of a car together hundreds of times. Partners.

Jefferson and Palma.

Carver wondered why they were here and not down the coast in Hillsboro Beach.

They didn't seem glad to see him. He wasn't sure if he was glad to see them.

Chapter 33

Jefferson sat down across from Carver at the square table with its red-and-white-checked cloth. Said, "Just order something to drink. I don't want you having a full belly."

They were in Lobster Jack's, a trendy seafood restaurant on the dock. Sitting at a table near the leaded-glass window so they could look out at the *Bold Entrepreneur* gently rising and falling in unison with the other boats in port. It was a hypnotic sight, this slow dance of boats in the sunlight, in perfect rhythm with the lazy, metronomic tempo of the sea. A ponderous, relentless beat as old as the planet itself.

Jefferson and Palma had told Carver to stay in the Ford, then instructed him to make a U-turn and park in the restaurant's side lot. They had trudged back to their gray Dodge and then followed him.

In the parking lot Jefferson had said something to Palma, who was driving, then got out of the Dodge, hauled his duffel bag out from the back seat, and walked with Carver into the restaurant.

They were alone at the table. The long duffel bag, the one

that had contained the rifle beneath the motel bed, rested on the floor near Jefferson. The restaurant was cool. Paddle fans mounted on thick beams crisscrossing the ceiling rotated slowly. Carver didn't know where Palma had gone. Didn't ask. He assumed the other DEA agent was somewhere where he could watch the *Bold Entrepreneur* even more closely.

A blond, bespectacled waitress who looked like a college student, wearing a frilly red-and-white-checked apron that matched the tablecloth, sauntered over. Asked could she help them. Carver thought, If only you could. Jefferson told her just coffee. Carver said the same for him.

Lobster Jack's was paneled in waxed oak and had phony Tiffany-shade fixtures on brass chains above each table. The fixtures swayed gently in the breeze from the ceiling fans. There were dead flies on the oak windowledge near the table where Carver and Jefferson sat.

It was the slack time between lunch and supper; there were only a few other customers in the place. A middle-aged man and woman who looked like tourists were wolfing down a late lunch or early dinner of lobster at the other end of the restaurant. There was an expensive-looking 35-millimeter camera with a long lens on the table near the man's glass of beer. An old man in pastel pants and pullover shirt sat three tables away, methodically eating a platter of oysters on the half-shell. He had white hair. Had on a white belt, white socks, white shoes.

Jefferson said, "This place serves a great lobster-tail lunch."

"No doubt at taxpayer expense."

"Uh-hm. Makes it taste better."

Carver said, "How is it you're here and not down in Hillsboro Beach?"

"Courtney contacted us not long after you did. Tipped us that the meeting was to be on Willoughby's boat, and the *Bold Entrepreneur* was sailing here to tie up and wait for Kip Farneaux."

Carver watched the white-haired man work an oyster loose from its shell. Dip it in sauce. "Kip Farneaux?"

"He's a rich textile man from Georgia. When he joins the party on the boat, they plan on chugging out to sea to talk over which side of warring Central American drug suppliers to choose as their source."

"It's trains that chug, not boats."

"Boats do whatever they do, then; get from one place to another on the water. This boat will, anyway."

"Would one of these warring drug suppliers be the people who blew up Bert Renway?"

"Most likely."

A fly buzzed in tight circles around Carver. Touched down on the back of his hand. Took off again before he had a chance to flick at it, leaving only a tickle. He wished it would join the dead ones on the windowsill. "When's Farneaux due to arrive?"

"Later this afternoon. They'll probably put to sea soon after dark."

The waitress came with their coffee. Placed the cups before them on saucers. Set a small silver pitcher of cream in the center of the table. Shot them a bright but empty smile and said if they needed anything else they should just ask her, her name was Linda. The pesty fly was on Linda's shoulder when she walked away. Carver was glad to see that.

When she was gone, Jefferson's eyes slid down and to the side to glance at the long green duffel bag next to his chair. Then he stared straight at Carver and said, "On the phone earlier this afternoon, you mentioned a rifle."

Carver said, "The one in the bag."

"How would you know there's a rifle in there?"

"Trade secret."

"Being in the same trade, we oughta share our secrets, don'cha think?"

"No, I'm not so sure."

"Why not?"

"The rifle."

"Oh." Jefferson's deep brown eyes didn't blink, but something changed in them. Some subtle shifting of mood, like a dim light in deep water. He said, "Gonna tell you about that rifle, Carver." A tinge of ghetto black in his speech again. Unconscious? Or was he trying to menace Carver? "You seen what kinda rifle it is?"

Carver nodded.

"Know what that means?"

"You were gonna tell me."

Jefferson sipped his coffee, put down the cup, and stared into the rocking dark liquid. "Remember what I told you 'bout what happened to my daddy the day after Martin Luther King was assassinated?"

"I remember. He was lynched."

"Yeah. Well, 'bout two years ago I was working this drug case and got on to the not-so-surprising fact that this group of wealthy and supposedly respectable Southern business-men was dealing dope."

"The Southern Christian Businessmen's League?"

"The same. The people that'll be on that boat, soon as Farneaux gets here." Jefferson stared out the window for a moment at the gently bobbing *Bold Entrepreneur*, and his face became an impassive ebony mask. Except for his eyes, where now something burned bright as hellfire. A preacher's son forever.

Carver said, "This isn't really about drugs, is it?"

Jefferson turned to look at him again. "Ain't you the perceptive bastard?"

"I have my moments."

"And this is one of them. No, it's not completely about drugs. While I was chasing leads and trying to establish the link between Central American suppliers and the SCBL, I ran across evidence concerning another crime. Nothing I can use to press a case. Nothing I can prove. Nothing anybody else'll believe, for that matter. Nothing they'll wanna believe. But I *know*, Carver. *Goddammit, I know!*"

Carver waited. Stayed silent. He'd seen this before and knew how it worked. Jefferson was rolling; what was in him, what he knew, had to come out. He needed to purge himself of it.

"The rifle in that bag, Carver, it was used to kill Martin Luther King."

Carver hadn't expected this. He put down his cup. Sloshed some of the hot coffee onto his thumb. Barely felt it. He remembered Jefferson slumped on the edge of the bed at the Sundown Motel, bent over the rifle and crying. "James Earl Ray's rifle?"

"Oh, no! Not Ray's. Ray didn't kill King, but he was part of the operation. He was a blind. A patsy used to divert attention from the real assassin. The SCLB helped him escape in his white Mustang—a car just like the real assassin's—then paid his way while he traveled all over the world. Till the dumb yahoo got himself caught goin' through airport customs in London."

"Why doesn't Ray tell the law this?"

"That was all worked out beforehand. He got what looked like a legal defense, only it wasn't really. He struck a deal with the court. Went through what the press called a 'minitrial' where a prima facie case involving only a few witnesses was heard. That meant a plea of guilty could be accepted unless contradictory evidence was presented. Ray's guilty plea was accepted, and a life sentence was recommended. The so-called jury then confirmed the sentence and that was that. If Ray'd pleaded innocent, he coulda been found guilty and executed, which was what he was tryin' to avoid. He bought the deal with his silence. Knew he didn't have much choice, considerin' the people he was involved with. The law doesn't weigh evenly on everybody, Carver. And it's not inflexible; it's like putty. And things can happen to a man in prison. Ray talks, even now, he knows he dies."

Carver was quiet for a while. Then he said, "Every political assassination, there's always a conspiracy theory."

"But this time it's true. How else you gonna explain where a small-time redneck like Ray got all the money he needed to go globe-hoppin' after the assassination?"

Carver couldn't explain and didn't try. It was something he and a lot of other people had wondered about before. There was an ocean of speculation about the Kennedy assassinations, both of which could have been, and probably were, planned and accomplished by lone assailants. But the King assassination, which was almost certainly the result of a conspiracy, had prompted less indignation and theorizing. Carver wondered if the reasons for such neglect were racial. Didn't like to think so but suspected they were. "But the rifle . . ."

"After King was shot," Jefferson said, "Ray fled from the scene, tossed a package loaded with clues onto the pavement, got in his car, and sped away. There was a Remington Gamemaster pump-action .30-06 rifle in the package."

"But not the rifle in the duffel bag."

"Right. That rifle I confiscated for myself from a certain

wealthy businessman's personal collection. Left him a duplicate so he'd never know. The thing is, the court never
established that Ray's rifle was the gun that shot King."

"You're kidding?"

"Nope. Look it up."

"What about ballistics tests?"

"None were made. County medical examiner, guy named
Francisco, testified the bullet was too misshapen to match
with a particular gun. There was a slight nick on the
bathroom windowsill of Ray's rooming house that was said
to match machine markings on the rifle barrel, supposedly
from when it kicked where Ray had rested it on the sill to
steady his aim. That's the only evidence that Ray's gun killed
King."

"Flimsy evidence."

"Not evidence at all in most courts, but enough in this
case. Makes you wonder, don't it?"

Carver wondered, all right. But some things he finally
understood. The fire that raged in Jefferson after the deaths
of King and his father—deaths inextricably linked in his
mind—had never died completely and was about to burst
into fierce flame.

"It'll be poetic justice, is that it?" Carver said. "You know,
but you can't prove, who killed King, and you're gonna kill
the assassin with the same rifle he used to murder King. That
the way you got it mapped out?"

Jefferson said, "You could call it poetic justice. I don't call
it nothin' but revenge." Ghetto echoes again. "I'm not
kiddin' myself, Carver. Justice is why I *should* do it, but only
half the reason I'm gonna. Once I found out about how King
was really murdered, I haven't thought about much else.
Obsessed, I guess you'd call me. I don't fuckin' care, though.
I'm gonna goddamn do this." His voice cracked. "I *need* this."

Carver started to take a sip of coffee. Saw that his hand was trembling and lowered the cup back to its saucer. It made a delicate *clink*.

He said, "You know the name of the man who pulled the trigger."

"That's right," Jefferson said. "I've known it for a while."

"Maybe you oughta tell me."

Jefferson breathed out hard, as if he'd been holding his breath for a long time. "Sure. Can't do no harm now. Walter Ogden shot King. That's why he's still with Wesley Slaughter and Rendering, turning a top salary with perks. Earned himself a privileged position for life, did Walter. But his life's about over."

"But not just Walter Ogden's life."

"Right again, Carver. He was only the finger on the trigger. I never thought I'd have an opportunity like this. It's their greed gonna take 'em down. They killed Martin Luther King for ideological and economic reasons. Years later they saw even more money in the illicit drug trade and got into that. Couldn't stay out. That's why the core organization still exists. Why they'll all be together on that boat. Talkin' money, just like in the sixties. Only difference is, the money's bigger."

"You can nail them for dealing drugs," Carver said. "Isn't that enough?"

Jefferson shook his head sadly. "Not nearly."

Carver said, "What *is* enough? What's minimum? Taking Ogden's life?"

"Maybe it woulda been, but not now. You know, I'm kinda disappointed in you. From what I found out about you, what people said, I thought you'd understand this."

Carver hesitated, staring down at the table, "Yeah, I do understand." *God help me, I do.*

Jefferson smiled. If cats smiled at mice, they'd look like that. "There's a bomb on board that boat. Got a timer set to blow it at ten o'clock tonight, when, accordin' to Courtney, the *Bold Entrepreneur* will be well out to sea."

"How'd you get the explosives on board?"

"Courtney. Only she don't know it."

It took Carver a few seconds to realize the import of Jefferson's words. The extent of his madness. "Jesus! You're gonna let her die along with the others?"

Jefferson's eyes became dark pools of pain. "What's my choice? How'm I gonna get her off that boat without tipping the others?"

Carver looked out at the *Bold Entrepreneur* swaying in its berth. "I don't know."

"I lived for this, Carver! And the opportunity'll never come around again. You realize that?"

"Sure. But you said you and Courtney—"

"Dammit, what has to be will be!" Jefferson cut in. "I'm gonna *make* it be! *Me!* And it's *important*. You know that."

"Man with a mission. Like your father."

"Not quite like him. This mission's gonna be carried out. I swore that to myself a long time ago."

And something ugly and ominous stirred in a corner of Carver's mind. A cold dread took root in his stomach. "How come you're spilling this to me?"

"You found out about the rifle."

"Something more," Carver said. "I know it."

"Well, I guess I want you to know it. Owe it to you that you know. You're the one slipped the leash and made them mad. Made them wanna tighten the screws on you. You shoulda figured out how they might do it. Your goddamn fault."

No, no! Carver gripped his cane. Started to get up.

Jefferson reached across the table before he could attain balance and, slowly but firmly, eased him back down into his chair. The waitress and the old guy eating oysters stared for a moment, then turned away.

His throat dry, his heart slamming in his chest, Carver looked out the window again at the *Bold Entrepreneur* bobbing in the sunlight, wavering reflections from the water dancing over her white hull.

"That's how it is, I'm afraid," Jefferson said. "They got Edwina Talbot on board."

Chapter 34

Jefferson watched Carver across the table. Said softly, "Try any heroics and I'll put you in custody. You can bet I damn well mean it."

Carver stared back at him. And into the pure energy of an obsession that rationalized any sacrifice in exchange for justice on a cosmic scale. What was the life of a woman he hardly knew when it stood in the way of balancing the scales for the killers of Martin Luther King and, surely if indirectly, Jefferson's father? What was Edwina's life to Jefferson if he was willing to let the woman he himself loved die? If he was willing to use Courtney Romano as an unknowing instrument of death?

With effort, Carver composed himself. This wasn't the time to let Jefferson see the fear and desperation seething in him. He breathed in the bitter rising steam of a fresh cup of coffee and said, "There's no sign of her on board."

"No sign of anyone on board," Jefferson said.

Carver realized that was true, as it had been earlier when he'd planted the tiny transmitter on the *Bold Entrepreneur*'s hull. Ghost ship.

"Your friend Van Meter gave her to them," Jefferson said. "Called his man off the bodyguard job when we paid him to cooperate. Sold you out."

Carver didn't want to believe it, but he couldn't *dis*believe. *Women and money, they cause us to do things we wouldn't ordinarily.* Even Van Meter? Carver remembered the sexpot secretary Marge. The way the middle-aged receptionist at Van Meter's office had rolled her eyes at the sound of Marge's voice. Why *not* Van Meter?

"These people'll stay below deck until the boat gets well out to sea," Jefferson said. "They have an aversion to being seen and maybe photographed under these circumstances. Never know when a photo or a videotape might turn up in a courtroom. And they didn't get to be who they are by taking unnecessary risks."

"They have to eat," Carver said. He looked around at the supper crowd beginning to filter into Lobster Jack's. Fifteen, twenty customers now. Several more waitresses in the frilly red-and-white-checked aprons were gliding about the place, taking orders, balancing round trays with food and drinks on them. "Suppose they send someone over here to bring back food to the boat?"

"Ha! You don't know these rich cocksuckers. There's a gourmet cook on board, along with two crew members. All part of the crew of the *Sea Charger*, a larger yacht, owned by the SCBL once or twice removed. That boat's used to make drug pickups at sea. Folks on board the *Bold Entrepreneur* are probably sipping champagne and nibbling caviar right now while we sit here working on this horse-piss coffee."

"Champagne and caviar. Courtney's last meal."

Jefferson's body stiffened and he leaned back in his chair. But his expression didn't change. Something had been set in motion years ago for him, and its momentum was irreversible. Carver could understand that, which was why he feared it so much.

The waitress came over and refilled their cups for the third time. Jefferson pulled a crumpled pack of Viceroys from his pocket. Glanced at Carver. "Mind?" *I'm letting the woman you love be obliterated, but I wouldn't want to offend you with tobacco smoke or risk giving you lung cancer in twenty years without your permission.*

"I didn't know you smoked."

"Only now and again."

"When you're nervous?"

Jefferson gave Carver a brief smile. Dragged a blue Zippo lighter from the same pocket the cigarettes had been in and lit a Viceroy. The lighter worked on the first try; Jefferson had everything under control.

Or did he? The waitress hurried over and told him he was in the no-smoking section. Asked if he'd like a table where he could smoke. Jefferson told her no thanks. Said he was sorry, he hadn't known. He snubbed out the cigarette on the heel of his shoe and dropped the butt into his pocket.

Carver sat gazing out the window at the *Bold Entrepreneur* for the next hour or so, trying to imagine Edwina below deck. Just on the other side of that curve of pure white hull. What were they doing to her? She should be safe as long as they thought she could be used as leverage to control him. But how accurately could you figure somebody like Vincent Butcher? He was a sadist, a psychotic fascinated by sharp steel and what it could do to flesh. Maybe Wesley and Ogden couldn't control him.

At seven o'clock Farneaux still hadn't arrived. The *Bold Entrepreneur* continued to rock and bob gently at her moorings. A gull touched down and perched for a moment on the boat's navigational antenna, then flapped away into the graying sky, bucking the ocean breeze.

Jefferson was drumming his fingertips heavily on the table. The dull, relentless thumping was getting on Carver's nerves. He wondered what would happen if he simply stood up and limped toward the door. Would Jefferson shoot him in the back? Hardly.

But Carver almost certainly would be taken into custody, as Jefferson had promised. Cuffed and led from the restaurant. The diners at Lobster Jack's would get to see the apprehension of a notorious drug smuggler—at least Jefferson would flash his DEA credentials and tell them that. Or give them a similar story. Carver figured that was about how it would go. Gave up on the idea of simply trying to call Jefferson's bluff and walk to freedom and whatever he thought he could do to help Edwina. Jefferson probably had never bluffed in his life.

Carver drank yet another cup of coffee, loathing the bitter aftertaste of the stuff. But he knew he might need the caffeine to help keep him alert. For what, he wasn't sure. Something, though. Something. He *was* sure of that.

When the supper crowd had thinned, and the waitress had stopped giving Carver and Jefferson meaningful glances to let them know they were keeping the table occupied with only a potentially small tip, Carver said, "I gotta go to the bathroom. All that coffee."

Jefferson put down his cup and thought about that. Then he nodded. "I'll go with you. Gotta take a leak myself."

"I thought you DEA guys didn't have genitalia."

"I'll pretend," Jefferson said. "Get up and move, you wanna take a piss." He stood up himself. Stretched. Shook his head no to the waitress when she raised her eyebrows inquiringly as to whether they were finally leaving and wanted the check. The waitress was visibly building up a dislike for Jefferson.

Carver limped toward the rest room at the back of the restaurant. He wasn't surprised to see the facing doors labeled BUOYS and GULLS. He pushed open BUOYS and went inside. Jefferson was close behind him.

The rest room was large and done in pale green tile. An exhaust fan was rattling up near the ceiling. It was cool in there and smelled like disinfectant. A guy in white slacks and a navy blue T-shirt turned away from one of the four white urinals, zipping his pants. Left without washing his hands. The chef maybe.

Jefferson moved back while Carver stood at the end urinal and relieved himself, leaning against the wall with his palm, his cane hooked into his belt.

When he was finished, he zipped his fly and limped over to the nearest washbasin. It had one of those faucets that turn off automatically so no one can leave the water running and flood the rest room. Carver rinsed his hands and stood drying them under a blower that sounded like a vacuum cleaner.

Jefferson had stepped to the urinal and unzipped his pants. Carver waited until he heard urine splatter.

He moved fast, gouged the tip of his cane into Jefferson's back near the lower spine. Said, "I'll blow your fuckin' backbone in half you don't get both hands flat against the wall, feet apart!"

Jefferson started to turn his head. Carver slapped his palm against his ear. Jefferson placed both hands high on the tile wall, pressing hard with splayed fingers. Edged his feet back. Carver kicked at Jefferson's shoes, forcing his feet farther apart. Reached around and drew Jefferson's revolver from its spring-loaded holster. Stepped back.

Jefferson had spotted his pants some, but he'd stopped pissing. He said, "Goddammit, the cane!"

"Might have been a gun," Carver said. "Thing is, you get used to a man with a cane so it seems like part of him. You forget it exists. Then, when something that feels like a gun barrel pokes you in the spine, it takes you a few seconds to remember the cane."

"Long enough for him to get a real gun," Jefferson said. He pushed away from the wall and turned around slowly, almost lazily. He was smiling. "We both know you won't use the gun, though, Carver, so it might as well have the same firepower as your cane."

Carver said, "I'll use it. For Edwina."

That stopped Jefferson. He looked as if he'd been about to step forward, but his body took on a tense stillness. Poised but unmoving. Maybe love, need, was something he understood. Maybe what he was doing to Courtney was costing him more than Carver had thought.

Carver told him to move into the nearest toilet stall.

Jefferson hesitated, but he obeyed. Did as Carver instructed and leaned with both hands against the wall over the commode. Carver reached beneath Jefferson's coat and worked the set of handcuffs from their leather case near the small of his back. Then he made Jefferson sit down on the toilet seat. Forced his arms around behind him and handcuffed him to the plumbing. Jefferson might be able to jerk the pipe loose from its fitting and work the cuffs over it, but it would take him a while.

When Carver had stepped back out of the stall, Jefferson said, "Now what? You call McGregor? Get the area crawling with local law? Get your lady friend shot or used as a hostage?"

Carver was surprised. "You know about McGregor?"

"We know everything," Jefferson said, glaring up at him. Son of a bitch was serious. Government types!

Carver kicked Jefferson's ankles to the side and swung the stall's metal door shut. Punched the button on the blow dryer again in case Jefferson decided to make some noise to attract attention. Limped out of the Buoys' room.

Smiled at the waitress. Stood in line at the cash register briefly, behind a customer who needed change for a hundred-dollar bill. Paid the check. Got out of the restaurant. All peachy. No problem. Apparently.

"Now what?" Jefferson had asked. Well, *that* was something the DEA didn't know.

Couldn't know.

Because Carver wasn't sure himself.

Chapter 35

The Ford was still parked in the restaurant lot, but the gray Dodge was gone. Probably Ralph Palma was slouched in it somewhere watching the *Bold Entrepreneur*, forcing down a hamburger and coffee while the people on board the boat enjoyed their champagne and caviar. Jefferson had it figured out, all right, class-conscious bastard. No going back for him and he knew it. In love with his destiny and locked in a dark dance with death. Carver had heard that same music and knew its power to hypnotize.

As soon as he got into the Ford, he noticed the little square receiver for the transmitter he'd placed on the boat was gone from where he'd left it on the front seat. He bent forward and reached under the seat. The Colt automatic was still there, cool and heavy to the touch. It felt like doom.

He started the car and drove from the lot, down along the dock and away from where the *Bold Entrepreneur* was tied up. Made a couple of left turns and parked in the next block.

Between two low brick buildings, a dry cleaner and a bookstore, he could barely see the bridge of the *Bold*

Entrepreneur. He sat in the car for a while with the engine idling and the air conditioner blasting, watching the boat, admiring how the setting sun glanced orange-red off its brightwork, letting his mind turn over. Then it occurred to him that Jefferson might be free from the handcuffs by now. Might have gotten together with Palma to go looking for him. The Ford would be easy to spot.

Carver moved the Ford down a block. Then he got the Colt out from under the front seat and tucked it in his waistband beneath his shirt, next to Jefferson's smaller .38 revolver. A dangerous thing to do and an easy way to get your balls shot off, but it kept both guns out of sight.

He got out of the car and crossed the street. Limped back a block, to near where he'd been parked, and then went between the bookstore and dry cleaner and walked behind them.

He was in a kind of wide alley. There were dumpsters and trash cans along one side, but all neat and clean. A tidy stack of newspapers, bound with twine, sat next to one of the trash cans. Carver figured the truck that picked up the trash would suit the area, be new and bright, with a smiling, uniformed crew.

On the other side of the alley was a grassy area with palm trees and two bleached white concrete benches. Though the sun was low now, the temperature remained high. Probably in the nineties. Carver was sweating; he felt hot and oily. He limped over to one of the benches beneath the palm trees and sat down. He had a better view of the dock from here, through another line of gently swaying palms, and he wasn't noticeable himself.

He sat patiently, practicing what he was good at: waiting. Putting together what he was going to do. Trying to, anyway.

Farneaux arrived just before dark.

A long blue Lincoln coasted along the dock, past the *Bold Entrepreneur* at about twenty miles an hour. It must have let Farneaux out some distance from the boat, because it was a good five minutes before Carver saw a short, well-tailored man with iron-gray hair step jauntily from the dock onto the *Bold Entrepreneur* and quickly duck through a door and into a companionway beneath the bridge. There were lights on aboard the boat now; the portholes glowed, and occasionally there was shadow movement beyond the thin curtains. A loop antenna above the bridge began to revolve. Heightened activity.

The boat could set to sea now. All the players were aboard.

All but one.

Carver stood up from the bench and planted his cane firmly. Limped toward the line of palm trees and the dock.

Toward the gently rising and falling white hull.

Knowing what he had to do, even if he didn't know exactly how to do it.

Chapter 36

As Carver thumped across the rough plank dock he could smell the rotted-fish scent of the water beneath him. He was still a hundred feet from the boat when a man in dark slacks and an unbuttoned white shirt emerged from below deck and made his way up to the flying bridge. Another man followed him up onto the deck but walked toward the stern. He hopped nimbly onto the dock, bent over, and with a deft motion untied the aft hawser from its cleat. Swaggered along the dock toward the bow to untie that line so the *Bold Entrepreneur* would be floating free.

Busy with the line, he didn't notice Carver. He and Carver stepped on board the boat at about the same time. Carver almost fell and had to steady himself for a moment by hooking the crook of his cane over the low rail. The sudden movement and clatter of the cane caught the man's attention. Carver was in too close to be seen by the man on the bridge, and a generator was chugging away and covering softer sounds.

Startled, the man in the unbuttoned white shirt stared at him. He had bushy black hair trimmed short and wild, a chest matted with more black hair. Broad shoulders. Very flat-bellied and lean through the waist. Kind of guy who could give you trouble.

He cocked his head and dropped his hands to his sides. Took a step toward Carver. Said, "Help you?" His voice was neutral; he didn't know which way to play this, how he should act.

Carver said, "I'm supposed to deliver a message to Frank Wesley. Important."

That made the man even more curious. Over the chugging of the generator, Carver was barely aware of voices, loud laughter, from below deck. Where were Jefferson and Palma? He was sure they knew he'd come on board; he hoped they wouldn't charge in after him, fuck up everything.

The man moved closer. Carver smiled. Into this now. "You Mr. Ogden?"

The man started to answer, barely parted his lips, when Carver rammed the tip of the cane deep into his abdomen just beneath the sternum. Breath whooshed from the man and his eyes widened in surprise and pain. When he clutched his stomach, Carver whipped the cane across his throat, playing for keeps. The man dropped to his knees, bent over sharply, and rolled onto his side. He was gagging and trying to catch his breath all at the same time, unable to make much noise with his crushed larynx. One hand clawed at his throat.

Twin diesels clattered and roared to life, and the boat began to vibrate and head out to sea. Carver shoved the stricken man overboard, knowing he might drown, knowing that leaving him on board might be fatal to himself and Edwina. *Playing for keeps.* Over the roar of the diesels, he had to strain to hear the splash.

The deck's vibration running up his legs, into the core and

blood of him, Carver drew the Colt from his waistband. His heart was racing and he felt the odd exhilaration that told him he was ready. More than ready—eager.

He limped to the low door he'd seen Farneaux disappear through. Opened it. Saw a narrow set of polished wood stairs. Lifted the cane and used the strength of his arms on the railing to steady himself as he dropped through the companionway and below deck.

Landed on soft carpet and quickly found his balance with the cane.

Silence hit like a bomb. In the surprisingly spacious, plush area below deck, they all turned and stared at him. At the gun.

Walter Ogden was there, seated with his legs crossed on a red velvetlike bench that curved along the side of the hull. Four men in shirtsleeves, one of them Frank Wesley, were sitting at a round poker table, not playing cards but eating. Not caviar and champagne but steak and red wine. Except for Wesley, who had a glass of what looked like bourbon in front of him. A small black man who was actually wearing a tall white chef's cap was standing over the table, delicately holding a bottle of wine in both hands. His eyes riveted on the gun, he slowly sat down next to Ogden on the bench, cradling the wine bottle as it it were an infant he needed to protect.

Carver couldn't hear the generator down here, but it or power off the engines was doing good work, keeping the boat very cool. The smell of the sea didn't penetrate from outside. The carpet was thick and red, the color of the curved bench, and there were matching little red curtains framing the portholes, which were covered by white sheer curtains. On the paneled walls were fox-hunting prints, like those on Willoughby's walls down in Hillsboro Beach.

All four men at the table started to stand, as if they'd all reached the same conclusion with the same mind. Or maybe there'd been some sort of signal.

Carver waved the gun in a tight circle. Said, "Stay sitting, gentlemen."

They lowered themselves back into their canvas sling chairs, again in unison. Ogden, on the low red bench, hadn't moved.

Carver had what he thought was a bulkhead behind him, so he wasn't worried about his back. "Where are the others?"

Ogden said, "Farneaux's in the head." Still without moving.

A door opened and Farneaux, now with his suitcoat off, ducked his head and stepped in from what looked like a narrow teak-paneled hall with a bathroom off to the side. He had a puffy face and a yellowish complexion that suggested he was ill. When he saw Carver and the gun he looked even sicker. His eyes rolled. His slash of a mouth opened to trail a thread of saliva and then arced down in fear and disgust.

Carver said, "Where's Butcher and Courtney?"

Ogden seemed to be the only one with enough presence of mind to speak. "Resting."

"Get them in here."

Ogden didn't have to get up. He reached above his head and pressed a button mounted on the smooth white ceiling.

Within less than a minute, Courtney stepped through the same door Farneaux had come through. Her thick black hair was mussed and she had on red shorts and a khaki blouse. Red high heels. Looked like a hooker. Part of her act, Carver figured. She blinked as if she were tired. She appeared surprised for a moment, then her face went blank. Carver could imagine her brain spinning behind those calm dark Latin eyes.

Butcher followed her, ducking almost to a squat to get through from the low passageway. He was wearing white shorts and was barefoot. Didn't have a shirt on. He was fat, but below the layer of blubber muscles rippled like separate live things trapped in cellulite. Might have been a sumo wrestler. He was wearing the obscene rawhide necklace of cured earlobes around his fat, perspiring neck. One of the lumps of flesh was a lighter color than the others. There didn't seem to be a hair on his body, not even on his tree-trunk-thick, slightly bowed legs.

He gave his piglike little grin and said, "Well, looka what we got here." He'd been holding his right hand behind him. Moved it around now to show he was gripping a knife with a long, thin blade. "I got me a new charm on my necklace, Carver. But you know about that, don't you? How's the ear feel today?"

"Feels like it's time for you to shut up."

Wesley stood up and faced Carver. "To what do we owe the dramatics, Mr. Carver?"

Carver said, "Sit back down." He didn't like Butcher and Wesley both standing. Not to mention Courtney, who didn't yet know the game. His eyes shifted to the grotesque necklace. *A new charm.*

Wesley didn't move. Instead he said with something like impatience, "We all know it's not in you to squeeze that trigger. It takes a certain type of man to kill face-to-face. You're not that type. Butcher is. So let's waste no more time pretending."

"I have the gun," Carver reminded him.

"Means nothing."

"Guns always mean something."

"Not in this case. Because you're the product of your morality. Of too many books, TV shows, and movies that taught you how to behave. Made you what you are. You're a hard man, but you have compunctions, Mr. Carver, and they'll freeze your finger on the trigger."

"Can you be sure?"

"I certainly can," Wesley said in a condescending voice. "Because I know about people. How they think. What they become. How they can't help what they are and, under extreme stress, can't be anything different. Being sure, and acting on it, is how I've reached the pinnacle. Why I don't fall off."

"You might make a mistake."

"Haven't made one yet. Sheep never attack wolves; it isn't in nature's plan. No mistake here, Mr. Carver, except for yours."

Ogden stood up now. He'd been listening. Wesley had convinced him. He nodded to Butcher.

Butcher put on his dreamy grin and moved toward Carver. The boat rocked gently, as if influenced by his weight.

Wesley said, "You made the mistake by coming on board, Mr. Carver. But we can talk about it. Sit here at the table and sip fine wine and make our respective positions clear. Be men of reason. Agreed?"

Carver squeezed the trigger. Butcher's head jerked and blood sprayed. He remained standing but the top of his skull was gone. Red and gray matter patterned the teak wall behind him. There was a stupid, incredulous look on his face, as if he'd just been told a joke he didn't understand. No top to his head, he had to be dead, but he wouldn't fall. Hadn't even dropped the knife.

Carver shot him again, this time in the chest, and he dropped in the lifeless, limb-splayed heap of the dead.

Wesley sat back down.

So did Ogden. Farneaux was slumped in a corner, vomiting, stinking up the place. He'd been standing close to Butcher and his white shirt was spattered with blood and brain matter. The cook was shaking violently on the bench, his chef's cap cocked at a crazy angle on his head. He'd dropped the wine bottle but it hadn't broken on the soft carpet. Wine was gurgling from it. Everyone at the table looked sick; no one could take his eyes off Butcher.

They hadn't seen killing firsthand, none of them. They'd caused plenty of deaths since the King assassination, but their victims had been rival middlemen and burned-out addicts. Poor, trapped kids and desperate dealers they'd never met. This was different. This was someone they knew, even if they didn't like him. This was blood and bone and gristle. Violence right here with them and about them, where they could see it and smell it and couldn't deny or escape it.

Courtney was trembling like the cook, but her expression was still impassive.

Ogden was the only truly calm one. He said, "What the fuck you want out of this, Carver?"

Carver said, "Edwina Talbot. Get her."

Ogden didn't answer at first. Then he laughed. Wesley glared over at him as if he'd done something obscene.

Ogden said, "She's not on board. Never was."

Carver swung the Colt toward him. "I don't mind squeezing the trigger again."

One of the men at the table said, "Jesus, no! Don't!"

Ogden seemed unconcerned. "We don't have her. Didn't take her. If somebody told you we did, they were lying."

Carver looked at Courtney. Courtney, no longer trembling, said, "He's telling the truth. She's not on board."

Wesley was regaining his composure, though his face still

had a greenish tint. He swiveled in his chair to face Carver and said, "Search the boat if you'd like. It's not that large."

Carver told him to stand up.

Ogden said in an amused voice, "Minute ago you wanted him to sit down."

Carver gripped Wesley's soft arm and jammed the Colt's barrel hard into his temple. Wesley made an involuntary whimpering sound and backed with Carver into the narrow passageway, leaving the door open.

Quickly Carver checked the two staterooms and the bath. They were empty. Wesley was right; the boat wasn't that large, there weren't many places to look. And if Edwina were on board, Courtney probably would have said so. Somebody would have admitted it. Shooting Butcher had made the desired impression.

Carver shoved Wesley back out into the main room. Told him to sit down again. Wesley obeyed.

But the action seemed somehow to have cleared Wesley's mind. It was clear that Carver had miscalculated; Wesley saw that as a weakness to be exploited. He said, "You believe us now? That your lady friend isn't on board?"

Carver said nothing. Trying to figure it. Why he'd been lied to and what was the angle.

"Which means," Wesley said, "that we're guilty of nothing. On the other hand, you've forced your way on board and killed a man."

Carver said, "I doubt you'll radio the Coast Guard."

"Point is," Wesley said, "your heroic rescue turns out to be a farce. Where's that leave you?"

Carver knew where it would have to leave him. He'd known it from the moment he'd heard the powerful twin diesels as the boat nosed out to sea.

He said, "There a lifeboat on this thing?"

Wesley laughed, feeling the balance of power shift. "Only an inflatable raft, I'm afraid. Not a very romantic way for you to make your exit." The rest of the men at the table were gaining confidence along with Wesley. One of that prosperous group actually smiled. Nobody was looking at Butcher's body now.

Carver said, "Call your man on the bridge. Tell him to set the boat on course and to get down here."

Ogden shrugged and stood up. Leaned over an intercom and said, "Harry, set her on course and come below."

In a minute or so a pair of jeans-clad legs were descending the companionway. Rubber-soled deck shoes touched carpet.

Harry was only in his twenties, but he was solidly built and tough-looking, like the man Carver had taken out at the dock. He looked around and sized up what was happening. When he saw Butcher his face got hard. His eyes got older. He'd been around enough, this one.

Carver said to Courtney, "You know where the raft's stowed?"

She nodded. Still trying to understand what was happening. She knew it had to be Jefferson or Palma who'd told Carver Edwina was on board. Obviously didn't know why.

Carver instructed her to sit on the bench where Ogden had been. Then he motioned with the gun for everyone else to go through the door into the hall leading to the head and cabins.

Wesley said gloatingly, "So you yourself are going to take a hostage. You're getting in deeper, Carver."

Carver said nothing. He made Wesley lead the way so the rest would follow. Which they did, wordlessly.

When they were all on the other side of the door he closed it and jammed the table up against it. Wedged two chairs between the table and the opposite wall. They'd be able to force the door open eventually. But when they did they couldn't be sure Carver wasn't still out there with the gun.

He looked at Courtney and said, "They know about you." Which wasn't true but would gain her cooperation. Carver didn't want to take the time to explain about the explosives Jefferson had sent on board with her.

She stared back at him, then nodded. Had no choice but to believe him.

Carver said, "Let's get off this thing."

She stood and led him up the companionway and onto the deck. Though there was a breeze, the air was warm and thick. The motion of the boat seemed more violent up here, the night sea angrier. Whitecaps shimmered in the vast darkness.

Courtney opened a square hatch and dragged out a folded rubber raft, some collapsible oars.

She'd calculated this before. Within a few seconds she'd yanked on a cord and a CO_2 cartridge inflated the raft. It was good size, about ten by six, probably built to accommodate four to six people.

The *Bold Entrepreneur* was making only ten or fifteen knots. Carver and Courtney slid the surprisingly heavy raft overboard. Courtney immediately dropped down into the waves less than six feet from it and scrambled into the raft. Carver jumped into the water after her, making sure not to loosen his grasp on his cane. Sank for what seemed forever and then came up about twenty feet from the raft. He roller-coastered on a wave, stroked toward the raft, and found that the ocean was moving it away from him.

Courtney stared at him, as if making up her mind. Then she shifted position and raised one end of the raft to change its angle into the waves. Somehow steadied it in place.

After a struggle, Carver got close to it. Hooked it with the cane and dragged himself aboard, sprawling on his chest and stomach. Coughed up seawater. Courtney helped him get turned around. He was surprised by her strength.

Slumped on the undulating rubber bottom, he felt his waistband and discovered he'd lost one of the guns. Jefferson's pistol.

For a few moments he and Courtney sat watching the receding lights of the *Bold Entrepreneur*.

Then Courtney said, "They'll be out of where you put them pretty soon."

"We're not far from shore," Carver told her. "They won't find us in the dark."

She said, "Don't be so sure," and with a strong and skillful wrist motion extended the telescoped oars.

The wind seemed brisker now, and the sound of the unseen ocean was an endless and imponderable murmur of surrounding power. Now and then a wave would slap the raft hard, sloshing water on board and sending the oblong rubber craft spinning.

Carver and Courtney fitted the oars into the hard rubber oarlocks, then began rowing toward the low galaxy of lights that was the shoreline of Del Moray.

Chapter 37

When they got close to shore they saw the red and blue flashing lights, the commotion on the dock. Scurrying figures, arriving vehicles. Carver was pretty sure it was near where the *Bold Entrepreneur* had been docked and he'd thrown the injured drug runner overboard. He looked at Courtney, her compact body straining forward and back rhythmically, her features set in determination as she leaned into the oars. She couldn't know that in a little while the *Bold Entrepreneur* would be blown apart and everyone on board would die, as Bert Renway had died in Wesley's car outside Carver's office.

Carver's back and arms ached from rowing. His stiff leg, extended straight out so his foot was between Courtney's feet in the water sloshing in the bottom of the raft, was beginning to cramp. There was still a controlled desperation in their rowing, though he was sure that by now the *Bold Entrepreneur* was no longer searching for them—if it had ever searched. The sea at night was an arena that had concealed battleships.

He let up a little on the left oar as he rowed, altering the raft's course so it would land away from the red and blue lights and the people milling around on the distant dock.

Courtney glanced darkly at him. Realized what he was doing and didn't object. In fact, she changed the rhythm of her own strokes to help him angle the raft in toward shore. Above the rush and crashing of the sea, the plaintive wail of a police siren drifted out to them on the night. A lonesome call from another world.

When the raft was about three hundred yards from the dock, a spotlight picked it up. Carver was momentarily blinded as it pinned the raft in a wavering circle of white light. He saw Courtney wince and duck her head, averting her eyes.

Another spotlight found them. Another. With their heads lowered, they kept rowing. Carver was getting a cramp in his left arm.

Courtney said, "You fucked things up, Carver. How you gonna explain? Huh?"

"You'll find out around ten o'clock."

"Which means?"

"Just what I said." He decided he wouldn't tell her about the explosives. Jefferson had used her to plant them, but now she was safe. And Edwina was safe. Now Jefferson's plan didn't sound so unreasonable. Carver decided to let fate and Jefferson, and maybe justice, have their way with the *Bold Entrepreneur*.

The Del Moray police were all over the dock. As soon as rubber bumped wood, grasping hands were reaching down to pull Carver and Courtney up out of the raft. Carver dropped his cane, told the two cops yanking on his arms to ease up. Recovered the cane. Felt whole again.

Found himself standing on the dock beside Courtney, surrounded by uniforms. People were yammering at him but he wasn't listening; it took a few minutes for him to stop feeling the motion of the sea. For the earth to level.

The tall figure of McGregor shoved its way through the

uniforms. He looked confused and mad. Said, "Carver, we're gonna talk. You're gonna tell me what the shit's goin' on here, and you're gonna tell it straight."

Carver hadn't seen Ralph Palma, but the DEA agent was there beside Courtney. His suitcoat was slung over his shoulder and he was wearing a white shirt and dark suspenders. He gazed dispassionately at McGregor and said, "Sorry, but I gotta talk to both of them first." He flashed his credentials at McGregor, who didn't even glance at them. He knew who Palma was.

"You feds can't just charge the fuck in here and push the local law aside," McGregor said. "Ain't Constitutional." But there was no conviction in his voice.

"Watch me do it," Palma said softly.

McGregor started to say something else, then he clamped his mouth shut. He knew where power lay, and when not to draw a line. And he knew Palma was serious.

Carver felt Palma grip his upper arm. Holding Courtney's elbow with his other hand, the DEA agent led the two of them away from the knot of police and toward the gray Dodge parked near the edge of the dock.

"We're gonna get together later, Carver," McGregor called behind them. "Bet your sweet ass on that!"

Palma said, "He's a charmer, no?"

"No," Courtney said.

When they reached the Dodge they didn't get in. Stood beside it and stared out at the ocean. Listened to the waves lap against the pilings. Palma carefully folded his suitcoat, lining side out, and laid it on the car's hood. Other than that, the three of them hardly moved. Carver's arms felt heavy. Now and then he felt a twinge in his back.

After a while, Courtney said, "I need a smoke."

Palma said, "I got a pack in the car." He opened the door

and leaned down to fish around in the glove compartment, supporting himself with one hand on the seat.

That was when the car's dome light winked on and Carver saw the rifle lying on the backseat. The weapon that had long ago killed Martin Luther King but not the dream.

The rifle, but not the duffel bag.

Carver felt a cold, tight turning in his mind. A realization that was growing into something that angered and astounded him.

Palma had straightened up and slammed the car door. Was lighting Courtney's cigarette with a paper match, cupping his free hand to protect the wavering flame from the breeze.

Carver said, "Where's Jefferson?"

Courtney drew on her cigarette. Exhaled. The sea breeze snatched the smoke away from before her face. She was staring at Palma as Carver was, waiting for his answer.

Palma flipped the still-burning match away. It arced toward the water like a tiny shooting star and disappeared. He looked at Courtney, then Carver. Then he gave an odd kind of smile. A slow and elegant shrug.

Carver stood staring out at the black waves, hearing and feeling their weight and power even if he couldn't see them except as occasional whitecaps that caught the moonlight. He knew Courtney hadn't actually taken explosives on board the *Bold Entrepreneur*. And he knew why Jefferson had lied to him about Edwina being on the boat. Jefferson had let him escape at the restaurant. Knew he'd head for the *Bold Entrepreneur*. Had *sent* him. Sent Carver not to rescue Edwina but to save Courtney, or at least to give her better odds.

Carver had still been a step behind and not realized it. Been used.

But now he understood. Jefferson had understood him,

and Carver understood Jefferson. Wolf and gray wolf. Carver knew why Jefferson had wanted Courtney to have her chance to get off the boat.

And he knew what was in the green duffel bag, and why the rifle but not the bag had been left in the car. And what had happened to the electronic receiver that was missing from the front seat of the Ford in the restaurant parking lot.

There was a broken kind of roar. From farther up the dock a long, sleek speedboat shot into open water. It was the projectile-shaped boat Carver had seen docked earlier. The favorite of drug runners. The Cigarette.

Courtney had figured it out, too. She moaned, "Oh, God! No, no, no . . ."

Palma rested a hand very softly on her shoulder.

The speedboat bucked the incoming waves, its snarling twin engines racing whenever the stern cleared the water, then digging in solid when the boat settled back down.

It was headed straight out to sea now. Soon they could only hear it and see its long moonlit wake, curving like a silver ribbon away from the shore. Then the shimmering wake, too, disappeared and there was only the blackness of the night sky and ocean, a void as empty as eternity.

Palma said, "Those are fast boats. Catch anything that floats."

Courtney said nothing. Carver could see her shoulders quaking, as if she were cold in the sultry night.

After about ten minutes, she seemed calmer and moved away from Palma's hand, taking a step out toward the sea. Stood bent forward from the waist, poised.

Carver leaned on his cane, waiting. Squeezing the hard walnut that was worn to his grip. *About now. About now.*

"Any moment," Palma said softly. "Any goddamn moment."

Time seemed to drag to a halt, as if the planet had broken rhythm in its rotation. The stillness around them had weight.

For an instant the fireball that blossomed on the eastern horizon was brighter than the sun. Then the low and echoing voice of the blast rolled across the waves to shore, bouncing off the suface of the sea like wild and thunderous laughter.

The fireball lost its perfect rose configuration and contracted to a small, steady orange glow that lasted a long time and then flickered and disappeared, leaving only darkness beyond the coast.

Courtney's lips were compressed and her jaw muscles flexed. But she didn't cry. Not Courtney. Finally she turned away and walked along the dock, toward the flashing red and blue lights of the police cars. Toward the motionless, silent figures still staring out to sea. She moved slowly and smoothly, as if through water.

Beside Carver, Palma said, "I tell you one thing, that was all he thought about, ever. Like he was fuckin' haunted, you know? I loved him, but he was one crazy son of a bitch."

"Maybe," Carver said.

Chapter 38

～～ No one ever knew the real source of the explosion that destroyed the *Bold Entrepreneur* and killed everyone on board. The news media played it as a tragedy, and the feds pressured local law into agreeing. There were glowing eulogies for some of the victims. A televangelist who'd been the recipient of SCBL donations held a series of coordinated TV prayer and memorial services throughout the South.

Carver heard months later that the city of Atlanta had named a street after Frank Wesley.

No connection was made between the boat explosion and the DEA agent who disappeared fighting the illicit drug trade in Florida. Apparently Ralph Palma wasn't talking. Or the DEA didn't want it made public that one of their agents had acted illegally, murderously, and without proof. Finished business, and the kind of thing the government preferred kept confidential.

Carver checked out what Jefferson had told him, and it was true. The gun recovered after the Martin Luther King assassination was never linked directly to the bullet that killed King. A smokescreen of legal technicalities and wild rumors had obscured the very suspicious facts of both the murder and the time afterward. From somewhere, James Earl Ray had received enough money to travel all over the world before running afoul of customs at Heathrow Airport in London. From somewhere.

One day, not knowing why, Carver detoured from where he'd been driving and found himself at Beach Cove Court. Drove down Little Cove Lane to Bert Renway's mobile home. Renway, the little man who'd been made a pawn in a big game.

Everything looked the way it had when he'd first come here. He parked the Olds and limped over to the white double-wide trailer with trim the color of egg yolks. Started to knock on the aluminum door and then changed his mind. If someone did answer his knock, he wouldn't know them. He'd have nothing to say. He wasn't sure himself why he'd come here, except that it still bothered him, the way Bert Renway had died and why.

He backed away from mobile home, from the sun's heat glancing off the smooth white metal. Limped across a hard, weedy stretch of ground to the Willa Hataris trailer.

He stood in the shade of the metal awning and knocked on the door. Knocked again, harder.

No one came to the door and there was no sound from inside.

Carver gave up and started toward the parked Olds.

Halfway there, he saw a thin haze of dark smoke hanging above the Renway trailer. After staring at it for a moment, he hobbled over the rough ground toward it.

He stopped and watched the man standing behind the trailer. Probably the tenant or the new owner who'd just moved in. A small, gray-haired man wearing a sleeveless undershirt and baggy brown slacks held up by suspenders.

He was obviously clearing the trailer of Renway's posses-
sions. Using a rake handle to poke tentatively at a glowing
fire inside a wire barrel.

Burning trash.

Carver limped back to his car and drove away.

He smelled the smoke for miles.